GRIMALDI'S GARDEN

SUSAN KNIGHT

FOR KARL, JENNY AND LEO

First published in 1995 by
Marino Books
An imprint of Mercier Press
16 Hume Street Dublin 2

Trade enquiries to Mercier Press
PO Box 5, 5 French Church Street,
Cork

A Marino Original

© Susan Knight 1995

ISBN 1 86023 014 8

10 9 8 7 6 5 4 3 2 1

A CIP record for this title is available
from the British Library

Cover painting by Robert Armstrong
Cover design by Bluett
Set by Richard Parfrey in Caslon
Regular 9.5/15
Printed in Ireland by ColourBooks,
Baldoyle Industrial Estate, Dublin 13

The Publishers gratefully acknowledge
the financial assistance of The Arts
Council/An Chomhairle Ealaíon

CONTENTS

PART ONE

THE PIANO PLAYER

Once there was a garden. No, not a garden but the potential for a garden: a rough patch of soil, a couple of miserable trees that clutched at the sky with skinny arms. A hummocky rectangle of scrubby grass squashed between high tenements in a part of the city that was despised and hastily traversed by those with no option but to go that way. But old Joe, the Signor, looked at that patch of not-a-garden and could see what other more sensible people could not: a kaleidoscope of colour, a delirium of scents, an exaltation of birdsong, a little bit of blue heaven in the grey northern city. He slapped more money than he could afford down on the table and bought it.

Marian, lying on her back, looked up. For a relatively new house, the ceilings were a disgrace. Something would have to be done about those cracks and she didn't just mean Polyfilla. Maybe one of those thick textured paints would be the answer, though she'd heard they were more trouble than they were worth. Liam would know. She'd ask Liam.

Her husband finished what he was about and rolled off her with a grunt. He's getting quicker, thought Marian gratefully. She kissed his cheek, said, 'That was nice, dear,' and after modestly pulling down her nightdress, crossed to the en suite bathroom.

Something of a mixed blessing, the en suite bathroom. The bedroom really wasn't big enough for it but it made life so much more civilised and suggested that they lived in a much grander house when she mentioned it to acquaintances. Liam had done a good job, she thought as she turned on the bidet. Beautiful tiling, most professional.

Her husband Francis listened to the water swishing. Listened to his seed being flushed down the waste pipe, millions of tiny futile spermatozoa making their last unexpected journey. He turned over in bed and tried to sleep.

Across the city, not far away, the Englishwoman stroked her daughter's sleeping face. She tried to trace in the tiny features the likeness of the father but found she had forgotten. Her hardened hand gently brushed the child's soft skin. 'Not quite right,' they'd said at the health centre as kindly as possible. Poor little Starveling.

The house on which Francis was paying a mortgage at a variable rate of interest, where he lived with his wife Marian and his two teenage children, the house which Marian was constantly improving, was a narrow semi-detached in a modern development. It was cloned so effectively over a maze of indistinguishable streets that on first moving to the district some years before, Francis had occasionally, in his customary state of absent-mindedness, walked up the wrong front path and tried to insert his key in the lock of someone else's front door.

'For goodness sake,' Marion had exclaimed. 'No one has crazy paving like ours!'

It annoyed her when he said that the houses all looked the same. She kept trying to explain about the little personal touches that made all the difference. Shortly after he had got lost for the third time, before people could start to talk, she replaced the standard wooden front door with a sliding glass panel. The glass was patterned and frosted, so from outside you could only see imprecise shapes moving within. Francis never went astray again but only because he concentrated.

Ruth, the Englishwoman, did not expect to spend the rest of her life in Ireland but for the time being she was comfortable. She missed the cultural mix of other countries, the black, brown and yellow skins, the exotic tastes and smells. She knew it was not the best place for a painter to succeed in – the glorious visual sense of the ancient Celts seemed long lost to her – but she loved the grey light, the grey rocks, the wilderness that nudged even at the edges of Dublin city itself.

She taught art at a community centre where most of the students were middle-aged housewives, with a sprinkling of men, elderly or unemployed. She tried to coax them away from crude realism and showed them reproductions of modernists from Kandinsky to de Kooning to Kindness. They looked politely, then continued daubing at their vases of flowers, their bowls of fruit, their landscapes.

Her own pictures she tried to sell at market stalls, from the railings of Merrion Square, most people walking on, preferring to pause over the Dublin scenes, the vases of flowers, the bowls of fruit. But never mind if they didn't buy. Soon she would have enough work for what she really wanted, an exhibition.

'Can nothing be done?' the chief librarian asked with a sigh.

Francis looked at the book and said, 'We could try and flip through each one when it's returned but what would that prove. The culprit could always say it was already defaced.'

'Anyway,' Maureen, the assistant, added, 'we wouldn't have time.'

They would, of course, Francis thought. It was a small branch library and often empty. Their work was steady but seldom frenetic.

He turned the pages of the American detective novel. The words 'Jesus' and 'Christ' had been scored out whenever they occurred.

Marion, although she would hardly admit it, had her best ideas for home improvements while performing the sexual act. It was the one occasion when she had leisure to think, as she kept herself busy. An efficient woman, she was able to complete the housework quickly, leaving the place spotless for she was very houseproud and couldn't abide disorder. Now that the children were older, she had more time to herself and attended a number of weekly classes as she had done over the years. Souvenirs of many of her courses could be seen around the house and garden. The dried flower arrangements that she put in the hearth in summer, the macramé plant-holders in kitchen, living-room and main bathroom, the ceramic ashtrays – no one smoked in the house, though both children did so outside, secretly. She currently attended Ruth's painting class but was slightly disappointed. The woman was so vague, so short on the necessary facts, and rather slovenly in appearance. Her retarded child sat on the floor during the class, staring intently and emptily into space or else smearing paint on a large sheet of paper with its hands. It gave Marion the creeps. Still, she was pleased with her view of Ireland's Eye, painted from a postcard. When it was finished, she would take down the heavy mirror over the mantelpiece in the living-room and hang the picture in its place. The mirror could then go into the hall.

The moral guardian sharpened his pencil carefully. Such a task it was. He scored out the word 'motherfucker', sucking his teeth and making clicking noises. So much to do.

Francis had met Marion at French evening classes – she was intent on improving herself even then. He had proposed to her in French. It seemed easier than in English, as if the words didn't really mean anything. *'Voulez-vous m'epouser?'* He'd had to repeat it several times, because she wasn't sure she'd understood. Then she kissed him and told him he was very romantic (*très romantique*). *'Oui, François,'* she'd said.

He knew he was something of a disappointment to Marion. He was something of a disappointment to himself. It seemed he had managed to dream away the best years of his life. He looked at the two large people who lived in the house with him and his wife and wondered how they could possibly have any connection with himself. Certainly, however much they had gambolled on top of him when they were small, whatever the echoes of laughter down a long tunnel of time, there was none of that now. The boy, Gerald, would sit in his room, external sound blocked out by a walkman permanently tuned to a rock radio station, glassy-eyed in front of a computer screen, zapping at alien space ships, using a joy-stick to move a karate hero up levels of a crazy castle where floors fell away and knives came out of walls to spear you or a portcullis smashed down, chopping you in half, blood everywhere, pressing a button to spring back to life good as new, unaware that time was running out. Or else he would move down to the living room and sit in front of the television, where a succession of American teen-coms passed before his eyes, interrupted only by advertisements for building societies, bright cars, sweet fizzy drinks and denims with expensive labels.

The girl, Valerie, recently become large-breasted, large-buttocked, thick-thighed, spent hours on her appearance pulling half a headful of long permed hair up into a pony-tail on the top of her head. Then out she went to lounge on garden walls with an army of her identikit pals, going silent when someone passed them by and breaking into loud sounds again a second later. Francis feared these groups as he made his way home from work, staring at the ground, acting as if he didn't see them, looking up suddenly to catch his daughter's cold eyes upon him.

'Does that look like water to you?' Ruth asked, frowning at the thick blobs of paint.

'Well . . .' Marion replied.

'A lighter touch would give a better effect, spray on the rocks, you know.' Ruth took the brush and showed what she meant. But nothing could help. The sea looked like cement, the clouds like smashed concrete blocks, Ireland's Eye itself like a lopsided chocolate mousse.

'Do you really want your picture to look like a postcard?' she asked. (Here we go again, thought Marion.) 'I've a book on Turner at home. I'll bring it in and you can see how he handled it.'

She knew she was wrong. She knew they didn't want to be artists, just to divert themselves, to have a bit of fun. Her trouble was that she wasn't a teacher. She was an artist with an uncompromising eye. She was out of sympathy with her students.

Starveling lay on the floor absorbed in sucking green paint off her fingers. The class pretended not to notice as Ruth went over and took care of her.

When Francis was small, he had briefly owned a dog. His mammy and daddy had bought it for his birthday. He had called it Red, because of its colour.

For a few weeks he petted the pup and played with it, throwing balls for it to chase. Red would lumber after the ball on outsize paws, sniff it, try it for taste and then look back at Francis hopeful for ideas on what to do next. His mammy cleared up the dog messes and said she hoped Red would grow out of it, otherwise ... Then one day Red ran out of the house under a car and was killed. Francis's mammy refused to get another dog.

'I couldn't go through all that again,' she said, though whether she meant the shock and pain of sudden death or whether she was referring to having to clear up dog messes from dawn to dusk, remained unresolved.

Francis had always intended getting another dog but every time he broached the subject with Marian she recoiled in horror. 'They're so unhygienic,' she would say, 'You can catch terrible diseases from them.'

'Their hairs get everywhere, it's impossible to keep the place clean.'

'I know who'd end up looking after it. Me. No one else would bother.'

'What if it bit someone?'

It was undeniable that Ruth had seen something of the world but when she cast her mind back, all that remained were uncoordinated images like a heap of snapshots muddled together and unlabelled. She had hitchhiked through Sweden which seemed in her memory to consist largely of thick woodland. In Amsterdam she had shared a sleeping bag with a stranger in a park near the Rijksmuseum. She had caught a boat down the Rhine from Cologne, floating past sunlit vineyards, villages with high church towers hanging off the sides of hills. She had attended courses in Paris, Prague,

Budapest and Moscow, visited cathedrals, palaces – some genuine, some perfect copies of buildings destroyed in the war – gazed at ten thousand paintings in hundreds of museums, rummaged through markets, bitten into half a million buns. She had travelled down the east coast of America by Greyhound bus, journeying overnight to save the cost of accommodation – stopping off in Philadelphia where she had seen the soon-no-longer-to-be-president Jimmy Carter smiling and waving, Washington DC in the lashing rain, Richmond, Virginia where a black man offered her drugs, Atlanta, Georgia where a white skateboarder was the only other person on the streets and where she had seen a thrilling Sonya Delaunay exhibition. In New Orleans, a small elderly black tap-danced and clacked false teeth. New Orleans was full of American tourists buying tee shirts with facetious or obscene messages. She stared for a long time at the river boats on the Mississippi. On the way back north, she was so exhausted she passed without stopping through Nashville, Tuscaloosa, Chattanooga.

She had formed brief relationships with men met on her travels and as a result now had a permanent companion, conceived when a condom leaked. The Judgement as her mother called the child, Starveling her own name for the scrawny little thing, or else the Portable Baby. Still portable enough after nearly three years through her silence and stillness.

So it wasn't Starveling who made her loath to move on. Perhaps it was older age and the fact that travelling had after all been an excuse for inactivity. Keep moving to disguise the fact that you're standing still.

Or perhaps what stopped her at last in her tracks was the vague memory of Starveling's father, a sandy-haired Irishman she had coupled with in a graveyard in Aberdeen after a night spent drinking. She was almost sure that was when it had happened, lying on a tombstone in a mist, laughing and fumbling, spilling a bottle of whiskey over someone's dear departed.

It was the piano, he later decided, that finally brought him to breaking point. Francis had not even known he was approaching a crisis until the piano.

Later he came to suspect that the problem had been there for many years. What about the business of mistaking another house for his own? Supposing the key had fitted, turned in the lock. Opened the door. Wasn't that what he wanted? To try another life? And what about following people?

When Marion wanted things done in the house that she couldn't manage herself, she turned to the faithful friend. Liam, for many years the best mate of her elder brother, had always, the family tradition went, had his eye on her. But Liam was over-familiar, always there. She married the stranger, Francis, and though she wouldn't have said to herself that she had made a mistake, it was comforting to find that Liam was still around now that they were back again in the old neighbourhood.

Liam, a bachelor of forty-three, still lived with his mother, was clean-living, sporty and good with his hands. He had entered with enthusiasm into Marion's plans, done most of the crazy paving in the front garden, the patio in the back, crushing grass and daisies under concrete slabs on which Marion had then placed large pots of geraniums, a white plastic table and chairs for summer meals 'al fresco' which the climate seldom permitted. Liam had even tried to forge a friendship with Francis to show there were no hard feelings, suggesting they go for a few jars together one evening. It was not a success. Without Marion, the two men found they had nothing to say to each other. Liam tried to bring the conversation round to football but found Francis unbelievably ignorant. Francis was equally put off by Liam's uninformed Catholicism, his uncritical support for what Francis regarded as a political party of gombeens. They stared at their pints and drank faster than was good for them. 'Poor Marion!' Liam's mammy commented with satisfaction when he told her about it.

When Francis thought about himself, which he tried not to do too often because it was so depressing, he came to the conclusion that somewhere along the line he had got it wrong. And he had been getting it wrong ever since. As an only child, he had been over-protected as they say, so that the corners that might have been knocked off him in the ordinary way had stayed with him, causing him to bump into things constantly, to walk around in a state of self-conscious physical and mental clumsiness.

Just above medium height, with a permanent inclination of the head and shoulders that seemed to apologise for this, he had the air of one listening to confidences whispered in the hushed atmosphere of the library where he had worked for so long. He peered short-sightedly through spectacles that were constantly sliding down his narrow nose. Now his hair was starting to go, though so far it had kept its colour. His most outstanding feature was his hands with their incredibly long nervy fingers.

Of course he had been bullied at school. He was bad at sports, liked books, was very shy. So he developed a skill for disappearing. The bullies started not noticing he was there. Sometimes he even wondered if he was.

In the library, he was not so much himself but rather the authority figure, the 'librarian,' and as such held his own. In the estate where he and Marion now lived with neighbours who were taxi-drivers, bus-drivers, postmen, builders, artisans, Francis was thought to put on airs. If he happened on someone he knew by sight, he would look away quickly but not out of snobbery. The truth was that he was terrified of rejection. He avoided catching anyone's eye in case they looked right through him, leaving him smiling foolishly at nothing. Gradually to look lost in thought became his defence. Often, he really was lost and increasingly it was becoming hard to find himself again.

Once Ruth had been with Starveling in Donegal. They'd been walking on a long sandy beach, deserted except for a few people up ahead of them, moving strangely. When Ruth got near them, she saw they were severely mentally disabled, uttering raucous sounds, attracted and terrified by the waves lapping the shore. A woman was walking in circles, chanting incomprehensible words and gesturing with her hands. Starveling stared at her. The woman stared back and even started to follow them along the beach, stretching her arms towards them. Ruth, filled with terror and convinced that the woman was somehow trying to reclaim Starveling, walked faster, nearly ran. The child, held tight against her, still gazed back over her shoulder. When finally Ruth dared to glance round, she saw the woman being led gently back to the group.

Ruth, in her thirties, was a large woman, whose choice of big baggy comfortable clothes made her look even larger. Once she'd had long hair down to her waist but she got tired of it, caught hold of the shears and cropped it all off. She knew she looked butch which suited her at present because it discouraged the amorous intentions of Irishmen, who seemed to prefer their women conventionally feminine.

The previous summer, a woman friend had invited her to Kerry, to a holiday home. On arrival, Ruth discovered the place to be full of lesbians, alone or in couples. Ruth had ended up sleeping on the floor of an unused bathroom, making a bed for Starveling in the bath. A melancholy American woman had made a pass at her but so readily took no for an answer that Ruth had felt almost remorseful.

Most of the time Ruth was glad to be celibate though she didn't consider it a permanent condition. Occasionally she could have done with a good screw but instead bought a bottle of wine and got maudlin drunk listening to old records.

There was an inexorable pattern to things. That was what Francis believed. That was how he justified his passivity. Once he had asked Marion to marry him and once she had accepted, he was swept along by the inevitable flow, the houses they lived in, the children they had, the holidays they went on, the small rituals of life.

Had he perhaps chosen an organising woman to remove responsibility from himself? He hadn't yet confronted the question. But more and more often he thought of his childhood, of the dog Red, and an imprecise moment when things might have taken a totally different course.

The business with the piano happened like this. One day, he went to the city centre: his eyes had been troubling him for some time and he was to collect new glasses. When he tried them on, everything came into sudden sharp focus. He looked in the mirror and almost failed to recognise himself. Partly it was the contrast between the new dark steel frames and his old brown plastic ones, partly it was seeing suddenly how old he looked, sharp lines scoring his skin, thin hair, scraggy neck. He walked out of the optician's in shock. He went to a café where the tables stood under an artificial tree covered eternally in pink blossom, sat down with a coffee and thought. He was unable to come to a conclusion. Around him people laughed and chattered or sat silent, reading or staring into space. So many lives, so many.

He walked out of the café and found himself behind a woman in a silky purple dress stretched tight across her buttocks, on her head a black hat with a peacock feather that bobbed as she tottered on ridiculously high heels. Francis had never seen a woman dressed like that, had never seen such a hat. He began to follow her out of curiosity. Or out of something stronger perhaps, a compulsion as he thought later. Certainly he had never followed anyone before: it was totally out of character, he would be more inclined to take the opposite direction. She walked the length of Dame Street and up past Christ Church cathedral, dodging the traffic at the intersection and continuing into the Liberties. This was a part of the city, the oldest part, that Francis had never explored on foot, only driven through occasionally. The woman walked on, her feather bobbing, Francis trying to be inconspicuous behind her, not sure whether following someone like that constituted an offence.

The street was empty. Francis, feeling exposed, was about to turn back when the woman went into a junk shop. He approached and peered through the glass, browned with dirt, glimpsing within heaps of old furniture, clocks, mirrors. An ornamental hatstand stood in the open doorway, a greasy cap hanging from it. The shop was narrow and deep and Francis couldn't see the woman at all. He wandered in and started to examine a small table with rickety legs. Suddenly, the opening notes of a tune played on a slightly off-key piano came from the rear of the shop. He made his way carefully between the chairs and stools and chipped, glass-fronted cabinets towards the music. The woman, her peacock feather still bobbing, was sitting with her back to him at the piano, playing, watched by a fat and grizzled old man who nodded silently at Francis.

Suddenly she started singing in German, her voice deep and cracked. It made Francis shiver to hear the poignant melody, even more so than if the piano had been in perfect tune, the woman's voice true. She played the piece to the end, then stood up, tapped the old man on the shoulder and walked out past Francis. He saw that she was old, that tears were running down her collapsed cheeks.

The old man shook his head after her and turned to Francis.

'What can I do you for?' he asked.

Francis looked at him uncomprehending, then asked, 'How much for the piano?'

'Two hundred and fifty.'

'Can you deliver?'

'Depends. Where are you?'

Francis told him and gave him all he had, thirty pounds, on deposit.

'What piece of music was that?' he asked.

The old man shrugged.

'Search me,' he said.

The narrow town house in which Francis lived with his wife and children had not been built with pianos in mind. The architect's mandate had apparently been to design the houses in such a way as to fit as many as possible on to the plot of land owned by the development company.

The living room was wedge-shaped, nine feet across at its widest point and six feet at its narrowest. A long couch stood against one wall, the television against the other. When the piano was delivered, Francis pushed the television down to the narrowest end of the room, leaving the couch facing tightly up against the piano. Gerald went up to his computer in a huff, Valerie disappeared out into the night to tell her friends that her dad had finally flipped. Marion threw a fit when she came home from her car-maintenance course and found Francis seated on a stool in front of the piano, trying to pick out a tune.

'What is it?'

'A piano.'

'I mean, what's it doing here?'

'I bought it.'

'What! How much?'

'Er . . . Two hundred and fifty pounds. Free delivery.'

'Two hundred and fifty! What about the microwave I've been on at you to buy that you said we couldn't afford.'

'We have an oven already.'

'Not a microwave. Everyone has one these days. Have you any idea how much easier my life would become if we had a microwave?'

Francis thought privately that Marion already had quite an easy life but considered it judicious not to say so.

'What about the children? They live here too, you know. How can they watch TV? They'll get cricks in their necks.'

'They watch too much television. Especially the boy.'

'Gerald. His name happens to be Gerald.'

'Yes, him.'

'You can't even play the damn thing.'

'I can learn.'

'At your age. Don't be stupid.'

'You go learning all sorts of things.'

'Not to play the piano. That's for children.'

'Our children could learn.'

'Hah!'

Francis was trying to remember whether the library held any music tutors. He picked out 'Pop goes the Weasel' on the white notes.

'Even the sound is wrong,' commented Marion from the kitchen where she was making coffee.

'I can get it tuned.'

She re-entered the room, clutching a mug. She hadn't made any for him.

'It's so ugly.'

'I'll clean it up.'

'It doesn't suit the room . . . It doesn't suit the house . . .' (This was quite true. With its dull, shabby wood and broken candle-holders it looked totally out of place amid the bright veneers, the sprigged wallpaper, the satined and glossed paintwork, the tufted couch – like a tramp, like an interloper.) 'It doesn't suit us.'

She burst into tears. She was puzzled and hurt. Why had he done this to her? She insisted the piano be sent back. He saw the tears as blackmail and refused. It was a long time since they had had a row. Not because they got on so well but simply because their lives didn't cross to any great extent. Francis had forgotten that Marion could get quite nasty.

Later, trembling with emotion, Francis went out to the pub, passing through a horde of amazons who jostled him and burst into peals of laughter at his back. It was horrible. The whole thing was horrible. He was a stranger in this familiar world, as ill-fitted as the piano. When he came back, after several pints and closing time, the house was dark. Peering in at his piano, he found it pushed down into the wedge with no space for a stool and covered with a lacy cloth. The television was back in its old position.

Ruth's mother, a widow, lived in Kent. The garden of England, people said when she told them. It wasn't like that. It was a featureless suburb that in Ruth's childhood had appeared to be full of featureless people. Her father was shadowy, a man who absented himself a lot, drinking with cronies every night or locked in his 'study', the spare bedroom where he usually slept and where he pipe-smoked sweet Dutch tobacco. The scent could still give Ruth a jolt. She later thought her parents must have stayed together for the sake of herself and her sister and wished that they hadn't, for the house was cold and loveless.

But her mother, a religious woman, disapproved of divorce. She did numerous good works with a grim expression on her face, had a circle of virtuous women friends who collected clothes for down-and-outs, was a badge-wearing member of the Mothers' Union, complained about the vicar's wife who had a job and organised bazaars and cake-sales to raise funds for unmarried mothers (none of whom were in the Union) or church missions to Jews. She called the Israelis Israelites. When Ruth finished college, her mother had imagined, without asking her or without ever attempting to find out what went on in her daughter's head, that Ruth would come home to live and teach in a local school.

Instead Ruth went to Paris for a year and studied stage design, an excuse for having a good time and continuing to be a student.

'Thank God,' Ruth's mother would say to her friends or even, as she got older, to complete strangers in Ruth's hearing, 'that I have one good daughter.'

Linda, Ruth's sister, a cheerful girl several years her junior, had become a dental technician before marrying the only boyfriend she'd ever had, settled down, not too near her mother, not too far away, and reared two healthy children.

After Starveling was born, Ruth's mother assumed that the

child would be given up for adoption. She had written to tell her daughter that the vicar, in complete confidence of course, had recommended an appropriate organisation. When Ruth announced she was keeping the baby, her mother told her not to think of visiting her with it. She saw Starveling one or twice at Linda's, but refused to touch her as if she was contaminated. When it emerged that the child was slow, her mother's comment was that Ruth should have had it adopted while she still could. It was on this occasion that she referred to Starveling as 'the Judgement'.

Ruth in turn called her mother 'a wicked old woman'. She had never been back.

Francis was walking round the large peninsula on the north side of the city known as Howth Head. He had imagined that, out of town, away from people, in the open air he would at last be able to think clearly. But the only thought he had, buzzing round and round in his brain, was that he had made a terrible mistake. Once, long ago, he had taken the wrong road and was lost forever now in tangled paths as on one of his son's computer games. The trouble was that he had no lives to spare.

It was a warm day and the effort of walking made it seem more so. Luckily there was a breeze. He had parked his old Renault in Howth village, his destination, and had taken the bus back over the hill where he started his walk, past the Martello tower that gave a view out over the bay to the city, clambering over the cliff called the Red Rock and tracking the winding path that led past a small pebbled beach, littered with empty beer cans and other detritus. There was no one about. No sound but screaming gulls nesting amid the rocks. Soon he rounded a cliff and cut off all sight of civilisation.

Gradually he forgot his frustrations. He took off his sweater and tied it round his waist for convenience. He tunnelled through the rhododendron bushes and other thick plants that came over the cliff at the back of the gardens of the rich and privileged who lived on the hill. In places it was so overgrown he had to push through thorny shrubs that caught at his clothes. Flies buzzed round his head, the occasional blue or brown butterfly. Finally he came out at the furthermost tip of the peninsula, the lighthouse. He continued towards the village, on the lower walk that hung at times precariously to the side of the cliff, with a steep drop down to jagged rocks. A head bobbed in the waves below him. Not a swimmer, no. Not here. A seal, splashing and diving. He remembered that seals were thought to have originated the legend of mermaids. Looking now at the stubby pale brown head, he considered that the sailors who imagined them to be alluring fairywomen must have been even more shortsighted than he was.

Another head caught his eye, an extraordinarily red head below and in front of him on the cliff, moving with difficulty as if trying to swim up through the thick ferns. He could see that their paths were likely to cross and automatically quickened his pace to avoid a confrontation. He wanted to be alone. He didn't want to smile and say 'Fine day', or else walk eyes down, pretending not to see, prickled by a familiar fear.

He soon realised all he had gained by hurrying was to ensure the meeting. The boy – he could tell now it was a boy – had spotted him and, heaving himself up the last few yards, was actually waiting for him on the path. He was slight, in jeans and an inappropriately thick jacket, with a crest of the short, bright red hair standing up on his head. His face was very pale but had a zig-zag mark on the left cheek, below the eye. Francis thought it was painted on until he came close and saw that it was a livid scar.

'This was where it happened,' the boy said to him, 'They

jumped there.'

'Oh?' Francis said enquiringly, 'fine day' dying on his lips.

'The ones who died, last week,' the boy explained.

Francis remembered the incident faintly. A tragic accident. But there were so many casual deaths. He looked down at the postcard scene, the waves crashing on the rocks, throwing lacy spray up into the air.

'I knew them,' the boy said.

'I'm sorry,' Francis replied helplessly.

'I wondered if they'd left any signs.'

How ghoulish, Francis thought. Bloodstains, crushed fern where they had rolled, the contents of pockets?

'Did you find anything?' he asked.

'I heard their screaming.'

'Seagulls,' Francis said quickly. 'There's thousands of them.'

'Funny that people scream when they kill themselves. When it's something they've actually chosen to do.'

'I thought it was an accident.' Francis started to walk along the path, trying to get away from the spot, hoping the boy might go in the opposite direction. The boy walked with him.

'It wasn't an accident. I knew them . . . They were afraid of death, see.'

Francis didn't. He felt terribly uncomfortable. The continuing cries of the seagulls now sounded sinister. Hadn't someone said it was the dead calling?

'They were so afraid, they couldn't bear to live any longer in a constant state of dread.'

The boy stared at him with large flecked green eyes. He was terribly pale.

'Are you all right?' Francis asked.

'I feel . . . ' the boy staggered and Francis caught hold of him as his eyelids flickered and he went limp.

The path was wider here and Francis gently laid him down on a bank of heather. He opened the jacket. The boy came round.

'Sorry,' he said.

Francis tried not to panic. It was at least a twenty-minute brisk walk to the village. He couldn't remember any nearby houses though there were probably several, concealed by the rocks. It would be unthinkable to leave the boy by himself. He looked round the cliffside. No one.

'Can you make it?' he asked.

They walked together on the path, the boy's hand in his. It was a curiously pleasurable sensation to feel the trustful nestling, as if he held a tiny creature. Francis remembered long ago, taking one or other of his children on an outing, holding hands like this.

'You're kind,' the boy said.

To change the subject, Francis started talking about himself, the first thing that came into his head. He made a joke of the piano which he now imagined he would have to sell back to the old man, probably at a considerable loss. Maybe, he thought aloud in a wave of philanthropy, he could even find the woman with the peacock feather in her hat and present it to her.

The boy looked at him. 'You could put it in my house,' he said. 'You could come and play on it whenever you wanted.'

'That's very nice of you,' Francis replied, 'but I'm sure your parents would object.'

'I don't live with my parents,' the boy said. 'It's my grandmother's house.'

'Well then, she'd object,' Francis smiled.

'No, she wouldn't. She likes music. And in any case, she's dead.'

They walked in silence.

'If you want,' the boy said.

Francis was exceedingly glad to reach the village and find it just as expected. Three years had not passed as when the soldier met the devil in *The Soldier's Tale*. Twenty years had not flown by as when Rip van Winkle feasted in the cave of trolls. On the other hand, he regretted the ending of the walk, he was sorry to let go of the boy's hand.

He insisted they go to a pub for a drink, meaning coffee or orange juice. The boy ordered brandy. Surely he wasn't old enough. Still, he probably needed it. Francis bought a brandy for the boy and a beer for himself.

The man, the moral guardian, walked systematically through the city streets, ripping down posters advertising a meeting on 'A Woman's Right to Choose'. When he couldn't rip them off, he defaced them with an indelible marker bought especially for the purpose. No one paid any attention to him.

How stupid he was! How lucky he had not given himself away!

Even after another brandy, the boy was still dead white, apart from the livid zig-zag scar, and Francis had insisted on driving him home. It was not until they were standing in the hallway of the grandmother's house that he had said rather self-consciously, 'Actually my name's Francis.'

And the boy, the boy, had replied, 'Hello Francis. I'm Sonya.'

Incredibly red, incredibly short hair, an androgynous face, bare of make-up, a quirky little mouth that turned down, a slight straight body. A girl.

Later he thought, when he was able to think, that it was providential that he had believed her to be a boy. He would have behaved very differently if he had known the truth. He would have run a mile. And then nothing of what happened would have happened.

'You can bring the piano here and come and play it whenever you want.'

It was a large old redbrick house in its own grounds, dark green paint emphasizing the gloom, a smell of generations of dust. The room Sonya was showing him as suitable for his piano was on the side of the house. Bushes rubbed against windows that at the top were inset with red, green and blue panes of glass, stylised flowers.

'I don't know,' he said.

'Your wife doesn't want it in the house, right?' the girl asked.

'No.'

'Bring it here while you're making up your mind. I've always thought this room needed a piano.'

It was long and full of huge mahogany dressers.

'That thing can go in the hall.' She pointed at a sideboard. 'Then there'd be room. Come on, let's shift it.'

It was a struggle. The sideboard was solid and had to be emptied, enormous tureens and piles of plates and soup bowls carefully positioned on the floor. Drawers were removed. Francis found an old piece of carpeting and managed to get it under what remained of the sideboard and then pull it into the hall. A ghostly patch shone on the dark wall where light had been stopped for so long. It seemed like the outline of his piano. He could already see it there. He could hear it singing out and knew that it would look much more at home here than in his own sparkling house.

'It's perfect,' the girl Sonya said.

He could even get candles for it.

'All right,' he said. 'All right.'

She made two coffees in the old, primitive kitchen, brewing and straining the grounds through an unsavoury-looking bag. The

27

place was in chaos, every surface piled with clean or dirty ware and pans, opened packets of food, fruit and vegetables, magazines and books.

'Do you live here alone?' he asked.

'Generally I have people in. There's an extension out the back but the woman who's living there at the moment is moving out soon . . . My cousin sometimes comes when he's in Dublin, but he prefers a fancy hotel.'

She laughed for the first time. Extraordinarily, the corners of her mouth did not lift but seemed to turn down even more.

The coffee smelt delicious and tasted almost as good. Sonya gave Francis a key, so that he could bring the piano over whenever he wanted.

He left at last. Marion did not speak to him until he told her that the piano was going. Then she smiled briskly and kissed his cheek. He didn't think it necessary to tell her in detail what had happened.

There was a demonstration. A life-sized photograph of a statue of a miracle-working Madonna was taken in procession through the streets. Among the large crowd, the moral guardian walked tight-lipped as onlookers nudged and giggled and catcalled. They said the photograph wept just as the original statue did when in the presence of great evil. The guardian was expecting the Madonna to weep, for the evil in the city was very great. He stared intently at her, concentrating his powers. The sun flashing on the shiny surface of the photograph blinded him temporarily. He stumbled.

Later, blossoms fell from the sky. It was a miracle, they said. But what did it mean, the moral guardian wondered. He grabbed a few of the blossoms and put them in his notebook. He would think about it later.

Ruth did not want to move out of Sonya's extension. It was a wonderful place for a painter to work. Unlike the rest of the house, it was bright and airy, with a large skylight set in the roof. True, when Ruth had first arrived, she had had to clamber up precariously and scrape off the green mould that had accumulated on the glass, but once that was done, the place was perfect. Sonya was easy-going about rent, charged little and didn't make a fuss if there were problems. Ruth was, however, scrupulous about paying her share of the gas and electricity, and putting coins in the box whenever she used the telephone.

The trouble began when Starveling learned how to walk. She took longer about it than she should have done. She was well over two years old before she got up off her bottom but once she started she couldn't be stopped. She was soon even able to push open the door and wander off into the huge back garden that had become overgrown. One time Ruth, immersed in work, had failed to miss her for what could have been more than an hour. Calling out the back door at last, she finally heard a tiny sobbing in the far distance. When she tracked it down, she found the child had fallen into a kind of pit that looked horribly like a grave. It turned out to have been dug by an old man who had been growing onions and other vegetables there for many years with the permission of Sonya's grandmother. From time to time he turned up at the kitchen door and left something, a cabbage, a couple of leeks, a bunch of carrots. Sonya accepted them apparently without knowing or caring that they had been grown in her own garden.

But there were all kinds of dangers, briars, stinging nettles, a hedge that could be pushed through by a small person and which gave access on to a road, trees that were easier to climb up than down, a wreck of a shed, with broken glass windows, rusty nails – a mother's nightmare.

When Ruth tried to confine Starveling in a play-pen, the child howled all day. When she let her out, Ruth was jumping up every two minutes to check that she was all right.

It was no use. Ruth finally had to decide to rent a pokey old artisan cottage in the inner city, with access to a small paved yard surrounded by a brick wall. She bought a plastic slide and all day long Starveling climbed up the steps and slid down. Up and down, up and down.

It was usual for Ruth to mount an exhibition of the work of her pupils at the end of the school year, in May or June. As well as her Ireland's Eye picture, Marion was planning to show her first reasonably successful work, a still life with a bottle of wine and a bunch of grapes. A school hall was to be used for the show, which took place over a weekend. Ruth found she liked her pupils better when they were helping good-humouredly to set the thing up, clearing chairs and tables out of the way, heaving screens into position, hammering nails.

Most of the pictures had been framed at the pupils' own expense and looked when hung, Ruth grudgingly admitted, better than she had expected. She put up a couple of her own more accessible landscapes alongside them, just for fun.

The grand opening was cheerful, with a glass of wine and canapés made by the ladies. Marion contributed tiny vol-au-vents stuffed with mushroom cream. Francis was late – he was off somewhere – and people assumed that the man whose arm Marion was holding was her husband.

Liam looked around, mightily impressed with Marion's efforts and offering to buy the still-life. She said he could have it as a present. He paused in front of another canvas.

'I wouldn't give you tuppence for this one,' he said. 'I could do better myself.'

'You should come to the class and try,' Ruth smiled at him, moving off.

Marion giggled, 'Liam, you're dreadful. That's my teacher and that's her picture.'

'What's it supposed to be?' Liam asked, staring puzzled at the sweeps of colour.

'It's called Wicklow III,' Marion said, peering at the label. 'She doesn't think pictures should look like postcards.'

'Well, she's succeeded then,' Liam commented. 'Imagine sending that to anyone – Wish you were here. Wish I wasn't.' He laughed at his joke and swallowed his white wine grimacing, a pansy drink.

Later, Francis arrived, flustered. He'd forgotten about the exhibition and knew he was in the wrong. He told Marion he'd been delayed in town traffic, when actually he'd been trying to play his piano.

There was no wine left and only a few canapés on soggy crackers. Ruth had left and the rest of the class were discussing adjourning to a pub. Francis glanced round at the paintings which he found horrible. Only Ruth's own wild and windy mountains caught his eye.

Back in early childhood Francis had been given piano lessons. Now he found he could remember how to read music. He went to Walton's music shop and browsed through the manuscripts. The elementary books looked boring. He picked out some Bach preludes.

Sometimes he went to the grandmother's house in his lunch break. More often in the mornings when there was late opening at the library, or at the weekends.

'Are you sure I won't drive anyone crazy?' he asked Sonya.

'There's nobody here much during the day,' she told him, 'except me, and I don't mind.'

Sometimes he was aware of other people moving around, a toilet flushing, someone boiling a kettle in the kitchen, a door slamming. He never actually saw these people and wondered fancifully if they could be ghosts, the dead grandmother and her family.

As for Sonya, she told him she was an actress, which accounted for her irregular hours. She wasn't working at present, she told him, but had something coming up.

Often he was totally alone in the house. He would let himself into the dusty hall and feel the silence wrap itself round him. Then he would sit motionless at the piano, forgetting time, forgetting everything, light filtering through the stained glass, dappling him red, green, blue.

PART TWO

PANTOMIME

How they laughed, the rude mechanicals, at the sight of the old and greedy merchant Pantalone constantly being cuckolded by his young wife, at cruel Pulcinella, son of two fathers, deformed in body and mind, brandishing his cudgel, at the imaginary adventures of drunken, amorous Scaramuccia, at the bragging Captain Rodomonte, offspring – as he would have it – of thunder and lightning, near relative of death and close personal friend of the devil of hell, at ribald Arlecchino with his string of sausages, at tender Pedrolino constantly being punished for something he didn't do. How they whistled and shouted obscenities at the young boys dressed as women before women were allowed to appear on stage, and later at the women actors themselves: Cantarina and Ballerina, Silvia, Camille, Fiorinetta. How they shivered at sinister Brighella, the procurer, with his insatiable taste for tender young girls and murder.

How the small eyes of old Joe, the Signor, glittered as they cheered him.

It was a good summer in Ireland: plenty of warm and pleasant days, soft breezes, sun baking back gardens and turning white skin pink and freckled. The people who stayed in the country had the satisfaction of scoring over the sun-seekers who went to the

33

continent, where the weather was, as they say, mixed.

Ruth spent many days at the beach with Starveling, lying under the dunes or walking between Portmarnock and Malahide, marvelling at the fossils and collecting shells and bits of coloured glass that the sea had worked into jewels. She was ashamed to be so lazy for so many months, but knew it was doing her good to relax, imagining herself like a field lying fallow, replenishing its resources. In the autumn, Starveling was to attend a sympathetic local playgroup with flexible hours, so Ruth would have more time for herself. She began to look forward to starting work again.

Francis and Marion took their teenage children camping in Brittany. It had been stormy, the worst summer for a long time, the camp staff brightly told them. Over several nights, rain and wind battered their chalet tent, then calmed to a grey drizzle. Swimming in an icy pool between showers with a breeze raising goosepimples was considered definitely uncool by the children. Then Valerie found a gang to wander round with. She would disappear all day and come back late, smelling of beer and cigarette smoke, with love bites on her neck, her lips swollen.

Gerald fed francs endlessly into a games machine, battling against himself to fill all the places in the top ten scores that were displayed daily on the screen. He became so adept during the two weeks that a small group would gather round whenever he played, watching his single-minded struggle. Valerie, passing with her friends, would grudgingly boast, 'That's my brother.' Then the name 'Adrien' started appearing on the scorer, often above Gerald's own. He looked out for Adrien, hanging around the machine waiting for his rival to appear, not sure whether it was the small tousled Dutch boy, or the larger older spottier German. He never asked and the end of the holiday came before he could find out.

Despite the lack of sun, on dry days Marion would pluckily smooth lotion on herself and sit by the pool for hours, reading blockbusters or chatting with other Irish women. One came from Dublin and knew the sister of someone Marion had once worked with. A small world. Other times, the women took it in turns to drive each other to the supermarket in town where they would happily spend a morning discussing prices and produce — what exactly do you do with artichokes? — and have a *café crème* and a *gateau* in a cafe by the beach. Marion would place the order with the *garçon* in her best French ('. . . *et l'addition, s'il vous plaît.*'), impressing her companions. Sometimes Francis accompanied her. There was a shop he liked to browse through, overflowing with Far Eastern junk, carved elephants, grotesque masks, little sad-faced wooden figures. He bought one of these for Sonya because it resembled her. Francis liked Brittany, though the coastal landscape reminded him too much of Ireland to be quite foreign. National identity seemed almost totally submerged despite the fact that the use of Breton first names was no longer banned by law — Jean was once more Yan, Jacques Jakez — the black and white national flag fluttered from flagpoles and the names of towns and villages were displayed in both French and Breton on road signs, with the French name sometimes defiantly scored out. He unsuccessfully sought the discordant Breton music he had heard once in Dublin: it was impossible even to buy recordings in the small towns. But the Celtic past remained, whispering its secrets. Often he went for walks, through the long alignments of standing stones that legend said were the enchanted soldiers of an invading Roman army. He dragged the family miles across country in the creaking Renault to see ancient passage graves, rocks carved with obscure swirly designs like the finger-prints of giants impressed in stone, similar to those at Newgrange or Knowth.

Sonya held a party during the summer and invited everyone she knew, from Ruth to the old gardener, the neighbours on the left who didn't mind the wilderness but not the neighbours on the right who were always calling in the guards, actor friends, musicians. Even a woman she had started chatting to in a café on the previous day came with her husband and stayed bemused for an hour, knocking back the punch as if it were fruit juice, though someone had poured a bottle of poteen into it. Only Francis wasn't there because he was still in Brittany. People brought drink and salads − and other people − and roamed though the house and garden. Ruth took refuge from the crowd in the dining room − and noticed the piano newly installed there. She asked Sonya if she was learning to play it.

'A man owns that,' Sonya said and slipped off to greet some new arrivals.

It was getting darker. Ruth lit the candles on the piano and sat on the stool, looking out through thick and uneven panes of glass into the garden where people moved in the lilac light as if through water. She knew a few of them but not well and anyway felt unsociable. She sipped red wine and wished as often before that she had learnt to play.

Later, after a lot more wine, she found herself in another room where the heavy rock music drowned out conversation. Most people had gone home but she was staying the night. Starveling was sleeping quietly upstairs and Ruth was about to join her. A fat man took all his clothes off and shouted above the music that everyone was bourgeois. His words were directed most evidently at a young woman sitting on the floor. Ruth subsequently found out he was a teacher at a local convent school and the young woman a recent ex-pupil. His wife sat on the couch smiling, paying no attention at all to her naked husband. The man next to Ruth commented softly, 'If I were that shape and that meagrely endowed, I'd keep my clothes on.'

'Oh, I don't know,' she said, 'he has a certain something.' She pulled a small pad out of her bag and rapidly sketched the bacchanalian form. She added two little horns, two little hooves and a bunch of grapes.

'Yes,' the man said, 'Yes. He does have a certain something.'

'It's in the eye of the beholder, as they say.'

She gave the picture to the man when he asked her for it then got up and walked out, not up to bed but into the wild garden, away from the noise, the torpor and hysteria. She had been drunk but was sobering up; she had been tired but had passed beyond tiredness into a kind of trance. She climbed an unpruned pear tree in the old orchard and sat there in the sad pre-dawn greyness until the sun came up and the new day dazzled, bright as glass.

Marion was crying because the hero in the blockbuster had just died of Aids (contracted irreproachably through a blood transfusion) and the heroine, who had loved him deeply, was being terribly brave. She would, Marion suspected, finally find comfort and maybe even love in the arms of the faithful family friend. She thought for some reason of Liam, and hoped he would remember to water the tomatoes and beans. Of course he would. He was totally reliable.

Valerie was crying because her boyfriend had left to go back to the north of England. They had exchanged addresses and telephone numbers and even blood, pricking their forefingers and holding them together at the wound without any care for modern precautions. She trembled even now at the memory of his hand under her bra or unzipping her jeans and fondling her inside her panties. Her hand grasping his rock-hard dick and him showing her how to rub it until the gunge spurted out and his dick went all soft and small and bendy again.

Certainties. The moral guardian looked at the man on television with unwilling fascination. The man was apparently talking but his lips weren't moving. No part of him was moving and he was staring fixedly at the camera. His voice was monotonic and robot-like.

'The poor soul,' the moral guardian's wife commented, looking up from her knitting, 'he won't last long.' The man was a scientist and he had recently discovered new facts about the beginning of the universe which he was currently propounding. He was also suffering from an advanced stage of motor neurone disease and could talk only through a voice box.

The moral guardian stared at the man's unmoving face and the man stared back at him.

'His wife left him, you know.' The moral guardian's wife finished a row and examined her work. 'He kept running his wheelchair over her feet.'

'Be quiet,' the moral guardian snapped, 'I'm trying to listen to what he's saying.'

There was a lot about irregular waves of energy, singularity, big bangs, finite time. A time before time. Unimaginable.

'What I can't see,' the moral guardian's wife said after a while, starting to purl, 'is where's God in all that? Where's God?'

Two days after the party and still recovering, Ruth lay on Portmarnock beach in an old and skimpy bikini. She was at the far end of the strand, where no one goes, far from the ice-creams and the pots of teas. Starveling was splashing in a warm pool left by the tide and heated by the sun. Ruth squinted at the sea where red-sailed yachts were gaily dipping and bobbing round Ireland's Eye. Gulls landed in the shallows, only to take flight a few moments later when Starveling tottered towards them, stretching out her arms to try and catch hold of them even when they were already high in the sky. Ruth's bikini top cut into her flesh. Glancing round, she saw no one in sight and took it off. Not that she cared; only at times she felt vulnerable.

Another theory was that the alignments of standing stones once formed a calendar, the way Stonehenge is supposed to predict eclipses of the moon, the way the rays of the rising sun fall on a stone at the centre of the passage grave at Newgrange on the day of the winter solstice. Interpretations, theories but the heart of the problem was a mystery and would remain so maybe longer than the unravelling secrets of the universe. The mind of man deeper and darker than the mind of God. Francis brushed his hand lightly over a carved stone.

A shadow cut the sun from Ruth's closed eyes. She had almost dozed off, hypnotised by the sound of lapping waves. It was Starveling making anxiety sounds. But Starveling would have thrown herself across her. Ruth opened her eyes.

The child stood held by the hand of a man-shape, silhouetted against the sky. Ruth sat up abruptly, feeling very naked. She grabbed a towel. 'Sorry,' the man said. She looked at him with hostility. He was wearing a straw hat with holes, a faded tee shirt and ragged shorts. Nevertheless, this was no tramp. Not in those designer sunglasses.

'Goodbye,' she said.

'No, I've been looking for you.' He took off the sunglasses but the hat still shaded his face. 'Sonya said you'd be at the beach, but

I was about to give up . . . Then I saw the child.'

She didn't know who he was. Starveling ambled back to her pool and lay down in it, kicking her legs and screaming with delight.

'Ruth,' he said. 'You signed the sketch.'

The man from the party.

'Tom,' he introduced himself. 'I'm sorry. I didn't know this was a naturist beach.'

Later he would tell her how startlingly beautiful she had looked at that moment, her heavy breasts, her damp hair, her large, well-proportioned limbs, like a fleshy Dutch nude in a Rembrandt or Rubens, like the actor, Marianne Sagebrecht in the film *Bagdad Café*, more at ease without clothes than bulging uncomfortably in them.

'You disappeared from the party just when I was about to make my move.'

He was a journalist, separated, she later found out, lean and graceful, with an excessive amount of large white teeth.

He sat down beside her as the afternoon light turned gold. He picked a stalk of spiky grass and traced patterns on her arms. The sensation was between a scratch and a tickle, pain and pleasure. Ruth sighed deeply, her body rose like a wave. They would have made love on the beach among the shimmering dunes were it not for Starveling who circled them warily, sensing something strange. Later Ruth's bed filled up with sand.

The moral guardian had followed the news about the moving statues with great interest. He had even travelled to Ballinspittle to stand with the throng staring at the Madonna for hours, dizzy with hunger and tiredness. People next to him cried out as she turned her head towards them and moved her hand or opened her lips, blessing them, or rose several feet in the air. He saw nothing, only a garishly painted concrete statue with insipid features, rigid and still. It wasn't fair. He wanted so much to see her move. Why was he denied the blessing? Hadn't he done enough yet?

He had taken his wife to Medugorje before ethnic war cut the place off even from the most pious of pilgrims and she had fallen on her knees at the sight of the sun dancing. He had told her not to stare at it or she would go blind. She replied that she could plainly see the face of John F. Kennedy in the sky. The moral guardian looked up and saw a motionless ball of fire set in vivid and uncompromising blue, the earth spinning round and round it and pivoting on its own axis.

But the blossoms had fallen from the sky, hadn't they? He had the proof. Opening his notebook, he half-expected to find nothing or dust. The petals had squashed against the pages bleeding into them. It had been a windy day, he remembered. The blossoms could have been blown from a garden or park, tossed high in the sky to fall at last on believers and sceptics alike.

Away in Brittany Francis had missed his piano. On his return he tried to make up for time lost, practising every spare moment but making slow progress with the Bach pieces which were described as 'simple' but which were often as intricate as embroidery. At last he considered taking lessons. He wrote down a telephone number from the noticeboard in Walton's music shop.

Sonya seemed glad to see him back. 'You missed my party,' she said. 'It was wild. The guards came.'

She was delighted with her little wooden figure. 'I'll hang it in my room,' she said. He had never seen her room, never seen any room in the house but the old dining-room and the terrifying kitchen. And of course the lavatory – old thunderer, so called because of the alarming sounds it made when flushed. It was on the first landing, along with a prehistoric bathroom where an old iron bath stood on curved legs. Since his last visit the bath had been painted inside with the figure of a mermaid, green hair entwined with seaweeds, her tail curling under the large brass taps, a blankness in her pearly eyes. 'My friend did that,' Sonya explained. 'The one who lived in the extension.'

Liam informed his mother that Marion was complaining she never saw Francis these days. 'Probably got another woman,' Liam's mother commented. Liam, who had never had any woman, laughed merrily.

Valerie wrote a couple of passionate letters to her English boyfriend and got a scribbled postcard in reply which she showed to all her girlfriends. 'Irish boys are crap,' she told them, shivering at certain memories. In bed at night she rubbed her nipples and put a finger up inside herself, whispering dirty words into the pillow.

Borrowing Tom's beautiful Zeiss camera, Ruth went alone one day to Malahide and took a series of close-up photographs of the strange rock formations there, the fossils that looked like prehistoric jelly fish, the pebbles, weeds, lichens. Part of it was for her own satisfaction, part was for her new classes, about to start. She felt her students needed to be educated in looking, that, all right, so you want to depict something real, it doesn't have to be a vase of flowers or a cottage nestling in the mountains or waves shattering on a chocolate mousse. The photographs showed a real world of obscure forms. She had collected pictures of molecules, images from space, magnified crystals. She would get her students to bring in their own examples, forcing them to look and think.

She sat, gazing across the estuary at the long beach that led to Donabate, that you could surely walk across when the tide was out, sinking to your knees in the wet sand. Elderly couples strolled past, arm-in-arm; children played ball games in the distance; someone was flying a kite like an enormous orange butterfly. Suddenly, a mist came up, a wet greyness rolling in. Children, butterfly, everything was suddenly gone. Ruth walked out towards the sea, bare feet slapping the hard ridged sand. A white dog came running past her, as though materialised from fog. It quickly disappeared again, its paw-prints already dissolving in small pools. Droplets of water pearled her hair and skin. Sounds were muffled, the distant lap, lap of the waves. It was the end of summer. Going home as darkness fell, Ruth smelt aromatic smoke from a turf fire.

For his fourteenth birthday at the end of August, Gerald asked for and received a computer game which enabled him to play God. He could create a world, build it up and then destroy it by plague, earthquake or drought, or even cause an asteroid to collide with the planet, sending it out of orbit, hurtling into space. Then a message would come up on the screen: 'The planet has now entered a black hole and has been crushed to an atom the size of a pin-head.' Like a leader corrupted by power, he could organise lesser devastations, nuclear war, biological war; he could sell arms to one state enabling it to wage war on another; he could pursue a policy of disinformation causing governments to fall; he could build armies, brothels, prisons. He was omniscient and omni-present. The tiny figures on the screen moved as he directed them: he could decide whether to control them totally or whether – and the game was more challenging with this option – to grant them a measure of free will.

The picture of Ireland's Eye hung over the fireplace where artificial coals burned with a gassy flame but were not consumed.

'Like sinners in hell,' Francis thought.

At least Marion had not returned to her painting class.

'The teacher wasn't up to much,' she said.

She was now busy weaving, continuing Italian and doing aerobics in a shiny pink leotard with leggings.

Francis had found his music teacher rigid. She was a young woman who believed in doing things by the book and was horrified to hear that he wanted to start on Bach. She sent him off to buy a Grade 2 tutor and a manual of scales. He diligently practised the Carl Czerny pieces but they gave him no pleasure. Even less did he derive from the scales and arpeggios. When he finished the four lessons he had paid for in advance, he forced himself, sick with nerves, to announce to the teacher that he was not continuing. She took the news calmly and Francis failed to discern any regret on her face.

With a sigh of relief, he picked up his Preludes again, and though he could only stumble through them, he felt at times the same mystery as when he drew his hand over the standing stone.

He hardly ever saw Sonya these days. She was rehearsing for a play at last, a new play to be put on by a company with less than two pennies to rub together.

'Part of the theatre festival,' Sonya told him, though they weren't in the official brochure.

At least it proved she really was an actor. He had started to wonder.

Was it imagination or were her new classes immeasurably better than last year's? Ruth found them a joy to teach: the students were open to new ideas; they liked her photographs and brought in pictures of their own or found objects that challenged conventional perceptions. A jam-jar, when held to the eye like a telescope, blurred outlines, making colours run together. A microscope, the property of the child of one of them, gave close-ups of an insect's wing, a piece of fabric, a petal. Tom lent her his kaleidoscope that instead of containing the usual coloured glass beads was open-ended, its mirrors cutting and multiplying beyond recognition a section of face, the classroom, the view from the window. It never occurred to her that because she was happier in herself she was a better teacher and the students were merely responding to this. Her own pictures reflected her well-being, the colours were richer, the forms more harmonious. She painted one for Starveling of a white dog in a mist rearing up on his hind legs towards an enormous orange butterfly.

It wasn't that the moral guardian was stupid. Not at all. That was his problem. That was why it was hard for him. Life was much simpler for stupid people.

His wife was stupid. In his experience, women in general were stupid. Evil and stupid. There must be a reason, he thought, why 'Eve' and 'evil' sounded so alike. 'Evelyn' – there had to be a connection. Women were responsible for the way men behaved. Once he had heard a mullah – on television, of course – describe women as provocative and he was right. They brought men down; they weakened them. Delilah cut off Samson's hair.

The Muslims had the right idea, ordering women to cover themselves. Throughout the summer, the moral guardian had looked angrily at girls in shorts, waggling perky little backsides. Women wearing only tee-shirts over breasts that hung and wobbled like jelly, their nipples sticking out sharply. Skirts slashed up the back revealing the inside of bare thighs as they walked. It was disgusting. The moral guardian choked with loathing. Even his own old wife, whom he hadn't touched for years, wasn't above displaying her wrinkled dugs to him as if to incite him to that act which had been performed by them in the past with a view to the procreation of children. No children came. The woman was barren, as the Bible said. Less than useless.

Strangely enough, the books he was reading at the time, even the so-called classics, the books everyone praised, seemed to feature prostitutes or women who were no better, women who sapped their men, drawing the virtue from them. Legibly printed and neatly enclosed within little boxes, he wrote copious comments in the margins.

'Women bring God's wrath down on men.'

'Women are irrational and should submit in all things to men.'

'Women are provocative. They should cover their nakedness, not flaunt it.'

'Women are the Devil's instrument. They have the blood curse.'

'Burn, witches. As you will in hell.'

In the library, Maureen showed the books to Francis. She was laughing.

'What a nutter!' she said. Francis read the words and saw nothing to laugh about.

Most of Tom's friends were other journalists. When they met they discussed current stories and personalities – politicians, business-men, scandals – that Ruth, who never bothered with newspapers, knew nothing about. Sometimes they left her alone with her thoughts; sometimes the more gallant ones tried to draw her into the conversations where she betrayed her utter ignorance.

'She's a Brit,' Tom would say, challenging her, 'Her mother's a black Protestant.'

And Ruth would laugh because that was what was expected of her.

One night they met the fat teacher, Fionn, and his wife, Maeve, who, Ruth now discovered, were friends of Tom's. Maeve had borne six children, all boys, and looked like Mother Earth with a serenity, Ruth thought, that possibly came straight out of a pill box.

When Tom, as usual, introduced Ruth as a Protestant Brit, the fat teacher turned to her and remarked, 'Do me a favour. Get out of this country and take the troops with you.'

Another time Fionn said to her, 'Imagine there was a button on this table. Imagine I could press this button and eliminate all the Brits, every fucking one. Do you think I'd hesitate? Do you?'

He banged his fist on the table and eliminated her.

Nobody noticed, except perhaps Valerie, who couldn't care less, that Gerald was becoming even more introverted, even more remote. Marion was simply glad he was going out more, assuming he had made some friends. Neither she nor Francis observed that when he returned home he was unnaturally excited and his eyes glittered.

The first night of Sonya's play was a jolly enough occasion. Most of the tickets had been given free to friends – who were determined to enjoy themselves – or to reviewers from the press, a couple of whom actually turned up. But because it was theatre festival time, these reviewers were not the first- or even second-line critics, who were busy attending more prestigious shows. One was an agricultural correspondent whose wife had wanted a free night out. The other was a very young sub-editor who had only been to the theatre once before in her life. Neither was terribly impressed. The agricultural correspondent's wife was so shocked by the bad language and simulated sex that at the interval she installed herself in the lounge of the nearest respectable pub and refused to go back. The agricultural correspondent, who after all was working, sat on miserably through an endless second act taking pages of notes, none of which he subsequently used and anyway in the end there was no room in the paper for the review. The sub-editor praised the acting of one of the men because she fancied him but conveyed that everything else about the play was total rubbish.

Tom thought so too, snorting derisively.

I told you it wasn't up to much,' Ruth said, 'They devised it themselves but none of them is a writer. There are good ideas in it but it needs shaping.' She wanted to be charitable, having had a hand in the show, designing and making the set for no more than the cost of the materials. Just painted flats but well done, not tacky. Tom had told her off over it.

'You'll never get anywhere if you keep doing people favours.'

But at least they got free tickets, though Tom would have joined the agricultural correspondent's wife after the interval if he had been allowed.

'Darling, you were marvellous,' he assured a glowing, irony-proof Sonya after the show. 'Isn't that what I'm supposed to say?'

Ruth kissed her friend and squeezed her hand.

Francis didn't think much of it either but he went on the last night when the hall was nearly empty and the actors were demoralised after a bad run. Sonya's acting was not impressive; she spoke either too softly or too loudly and her arms sawed the air. Part of the problem was doubtless the direction but the play was far too long and possibly unsalvageable. The only good thing about it, Francis thought, was the set.

Liam, engaged in installing a dimmer switch in Marion's wedge-shaped sitting-room, looked at the tomes scattered around and marvelled at Francis. His own reading matter extended not much further than the evening paper. He opened a biography of Montezuma and grimaced at the illustrations. He fingered *A Brief History of Time*, flipped through *The Man Who Mistook his Wife for a Hat*. (How could anyone do that or write a book about it for that matter?)

'Your husband!' he exclaimed to Marion, not for the first time.

She gave him his mug of coffee and a plate of homemade spritz biscuits, one end of each dipped in chocolate. 'He never reads them,' she said, 'They're just for show.'

'Oh,' said Liam.

'Well,' she went on, biting a biscuit and making a mental note that they were slightly too crumbly, 'I'm sure he means to read them. He starts them, then puts them down and picks up a detective novel and somehow never gets round to finishing the heavy stuff.'

Liam was glad of the feet of clay. Really, Francis wasn't up to much at all.

'So Andy's coming back after all this time,' he said with satisfaction.

'Yes, for Christmas. Mam and Dad will be pleased. They haven't seen him for nearly five years.'

Andy was Marion's brother, made good in Australia.

'Is he bringing the wife and kiddies?'

'No, Liam,' Marion leaned forward confidentially and put her hand on Liam's. He giggled uneasily. 'I'm afraid . . . well, I can tell you, as a friend of the family, as Andy's best friend . . . '

'Yes?'

'They're getting a divorce. One reason Andy's coming over is to tell mam and dad in person. Less of a shock you know.'

When Liam told his mother the news, she shook her head and pursed her lips as if she had been expecting nothing else. As for Liam, he went to bed softly whistling to himself.

Tom, it has to be said, was a bit of a hack. He usually managed to keep his own beliefs out of the workplace. He only rocked the boat when the tide was turning and was chiefly distinguished for a flippant style and clever manipulation of clichés. Ruth began to suspect that the place he kept his politics was in fact the pub. He and his mates would get more and more radical as the night progressed and the empties piled up on the table. By forcible ejection time they were ready to start a revolution but generally bought a few six-packs instead and went home.

He had a flat on the southside of the city, with a fashionable Dublin 6 address. Ruth didn't care for it; it had a colour-supplement look about it and indeed Tom's previous girlfriend was a designer and had done it over in grey, white and black. A dove grey carpet that Ruth was almost afraid to walk on went wall-to-wall. The large padded couch and two armchairs were of black leather with one red cushion on each, like spots of much-needed blood, a metal chair not for sitting in stood against a wall, an expensive music centre had its own stand next to a yucca plant. A glass-topped coffee table was too casually strewn with magazines – *Time, Newsweek, Business and Finance*. A grey clock melted on the white wall in imitation of something out of a Salvador Dali painting. On another wall, a large black and white photograph looked like a desert landscape but on closer inspection turned out to be a close-up of part of the female body, cleverly angled somehow across breasts and buttocks. Ruth was forever staring at it, trying to work it out until Tom pointed out it was two women entwined. She decided she hated it.

'You don't like the flat because you're jealous,' Tom told her with satisfaction, 'Because it's Jessica, her taste, her personality.'

That was partly true but Ruth didn't think she'd like it anyway. Above all she loved comfort and everywhere comfort was sacrificed to style. The minimalist Japanese bedroom contained a futon, a hanging scroll depicting a bird on a branch of flowering cherry, a lacquered screen concealing a wardrobe, and a bonsai tree. The futon was possibly good for the back but terrible for love-making. The spotless kitchen would put you off cooking in case you dirtied the surfaces, though Tom, who was a good cook, managed well enough. He was by nature reasonably tidy but also had a woman come in twice a week for a very modest amount. She thought Tom was a dote.

The Tom Ruth thought she knew couldn't live properly in this flat, except in the crammed study, where papers and files lay in heaps round the word-processor, on the floor, under the window with its view over red-tiled roofs. A slightly tattered chaise-longue stood against one wall and Ruth betted to herself that Tom slept more comfortably there than in among the *japonaiserie*. A bookcase overflowed: Tom Wolfe, Saul Bellow, Norman Mailer, Gore Vidal and Truman Capote in outrageous proximity – Ruth remembered reading somewhere that they hated each other's guts – Dermot Bolger, Roddy Doyle, John Banville, Martin Amis, Salman Rushdie's *Satanic Verses*.

She was amazed and touched also to come upon her sketch of Fionn, framed and hung on the wall alongside family photos and cartoons.

After the break-up of the marriage, Tom's wife had gone back to Galway but occasionally brought the two girls to Dublin to see their father. Tom was due to have them for a long weekend and suggested Ruth join them with Starveling.

She could hardly wait to see a six-year-old and an eight-year-old disporting themselves in the immaculate apartment.

It was unfair of Marion to say that Francis never read the tomes he brought back from the library. Out of a sense of duty, he usually managed to get at least a third of the way into them and often skimmed the rest. Thus the book on druids, though never finished, left Francis with a certain superficial expertise on the subject.

It was true, however, that he would turn with relief to detective novels, his mood dictating whether he preferred a cosy whodunnit in a rural or academic setting or the hard-boiled violence of the American school, Commander Adam Dalgleish or Steve Carella, Dame Adela Lestrange Bradley or Travis McGee. Reading one such, already treated to the attention of the moral guardian, he was amused to discover that though most objectionable words had been totally eliminated, the hawk-eye had let pass *merde!* and *fou-le-camp!* Not a French speaker then.

Francis also enjoyed puzzles and annoyed Marion late into the night with his logic problems and his crosswords without clues in which numbers stood for letters. Sometimes three, two or one letters were given and then it was easy enough to work out the rest, allowing for a basic knowledge of letter frequency – E being, of course, the most frequently occurring letter in the English language, followed by T – and the fact that Q is always followed by U. One puzzle in which no letters were given kept him awake till after one at which point Marion exploded. He had found E and then made no headway at all. E blank blank E blank E blank blank. It should be easy. As he lay in the dark, his head buzzing with letters, it suddenly came to him. It was a trick. He had fallen into the trap. The answer was *infinity*. As it turned out, there was only one E in the whole puzzle.

Tom had a nice car, fast and new, and sometimes took Ruth and Starveling out for trips into the country. When his daughters came, they drove north out of Dublin to Malahide, where there was a castle in spacious grounds with a wooden adventure playground and a model train museum. Around the elaborate rail system that filled half the room ran whole trains, stopping at signals and stations. Starveling was fascinated and pressed her face to the glass. The rest of the room was taken up with display cases containing toy trains with tiny compartments where matchstick-sized people read newspapers, ate meals, looked out of windows as people do on trains. On a continental sleeper, a naked woman stood in front of a mirror, pulling her long hair up on top of her head.

The girls, attired in frilly frocks with snow-white ankle-socks and black patent leather shoes, giggled a lot and demanded a constant drip of ice-cream, chocolate, drinks, attention. They peered at Starveling and giggled some more at each other. Ruth disliked them irrationally – they were too young to know better – so she transferred her aggravation to Tom, who, she felt, should have prepared them.

'Come on,' he said, 'Hannah doesn't notice.' He always called Starveling by her given name.

'I notice,' Ruth said, 'And it upsets me.'

'Well, you'll have to get used to it,' Tom replied, 'because it's going to keep happening.'

Starveling thought the girls were wonderful and tried to do everything they did, following them round the playground, down the slide, across the swaying wooden bridge, into the little house.

'She's coming, she's coming!' the girls shrieked at each other as Starveling tottered after them, chuckling, stretching her arms towards them, delighted with herself and the great game and her new friends, not knowing and never to know that she had been fixed unmercifully forever in the role of monster.

At first, the fact that Francis seemed to have lost interest in sex relieved Marion more than it worried her. On holiday in Brittany, in the tent, she had put it down to modesty. Everything, everything, was audible from the next tent and Marion assumed Francis had no desire to put on a similar sound-show for the benefit of the rest of the campers, never mind their own children.

On their return to Dublin, he made love to her once, perfunctorily, drumming his fingers on her back in a strange way. After that, nothing. Gratitude gave way to anxiety. Was she no longer attractive then? She would lie awake worrying about it instead of planning improvements in domestic arrangements. Not that the house suffered, of course; she was too much of a professional for that. But the dimmer was the last of the innovations. He was out so much and when he was home, he was abstracted. Not that he was unpleasant to her; he was always polite. And when she rolled towards him in bed, he responded in a friendly way. But not as a lover.

One morning quite early, Francis walked up the overgrown path to Sonya's house, only to hear music ringing out of an open window. In the long dining-room, a little old lady sat at his piano playing a reel, a broad smile on her face, her tiny feet hardly reaching the pedals, let alone the floor.

Francis applauded her when she finished.

'Thank you,' she said. 'Are you the young man who owns the piano?'

'I suppose so,' he replied, amused to be considered young.

'I used to play quite well,' she said

'You still do,' he complimented her.

'Well, I'll leave you to it,' she got up, a fairy-story old lady with her white hair and lace-collared lavender dress.

'No, please play,' Francis said. Who was she?

'One more then,' she smiled. 'Do you like "Haste to the Wedding"?'

'I'm sure I do.'

She played, tapping her tiny foot against the leg of the chair, her fingers whizzing over the keys.

'I'm getting the hang of it now,' she told him when she had finished.

'Play whenever you like,' he said. 'Are you staying here?'

'Oh yes. I'm Mary's grandmother.'

When he looked blank, she chuckled. 'Or what does she call herself these days . . . Sarah . . . Sophie . . . '

'Sonya?'

'Yes.'

'Her grandmother . . .?'

Sonya had told him her grandmother was dead. Her grandmother said Sonya was Mary. It was very confusing. Francis played a prelude that he usually found quite simple. His fingers tumbled over each other. He couldn't concentrate.

'How many grandmothers do you have?' Sonya asked him later when he confronted her in the kitchen. She had returned from a rehearsal.

'None.'

'Of course you do. Everyone does.'

'I had two. They're dead.'

'Don't say none then.'

'All right. I had two.'

'So do I. So does everyone.'

'You mean this is grannie number two.'

'I mean the grandmother who owned this house is dead. Charlotte Isabel is staying here temporarily having been kicked out by the son whom she was living with because his wife hates her and kept interfering with her things.'

'She says.'

'Yes.'

'Your uncle and aunt.'

'I suppose so.'

Sonya looked away as she did when she didn't want to pursue a subject.

'So what's all this Mary business?' he went on.

'I don't know what you mean,' she said.

The trouble was that Tom liked to go out drinking most nights and wanted Ruth to come with him. She could get Sonya to babysit sometimes or her neighbour's daughter, who was a kind and homely girl. But while Sonya wouldn't take money, the neighbour's daughter had to be paid and Tom never offered to contribute. He was into equality of the sexes, too, and expected Ruth to buy her rounds. While Ruth agreed with this, she was finding the financial burden quite heavy, especially as Tom often ate with her, had a healthy appetite and gave her nothing towards the cost of the meals.

She also got very tired, drinking late, then making love into the night. Starveling woke at six. Ruth could just about manage her teaching but couldn't work at her own pictures.

When she told Tom she was having problems and suggested they stay in and only go out at weekends, or he go out without her, he got sulky and because she was fond of him and didn't want to hurt him, because of the sex and companionship, she gave in. But she was often irritable and weepy with frustration.

Tom was pleased to see Sonya when she arrived for babysitting purposes but resented it when Ruth arranged to go and see her without him.

'That kook,' he said, 'That head-case.'

He made fun of Ruth's students, which she resented. She did it herself, of course, but that was different. When Tom did it, he was somehow belittling not just them but Ruth herself and what she did. So she started defending them, which was grist to his mill.

'How were the Raphaels of Raheny today?' he would ask, 'The Donatellos of Donaghmede? The Bayside Botticellis?'

And when he had pushed Ruth to the brink, he would grab her and try and force his tongue into her mouth and she would fight and he would get excited and kiss her ear and lick her ear and she would rise like a wave needing to break and forgive him everything, everything.

They watched TV a lot, the moral guardian and his wife. They had no shared social life as such and never went out together in the evenings. In any case, the moral guardian considered the TV instructive, even if most of what was shown was totally reprehensible.

Thus they found themselves one night watching a film about an occasion when the Devil came to earth, in disguise of course, and seduced three women in a small American town. They proved only too eager to learn devilish ways from him and then, as women do, turned what he had taught them against him. Finally he was driven by a mighty wind into a church where a sermon was in progress. Far from being struck down by the sight of the crucifix as devils usually are, he started haranguing the congregation, denouncing womankind as God's mistake.

'You think God can't make mistakes,' the Devil said. 'Of course He can. Only His mistakes are called *Nature* .' The Moral Guardian was riveted. It was exactly what he thought himself. Inconceivable that he should agree with the Devil, only of course it wasn't the Devil at all but an actor and the words were put in his mouth by some writer.

The women finally destroyed the Devil in a peculiarly horrid way – the moral guardian's wife couldn't stand it and went out to the kitchen to make tea. But of course, the Devil can't be destroyed and at the end of the film you knew he was still there and might one day return. 'I didn't think much of that,' the moral guardian's wife said, giving him his tea. 'Weird. But then of course that actor's a bit strange in real life. I read there recently that he . . . '

And so she went on, burbling as usual. One of God's mistakes.

Sonya's other grandmother, Charlotte Isabel Dove, was frequently in evidence now whenever Francis arrived to play on his piano. She would scurry out from some corner, often clutching a feather duster with which she whisked the dust off the furniture and up into the air. Or else she might be wearing a snow white apron and pink rubber gloves as if she had been scrubbing in the kitchen. Francis doubted whether she really did anything. The house never seemed any cleaner or tidier than before.

Although she smiled a lot, she was always full of complaints and was often searching for some item that she had misplaced, looking suspiciously even at Francis as if considering whether he might have stolen it. One day it was her cameo brooch, which she was actually wearing, pinned high up under her chin, but when Francis pointed this out to her she gave him a sharp glance as if he had just performed a particularly astonishing feat of prestidigitation.

Otherwise she was a pleasant old soul who enjoyed picking out a tune, reminiscing about her youth and even flirting gently.

She was quite a competent pianist as well – though she never played the minuets and sonatas that had been rapped into her as a girl – and was able to give Francis some practical hints such as how to hold his hands over the keys and the correct height of the chair – he ended up sitting on Volume I of *The Decline and Fall of the Roman Empire*, abstracted from a bookcase.

She was sleeping in one of the upstairs rooms, claiming that the extension would frighten her at night – leaves brushing the windows, creatures hopping or scurrying on the roof; you never knew who might be prowling around. Francis suspected that Sonya had encouraged the fears because she planned to rent out the extension and didn't want her grandmother to get too comfortably settled in.

Sometimes, guiltily, Francis tried to pump Charlotte Isabel about Sonya, or Mary as she insisted on calling her, but on this subject the old lady's lips were stubbornly sealed. This of course only served to increase his curiosity and make him wonder if there was after all a melodramatic secret attached to the girl.

Gerald was staring at the computer, rap music pumping into his head through his walkman. He had been sitting motionless like that for some time as on the flickering screen the city continued to throb with life, people walking the streets, entering buildings, driving in open cars while he sat with his trembling finger poised above the button of the joystick, the sniper on the rooftop selecting a target, ready to eliminate.

PART THREE

BURIED ALIVE

On stage, Old Joe, the Signor, was renowned for his 'expiring faces', ludicrously mimicking the last moments of life. But as is often the case, the source of the humour was a darkness within. Old Joe was morbidly preoccupied with death and was in the habit of seeking out graveyards and wandering around them for hours. Once he even played dead to see the reaction of his sons. Johnny leapt in the air for very joy, for Old Joe at home was not the gullible and foolish Pantaloon he played on stage but a violent and even sadistic father.

'Hooray!' Johnny shouted gleefully, over the supposed deathbed, 'Now we can have the cuckoo clock.'

The other son, young Joe, no less overjoyed at his father's apparent demise but smelling a rat, feigned deep and inconsolable grief. Needless to say, when the truth was revealed the one was rewarded and the other severely beaten.

The Signor also had a superstitious dread of being buried alive. That was why he made grisly arrangements to be decapitated before burial.

He was not alone in this fear. The Russian writer Nikolai Gogol, a nutcase if ever there was one, was also obsessed by it. In his case, moreover, the phobia was perhaps prophetic as, when his tomb was opened for whatever reason, Gogol's head was found to have twisted

*round and his face frozen in a hideous grimace that apparently accords
with a last gulping fight for breath. An expiring face.*

Tom had been on a trip to England and brought back a huge box
of fireworks for Hallowe'en. All over the city, children turned
pagan, stole anything that would burn to make giant bonfires on
any spare patch of waste ground. They planned their gear:
skeletons, vampires, terminators, zombies, witches, punks.

Ruth's kind neighbour's daughter had offered to take Starveling
out 'trick-or-treating' with her own younger brothers and sisters
and Ruth made her a little columbine outfit, whitened the face
that was held up to her puzzled, and pinked the cheeks and lips.
She showed Starveling the strange creature in the long mirror
inside the wardrobe and Starveling failed to recognise herself until
she raised a hand to her cheek and touched herself and white
came away on her fingers.

'You're only gorgeous, Hannah!' the neighbour's daughter said,
and pulled her out into the night, large-eyed, clasping her goody
bag.

Later, Tom was to pick them up and take them to Fionn's for
the fireworks and barbecue.

Ruth sat alone in the silent cottage, staring into the red glow
of her turf fire until disturbed by the first of a succession of midgets
hammering on her door, demanding that she help the Hallowe'en
party.

Valerie was getting ready to meet her friends (in a pub, though
her parents didn't know it) and go on to a disco. She had another
boyfriend now, less experienced than her holiday romance who
had stopped writing altogether. She still sighed for him at times
while Deco fumbled at her hooks and eyes with clammy hands.

She locked herself in the bathroom and took so much time in a bath full of perfumed oils that Gerald had to use the en suite cubicle in his parent's bedroom.

'We ought to have a downstairs loo,' Marion commented.

Francis stared at the television in the dimmed light of the wedge-shaped living room. It was another mindless programme about a detective who was so fat he looked as if he was about to explode. Marion didn't know what Francis saw in it.

'Don't you think so?' she said. 'A downstairs loo.'

'For God's sake, Marion, where would we put it?'

He stood up.

'You're not going out?' Marion asked him.

'I thought I would,' he said. 'Won't be long.'

He smiled at her but his eyes wavered.

'See you later.'

Marion always felt slightly nervous on Hallowe'en night. Not that she feared the spirits of the dead; it was the malice of the living she dreaded: the youths who stole the stakes and trellises from your garden to throw on their bonfires, who lit their bonfires under trees or near power lines, who put bangers in your letterbox for fun because your house was so much nicer than theirs. Not that any of this had ever happened to her. Not yet. She shivered nearer the gas fire to warm herself at the fake coals.

'Watch out, this one's a volcano,' Tom shouted from the bottom of the garden.

He lit the fuse and ran out of the way. After a few seconds, the firework exploded in golden sparks. Oohs and aahs burst from the kids, except Starveling, who gazed in silent awe.

'Here,' Fionn gave her a sparkler, which she dropped in shock. Ruth picked it up, still sparking and helped Starveling hold it.

Soon she was whizzing it round and round like the rest of the children, her whitened face gleaming with delight. Too soon it finished and first stunned, then heartbroken, Starveling could only be consoled by another and another until they were all gone. But then the rockets were a distraction, soaring into the sky and raining down multi-coloured stars.

The children ate burgers cooked on the barbecue, the adults kebabs with salad and garlic bread. As well as cans of beer, there was mulled red wine, spiced with cinnamon and cloves.

Tom was still attending to the Roman Candles, Silver Fountains, Catherine Wheels, surrounded by noisy kids. Maeve was pouring cups of coke for them, looking for the ketchup, cleaning a cut knee and wiping tears from a small, dirty face, as she smiled beatifically to herself. Fionn sat down next to Ruth, a can in his hand.

'Hello, Englishwoman,' he said.

Oh no, she thought. 'Aren't they beautiful,' she remarked, 'I've always loved fireworks.'

He was staring at her, a significant expression on his face.

'Of course,' she went on, deliberately not noticing, 'there's always a horrible element in everything. Did you know – well, of course you must know – the Catherine wheel is so called because St Catherine was killed on a burning wheel?'

'You and I . . . ' Fionn said intensely, 'you with your English ice, me with my Celtic fire . . .'

Ruth bit her lip.

' . . . do you know what we share?'

She dreaded what might be coming next.

'We share an existential panic.'

He put his hand on her knee.

'Do you understand me?' His face was very close to hers. 'I

63

think you do.'

He sat back suddenly, looking satisfied. Possibly he felt he had made another conquest.

'Why do you wear those ridiculous clothes?' he asked. 'You look like a clown.'

'If I didn't laugh at life, I would be in despair,' she half-quoted.

He shrugged. 'You, an artist, you should have some style.'

He talked as if he already owned her. In the next breath he would be telling her she should lose weight but would of course be insulted if she should say the same to him. Men were like that. Even Tom. She looked across to where he was busy setting the last few rockets, all to go off at once. He was showing a nine-year-old how to position the fireworks in the bottles and glanced across at Ruth and winked at her. She smiled back, filled with love.

Domenico and Alessandro Scarlatti, François Couperin, Jean-Philippe Rameau, Baldassare Galuppi, Girolamo Frescobaldi. New discoveries for Francis. He tried out the pieces with the right hand, then with the left. Sometimes there was a third voice, which made it more difficult but also more interesting.

Sonya was apparently out. The rest of the house was in darkness. He wondered if Charlotte Isabel Dove was in bed or gone or dead. He played by candlelight, the glimmer reflected in the window glass. Far in the distance he could hear the cracks and bangs of fireworks, see above the trees the occasional pink or green flare fall slowly to earth.

Under the flashing laser lights, to the throb of a slow song, Valerie and Deco clung together on the dance floor. She could feel his dick hard between them like a piece of pipe. His hands caressed her buttocks and pulled her towards him. She rubbed her body up and down against him.

'I got a johnny,' he whispered in her ear. 'I robbed it off me brother.'

She supposed sooner or later she'd have to go through with it. She glanced through her half-closed eye-lids, weighted down with mascara, to where her brother Gerald sat in a dark corner with a few fellas. Trust him to go to a disco and then not dance.

Coming in later from the car-park where going through with it would have to be postponed because Deco spurted as soon as she touched his naked penis, she noticed that her brother and the others were gone.

'I suppose the horny old bastard was chatting you up,' Tom said on the way home.

'Kind of. Not seriously.'

'Why not seriously? What's wrong with you, then?'

She couldn't win.

'I don't think he's ever serious. He adores his wife and that's why she's so blasé . . . She knows it doesn't mean anything.'

'That's not what I've heard.'

'From him? I wouldn't believe a word he said.'

'No. From informed sources. They say he thinks up very unusual punishments for certain nubile students kept late for detention.'

'That sounds very unlikely.'

'The girls are only too willing, apparently.'

'Tom, you're not serious. He's so unattractive.'

'When did that ever stop anyone? In any case, he has power. That's always a turn-on for some.'

'If the nuns heard about it, he'd be out on his ear, disgraced.'

'The nuns are in on it.'

'Hah!'

'Honestly. They're crying out for it.'

'As in Boccaccio, I suppose . . . the dumb gardener in the convent. That's another gratifying male myth.'

'Don't think I don't know what you're talking about. I saw the film too.'

Ruth laughed because otherwise Tom would start to sulk and accuse her of intellectual oneupmanship. For some reason, some obscurely rooted sense of inferiority, he always got touchy on this point. In fact she had been sorting through a box of books that she had been unable to shelve in Sonya's house and had rediscovered an old edition of the *Decameron* that she had bought years before in a second-hand shop in Colchester for its delicately hand-coloured etchings. Now the charming tales read before sleeping edged over into her dreams, tinting them light blue and pink and pale yellow.

To change the subject, she glanced at the back seat, where Starveling was slumped asleep. Her make-up had smudged and faded, her columbine suit was dirty.

'She had a great time.'

'All those repressed women, screaming for it.'

'They don't in general, you know.'

'What do you know, you cold bitch? You cold, Protestant bitch.'

She saw now that for some reason Tom was desperate for a row. He had been drinking, of course, but until that moment she had thought no more than usual. Why did he want to spoil a good night?

He drove down to Bull Island and out on to the beach where cars were stopped while their inmates talked or kissed or screwed or stared at the sea lit intermittently by a crescent of moon coming out from behind ragged clouds. He thundered along the beach away from everyone else, driving into the edge of the waves and stopped the car, trembling.

'He had his hand on your knee,' he said. Was that it? Was that all?

He threw himself at her over the gear stick.

'Starveling,' she whispered. 'You can't.'

He opened the car door and marched around to her side to pull her out.

'No,' she said. 'No.'

'I want to fuck you, you bitch,' he said, pulling her arm.

She ran to the sea and as he caught hold of her, threw herself down in the icy water and sobbed, salt to salt.

When they saw what had happened, the boys huddled in the dark alleyway ran off in confused terror. They couldn't be blamed, it was later said. They were victims, too. It was lucky they made so much noise and aroused the suspicions of a passing off-duty guard and his girl, who took a look down the alleyway to see if there had been a break-in.

The guard, who had a certain training, did what he could, while his girl went off to call an ambulance.

Marion sat alone in the town house watching television, not a scary Hallowe'en film, not by herself. A news programme about a war in a remote part of the world.

She listened out for returning footsteps, the car.

When the phone ran, she jumped with annoyance – one of the children wanting a lift home and Francis not yet back.

It wasn't the children. She listened carefully, trying to stay calm. Then she phoned Liam.

Jealousy. Ruth had never been on the receiving end before, not of such violent emotions. She had picked Tom out of the sea and led him back to the car. He was incapable of driving and so, though she hadn't sat behind a wheel for many years, though she hadn't a clue how to operate this model, though her brain was muzzy with drink and tiredness and unhappiness, she drove them jerkily back, across a narrow wooden bridge down the coast road to her little cottage. Starveling slept through everything, the darling, and merely opened her eyes on arrival without waking. Ruth kissed her and put her to bed without changing her.

She contemplated leaving Tom in the car, but he was soaked and it was a frosty night.

Baldassare. A strange name. Balthazar, probably, like one of the Three Kings. Baldassare Galuppi.

Francis played the little dance softly as it was very late and though he didn't think there were people in the house, he couldn't be sure. He had been half hoping, more than half hoping to see Sonya. Probably she was out with friends, at a party perhaps, having fun, laughing. He imagined her laughing, her strange little mouth turning down in that way it had.

He blew out the candles and, reluctant to switch on the electric light that would dissipate the magic mood, felt his way to the door, into the silent hall, a shadow passing over the huge mirror, out into the diamond night, crunching over the gravel path, still hoping she might suddenly come.

Marion was inexplicably gone. Before he could read the note, Valerie crashed down the stairs.

'Mam's been ringing and ringing,' she screeched, 'Gerald's in hospital . . . '

'What? . . . Calm down. What's happened?'

'You weren't here and he's nearly dead. You weren't here.'

The details only emerged much later. His son had left the

disco with a gang of boys. They had made their way to a dark alleyway, no doubt giggling in nervous anticipation. They had opened plastic carrier bags and removed various aerosols. Gerald had brought an air freshener from his parents' en suite bathroom, 'April flowers'. He had inhaled and choked and passed out. The other boys, unable to wake him up, had run off in terror. Luckily a passing off-duty guard and his girl had found him before it was too late. Marion and Liam were now with Gerald at the hospital.

'Liam?' Francis queried.

'Because you weren't here.'

Sonya came downstairs slowly. The piano player had gone at last, taking his jerky tunes with him. She smelt the pungent smoke from the extinguished wax candles. She stumbled into the dark room and lit one of the candles again with a match from a box she was gripping in her cold hand. She opened the window and watched the flame flutter wildly. It was the night the dead walked. Sonya sat on the floor of the room and waited for her dead to come to her.

Even if she had wanted to sleep, the snoring would have kept Ruth awake. Tom was lying on his back, his mouth open, performing a modernistic sonata on nasal tubes.

Ruth was exhausted but her brain was still whizzing round and round like a carnival carousel gone mad. She crept out to the kitchen to make herself a camomile tea which was comforting and allegedly soporific. Then she settled back into bed, lighting the lamp that Tom always claimed disturbed him so that when he stayed the night she was unable to sit up reading. Now, however, he was too far gone to be roused and she flipped through her *Decameron* to the last day and a story about a man who was constantly bothering a married woman with his attentions until she thought up a crafty way to stop him. She told him that she would only submit to his desires if he could give her a summer garden in the middle of January, clearly an impossible task. The man, however, hired a necromancer who went out into the snow and caused a beautiful garden to appear, full of herbs and fruits and flowers. Her bluff having been called, the woman confessed to her husband, who being, as the writer said, a man of honour, sent her off to fulfil her promise. The suitor, however, was honourable too and discharged her when he saw that she was motivated by duty and not love. Subsequently he and the husband became the best of friends.

Liam and Marion were sitting rigid in the hospital corridor, Liam holding Marion's hand. That was how Francis found them, like a sculpture, man and wife. Then finally Marion turned a face of blame towards him.

'Where were you? You weren't there . . . ' It was like a chant, started at home by Valerie, a chorus of Furies.

'How is he?' Francis asked.

'What do you care?'

'They're hopeful,' Liam said. 'They say we can go and see him in a minute.'

'We?' Francis thought, the family unit dissolving and reassembling.

'The doctor asked if we knew he sniffed glue,' Marion said.

'I didn't . . . Did you?'

'Don't be crazy! Do you think if I knew . . . ' Marion collapsed in tears on Liam's shoulder. Embarrassed, he patted her back and looked helplessly at Francis.

'Did you know?' Francis asked Valerie, white-faced now next to her mother.

'No,' the girl sobbed to cover the part-lie. All those other boys did it, Deco had said.

They went in to see Gerald, lying back linked to tubes and drips. His eyes were closed, his skin was bluish.

'He'll be out for a few hours,' they were told.

'Go home and rest.'

Marion didn't want to go home. How could she rest when her son was hovering between life and death? Finally Liam persuaded her.

'The hospital will ring when he recovers consciousness. There's no point sitting here all night.'

She didn't want to travel with her husband and quite frankly Liam could understand it. The man had made no attempt to apologise or explain his whereabouts. On the other hand, he was her husband and the father of the boy. Also, there were limits to the support Liam felt he himself could give.

Marion blasted Francis with blame all the way home and continued while he made them all a cup of tea. He was responsible. He had never shown any interest in the boy. Other fathers played football with their sons, took them to matches, tried to share their interests. Francis, on the other hand, did none of this and sometimes even forgot his own son's name. (He denied it, but softly. Let her get it out of her system.) Other fathers took responsibility for their children and she didn't just mean financially. It was easy enough to provide materially but what about spiritually and emotionally? When had Francis ever bothered about any of them? Valerie sat next to her mother through it all, staring at him resentfully. A new alliance.

The trouble was, Francis knew Marion was right or partially right. She had responsibilities too but he was not about to remind her of them now, as some of her bitterness clearly – he had read the early chapters of several books on psychology – emanated from her own sense of guilt. As she spoke, it was all he could do to prevent himself humming the undeniably catchy Galuppi melody and he thought with longing of the candlelit room.

'So where were you?' she asked suddenly.

And finally, regretfully, Francis told her.

Predictably, perhaps, Marion thought the piano was an excuse.

'I knew it,' she cried, 'I knew there was another woman. There had to be. You haven't had sex with me for weeks.'

Francis looked at her in amazement. And, embarrassed, at the girl Valerie, staring at him through smudged mascara.

'No,' he said.

'What age is she?' Marion asked. 'Come on, tell me.'

'It doesn't matter. It isn't important . . . I'm not . . . involved. Not like that.'

'What age is she?'

'I don't know.'

'Fifty? Sixty? Seventy?'

'No, of course not . . . Nineteen.' Sobs and laughter from Marion, a cold stare from the girl.

'But I'm not . . . sleeping with her.'

Marion stood up and pointed a shaking finger at him.

'If anything happens to Gerald,' she shrieked, 'it'll be because of you, because of your wickedness . . . You . . . fornicator . . . Get out of this house and go to your . . . nineteen-year-old. Go on. Go on.'

The phone rang like a scream. But it was only Liam, urged on by his avid mother, wondering if there was any more news. Marion started telling him about Francis. Liam tried to sound surprised but after all hadn't his mam seen it all along.

Francis fled upstairs, into the boy's room with its posters of rock groups Francis had never heard of, its sci-fi comics, its piles of computer games, its computer screen gleaming in the dim light like a dead eye.

He buried his head on the stranger's pillow.

In the morning, Tom rolled over on to Ruth and started making love while she was still asleep. The night before she had decided to end the relationship and had sat up rehearsing conversations in all of which Tom finally accepted the situation quietly. But now as his finger rubbed her clitoris, she tingled, she dripped juices like an overripe fruit, she lacked any power to push him away. They drank the wet morning sourness from each other's mouth and licked sweat from salty necks. Then Tom went down and put his tongue in her cunt. It was the only way she could reach orgasm, the small red tongue flicking in and out of her. She twisted herself round and took his penis in her mouth. Time pulled into an elongated thread as they pleased each other, her body rising and falling and rising ever nearer the unbearable peak, oh Jesus, oh God, until she pushed him away, crying 'No more, no more' and he turned again and put his penis inside her and came at last hard and fast and deep.

Afterwards she forgot all about the planned showdown.

Gerald recovered. Slowly. Marion, his mother, would sit at first by his high hospital bed, later by his own familiar divan, gripping his hand, staring intensely into his eyes until he wished she would go away. Sometimes Francis, his father, would stand behind her uncertainly, uneasily, looking away a lot.

Gerald didn't think much about his father. He had always had a shadowy identity for the boy – silent, preoccupied, often at work in the evenings when the children were home – and though occasionally in the past Gerald would have preferred a father who took more interest in him, at this stage of his life he was happy enough with one that left him alone. He didn't consciously feel let down by him at all, so that when his mother kept muttering that from now on things would be different, Gerald couldn't help hoping they would stay the same.

'What would you really like to do?' his mother asked. 'When you're better.'

Liam was there that day, an open-necked polo shirt under his jumper despite the late autumn chill, ready to spring into action, to take the boy jogging, swimming, canoeing, mountain-climbing.

'There's a new game out I'd like.'

'Yes? Yes?'

Gerald indicated the computer magazine he'd been reading.

'I don't know if it's available here yet.'

'Oh,' his mother's face changed, 'A computer game.'

'You need to get out more,' Liam cut in. 'Sitting in front of that screen all day ruins your eyes and softens your brains.'

'That's what I'd like,' Gerald said. 'That's what I really want.'

Sonya told Francis, in answer to his queries, that the extension flat was still free and that he could certainly move in if he wanted. The rent she required was embarrassingly low and he found that it would hardly inconvenience him at all to pay it above the money he habitually gave to Marion.

She didn't ask any personal questions and he didn't tell her any more than that he and his wife were thinking about a temporary separation.

But if Francis was hoping to be kicked out, he was disappointed. Marion, now that Gerald was no longer in danger, had stopped insisting that he leave and instead had taken the two of them along to a counsellor. This had been recommended by the hospital following Gerald's misadventure and Francis had been under the impression that it was his son who was to be discussed. It soon emerged, however, that it was the family that was under scrutiny and himself in particular. The questions, while not overtly accusatory, left him feeling he himself must take most of the blame for what had happened to his son.

But wasn't it too late to make amends?

'Not at all,' insisted the counsellor. 'Show the boy you value him as a person, give him the security of letting him know that you love him . . . '

The old woman was becoming worried about her husband, the moral guardian. He used to be just like anybody else but since he'd retired two years previously, he had become more and more peculiar. She put it down to the long hours spent in front of the TV or reading books. It wasn't healthy. And it wasn't as if he was enjoying himself. He was forever snorting in contempt at some programme or over a book.

'Listen to this,' he would say and read something out to her. Usually she had no idea what it was about and would respond with a 'Very nice' or 'My goodness' or something of the sort which would inevitably turn out to be the wrong response and make him even crosser. And now that the nights were drawing in and the weather was more often than not wet and cold, he no longer seemed interested in taking those long walks that gave her a welcome break from his cantankerous presence.

She sighed and put down her knitting. Retirement certainly didn't suit him even though during all those long years of working he had constantly complained that he never had the time to do what he really wanted.

'Coming to Mass, dear?' she asked.

He snorted in that horrible new way of his. That was another funny thing. In the last week or so he had stopped going to Mass, a life-time habit cut without a word of explanation. She'd get Father Byrne to have a chat.

When she came back from Mass, having postponed the awkward conversation with the priest – after all, maybe it was just a phase, a kind of change of life, men had those too, she'd heard – she found her husband in front of the television watching a foreign film. Most unusual. He was always giving out about subtitled films and bit her head off if she suggested he needed glasses, which he did.

When she asked what it was about, he snapped at her to keep quiet and she placidly resumed her knitting. And because the pattern was quite intricate – it was a lacy bedjacket in pink mohair – she couldn't really follow the story anyway. Indeed, she found the guttural, impenetrable language provided quite a soothing background for her work.

The moral guardian was watching a Dutch film about a man who performs an act of extreme courage, risking his life to save someone else. The universal acclaim that follows convinces the man, who had acted instinctively, that it is easy to be a hero. Much more challenging, he thinks, to be the opposite. He decides to commit a motiveless crime to prove his strength of will. He kidnaps a stranger, a woman, in a car-park and she is never seen again. Years later he is finally tracked down by her boyfriend, who has become obsessed with uncovering her fate. Ostensibly this boyfriend is the hero of the film but a much less interesting character in the opinion of the moral guardian. The man tells the boyfriend that he will show him what happened to the girl but first he must have a drink. The boyfriend guesses correctly that the drink is drugged but realises that unless he takes it he will never learn the truth. Curiosity overcomes him. He wakes to find himself sharing his girlfriend's fate. He has been buried alive. He starts to laugh.

'Was it a good film dear?' the moral guardian's wife asked him.

He started to laugh.

November. Perversely it was one of Ruth's favourite months, trees looming out of a grey mist with a few last orange or red leaves blazing from thin branches. The smell of decay and bonfires. Bright frosts that silvered the petals of belated rose buds now never to bloom. A melancholy time of year with tempests and floods and destruction.

Tom was going on a freebie to Brussels with a crowd of other journalists. Maeve in the pub one night told Ruth she should go with him.

'She can't,' Tom said too quickly.

'I wouldn't want to,' Ruth added.

'You should have a break though,' Maeve persisted. 'You're looking exhausted.'

Ruth didn't deny it.

'I'd take the wee one for a few days.'

'Ruth would hate Brussels. It's such a bourgeois town. And I'd be busy all the time . . . at conferences etcetera,' Tom said.

'Etcetera etcetera,' Fionn patted Ruth's arm. 'I'd be very careful about etcetera, Ruth.'

Later, she thought about the offer and phoned Maeve. A few days away by herself was just what she needed and Maeve was one of the few people she could trust to look after Starveling. Maeve's boys were nice, too, and casually kind, unlike Tom's daughters.

So Maeve took Starveling and Ruth headed off with wet gear,

a book of walks and a small rucksack to the mountains south of Dublin, to Glendalough. She found a bed and breakfast still open, run by an elderly woman with thirteen or so cats.

Glendalough was a place still possessed by the gods of prehistory. The sixth-century monastic settlement always seemed to Ruth an almost modern construction in the gloomy valley. On this solitary visit she walked a lot but also stood and listened as if at any moment she might hear ancient voices. The first day she climbed Camaderry in cold sunshine to the place where a line of trees seemed to career over the edge of the mountain like wild horses, gnarled and battered by the wind into unlikely shapes. She ran her hands over the rough trunks. She peered down the mountain side, across the black lake to the tiny wedge-shaped cave twenty feet above its surface where St Kevin had mortified his flesh as if the indifferent spirits of this place noticed or cared. Walking the next day through driving rain and a skeleton forest inexplicably blighted, she finally reached the incredible insurmountable wall of the Prison Rock that blocked off the valley end. It glowed in the dull light with the last purple heather, flaming bracken, shiny black granite viridescent with mosses, dripping, dripping. Down she plunged on the last day through a grove of pine as through a cave to the priory of St Saviour, white in a clearing, demon faces staring out of the stone. And everywhere such silence. Not even birdsong. Ruth tried not to think. She tried to clear her mind of all the trivia buzzing through it, to restore the broken link with the earth and the elements.

She didn't sit down in the open air and paint or sketch. It was too distracting when the curious – even this late in the year there were a few other visitors to the valley – peered over her shoulder and shrugged or giggled at the disparity between what their eyes told them and what they saw on her pad. In the evenings by the fire with the old woman and her cats, she felt constrained and ended up simply drawing the old face staring into the fire, recounting her life.

Not an interesting life, it had to be said. Banal even. The old woman was not a native of the area nor even of Wicklow and had found it, even after twenty, thirty years, impossible to be accepted by the dour local inhabitants. Or maybe she just felt it to be so, Ruth thought, another disappointed old person with memories of a girlhood when so much had still seemed within her reach.

Despite the counsellor's optimism and encouragement, Francis came to feel that it was too late for him to start again with his children. They were nearly adults. Without the foundation of early intimacy, it was like getting to know any new acquaintance. And would you bother if it was someone with whom you had nothing in common? Thinking it over, Francis found he was starting to blame Marion for the whole situation. She had controlled everything so effectively, she had managed everything so well, she had stolen the experience of fatherhood from him. That was when he was feeling sorry for himself. At other times, he put it down to his own weakness of character, his knack of taking the easy option, even his own selfishness.

Nevertheless, he tried. He took the two children out for a pizza meal and then to the cinema of their choice, an action-packed, crudely violent film that had him cringing in his seat while Gerald and Valerie placidly munched popcorn out of huge tubs (they'd only just eaten, for God's sake). He took Gerald to a match, both of them cold and wet and bored out of their minds. He tried to engage Valerie in conversation to find out what her interests were and was met with a wall of monosyllables that caused him at last almost to lose his temper.

Finally, one day while watching a American sit-com about a fat working-class woman and her even fatter husband, he told his son in the best tradition of the schmalz that was contaminating all language and relationships, 'Remember Gerald, I may not have been the best father in the world, but I'm always here for you.'

To which his son, intent on seeing how the fat couple would resolve their current problem, replied, 'Yes, dad. Sure.'

The year was already ending and Ruth was not much nearer compiling a collection of pieces for an exhibition than she had been in the summer. She had been unable to take advantage of the creative excitement inspired by her few days in Wicklow. There was simply no time. Her own work had to be squashed in somewhere between her classes, her responsibilities to Starveling and the exasperating complexities of her involvement with Tom, who had come back from Belgium full of assurances about how crazy he was about her.

It hadn't lasted. He had sat at her kitchen table the day after his return, a moody expression on his face.

'I didn't know you were planning to go away.'

'Maeve offered to take Starveling. It was a great opportunity. And I really needed a break.'

'It was to pay me out for going without you, I suppose.'

'Don't be stupid.'

'Whom did you go with?'

'No one.'

'Come on. Expect me to believe that.'

She looked at him. It was so typical of him to think that she had a mystery lover. It would of course be his first thought. Well, she was damned if she was going to offer any explanations.

He sulked. He wouldn't speak to her, staring at the television and drinking cans of Belgian beer. But in bed he rubbed up against her hopefully. And although she was tired out, because he was such a child, because it was easier to say yes than no, she let him make fierce love to her, resenting him and hating herself.

So her work suffered. Nothing she did satisfied her. Also she was worrying about money. The tiny income she received just wasn't enough, even with extras from the occasional sale or the even more occasional commission to design a stage set for some impoverished group of actors. After a few moments' thought, she started pinning up notices around the city and even invested in a three-day ad in Tom's paper (half-price because he reluctantly placed it for her) offering to paint or sketch portraits. She even briefly considered setting herself up in Grafton Street, providing instant images of passers-by alongside the buskers, the pavement artists, the people who wrapped coloured silks in your hair.

To her own surprise, she received several replies, mostly to the newspaper ad. As a result, she sketched the children of a man in Terenure who wanted a novel Christmas present for his wife. She charged him £50 and he paid so readily she wondered if she was underpricing herself. A company director looked slightly dubiously at examples of her work – she had done a couple of quick sample portraits of Sonya, Tom and Starveling, as well as the sketches of the old woman in Glendalough and her cats – but commissioned her anyway, no doubt because she was so cheap and offered to frame the picture for him, too. Because he was a busy man, he told her, he would have no time for sittings and slid a passport photograph across the table to her. She was having none of that and borrowed Tom's camera to a take a series of shots. As she daubed away at the portrait, evening after evening, Tom grumbled that she was selling her soul.

'I have to live,' she replied. 'At least I can worry about my soul on a full stomach.'

'Make sure he pays you,' Tom said. 'His company's in big shit.'

Which scared her into deciding to ask for an advance in future. The company director, however, paid without a query and even promised to recommend her to his friends.

And Ruth, who had diagnosed herself as suffering from artist's block, found to her surprise that she actually looked forward to the prospect of more such commissions.

The moral guardian didn't want to kill anyone. Not any person. But he would like to show himself capable of an extreme act, to prove that he no longer considered a vengeful god would punish him. To prove that he was his own god in the universe.

His wife was right to be worried about his reading. It had led him into strange by-ways. He was not merely watching foreign films, he was even reading foreign novels. They were different. No doubt about it. They had a different way of looking at things. They got under the surface. The only problem was the names. He found the foreign names confusing.

A movement in the garden – he was sitting in the back room facing out – caught his eye. The neighbour's cat, a large and ugly tom, was again defecating on his wife's beloved flower beds. Sometimes the cat even entered their house through an open window or door – how many times had he told her to keep everything shut! On those occasions it had sprayed its disgusting odour everywhere.

The guardian looked out at the cat, which looked back at him malevolently. Everything is permitted.

In the weeks of Gerald's hospitalisation and convalescence, Francis avoided visiting Sonya's house, convinced that somehow Marion would get to hear of it and there would be an almighty row. He was also still trying to spend as much of his free time as possible with his children until they became sick of the sight of his wistful and guilt-ridden face and wished he'd get lost. He never meant, however, for the abstinence to continue indefinitely and was, in fact, wondering how to engineer a resumption of his visits when Marion brought the subject up one day as the two of them were sitting in the kitchen eating supper.

'One good thing about Gerald's accident' (Marion always called it that) 'you've given up that silly business of the piano.'

'What?'

'We could always get a nice keyboard if you really want to play,' she said, her tone implying that no one actually believed it. 'Liam says they can be very compact. After all, that enormous great piano wasn't really suitable for this house, was it?'

'You can't put expression into keyboards. Keyboards don't have the same richness of tone.'

'I can't believe that heap of junk had any tone at all. Not the way you played it.'

She laughed. She really believed she was winning.

Francis looked at her – certainly an attractive woman, even in her forties, but intimidating somehow, the dark hair blow-dried and laquered into submission, the meticulously applied make-up, pearly green shadow on her eyelids, pearly coral on her lips, pearl varnish on her finger nails. She glittered discreetly. She had dressed up for some reason and wore the tailored navy suit with the shoulder pads and straight skirt that gave her a formidably military look.

'I can't give up the piano,' he said.

She gripped the counter.

'You mean, you can't give up the girl.'

'That's not what I mean. Let me bring the piano back here. I'll never see Sonya again.'

'Sonya?' she laughed as if he had made a joke. 'What a name! Sounds like a Swedish au pair.'

'Don't ... ' He suddenly felt dizzy and sick. He couldn't breathe. 'Please ... '

But Marion was remorseless. 'I'm not having that thing in this house and that's final.'

He couldn't argue. Not then. He felt terrible, as if something was pressing down on him, closing in on him.

Marion, seeing how grey and sick he looked, relented, suggesting a holiday.

'This time of year?'

'Just a few days down the country. To enable us all to get to know each other again. We've been through a lot. We all need to relax.'

'I can't get the time off. We can't afford it.'

'Just a few days. A winter weekend. I'd say for Christmas only of course Andy is coming, so we can't do that.'

The prospect filled Francis with unspeakable dread. He dreamt he was caught in a thick spider's web and woke up cold and wet and gulping for breath. The doctor diagnosed asthma which, he assured the patient, sometimes develops in middle age. Francis was given an inhaler. Then he dreamt he was asleep and woke up to find himself trapped in a wooden box. He groped in the dark for his inhaler and failed to find it. Marion had tidied it up.

'Can you hear something?' the guardian's wife asked, turning in bed.

The guardian said that he could not. Sweat was running down his face, his hands stung from the scratches the cat had given him before he managed to get it in the box. Afterwards he had started pruning the roses to provide an adequate explanation for the wounds. His wife was delighted that he was at last taking an interest in the garden – wasn't that what retired folk were supposed to do? He had even been digging the weeds behind the shed. She told him to be careful and wear gloves next time.

Next time. There would be no next time. He'd proved himself. Hadn't he?

The muted wails of the buried cat grew weaker and finally stopped.

A week later the heartbroken neighbour had almost given up hope that puss would ever return.

'I told her,' the guardian's wife said, 'maybe the cat's gone to live with someone else. Maybe someone else liked him so much they took him.'

The guardian buttered his toast.

'Mm,' he said.

'Of course, I don't really believe that myself. I'd say he was run over or else picked up by one of those vans they say goes round at night, collecting them for their fur. I didn't tell her that,' the wife concluded. 'No need to cause unnecessary distress.'

'No,' said the guardian, taking a bite.

Philip saw Ruth's ad in an alternative bookshop in Temple Bar and rang her immediately. He suggested they should meet and she joined him in the wine bar where he worked and where they did good salads at lunch time. She showed him photographs of her portraits and he explained exactly what he wanted. They came to an arrangement.

When Tom saw the work in progress, he exploded.

'You're painting from a photograph I hope,' he said.

'No, from life.'

'Jesus!'

'What about Hannah?' Tom asked later.

'She's at play school . . . Philip comes over on Monday and Thursday mornings. That suits both of us.'

'Monday and Thursday mornings. Christ, Ruth!'

'What's wrong?'

'It's fucking pornographic.'

She liked Philip. He was excessively camp but very very funny and her morning sessions with him were relaxing. The first time he brought a red velvet cover which he threw over her couch, took off all his clothes and lay back in an attitude of sexual invitation which she tried not to find distracting. Clearly the invitation was not extended to her but to some future viewer of the picture.

'I want Egon Schiele without the angst,' he announced.

After the first moments she was able to consider his explicit nudity merely as an artistic challenge. Unfortunately, Tom was unable to let the matter rest. The fact that Philip was gay merely released his latent homophobia along with a suspicion that it was all a ruse to put him off the scent.

He burst in one Monday as they were finishing up, imagining perhaps that he would find them doing it. Luckily Philip was already dressed and he and Ruth were innocently drinking coffee together. But Ruth was furious at the way Tom sniffed around, at his ill-concealed hostility. When Philip had gone, she flew at him.

'Never do that again . . . Don't you dare insult my clients. I need them. I need the money, do you hear . . . You have no rights over me . . . What I do is my own business and if you don't like it you can piss off.'

Tom was gruff but, taken aback, as apologetic as he could ever be.

On his next visit, Philip asked if she had managed to calm her macho friend.

'I was totally terrified, love. He was so fierce. I couldn't help thinking, what if he'd arrived ten minutes earlier, when I was totally exposed. The mind boggles.'

Ruth agreed. Her mind had been boggling too. She didn't, however, tell Philip the words Tom had used to describe him.

When the picture was finished – and really it was rather good, Ruth extracting a promise from Philip to allow her to show it at her exhibition, if and when – it was to be hung in the wine bar she found out was actually owned by his partner, alongside some disconcerting photographs that Philip told her were the work of 'a pet of a Rumanian who passed through our hands during the summer.'

'Don't they put people off their guacamole?' she enquired.

'Not at all. They make them even hungrier,' Philip grinned. 'Just wait till they see me. They'll be totally ravenous.'

At her next class she was approached by one of her few male students, a pleasant-mannered, diffident man who always wore a neat suit even when painting, like the surrealist René Magritte.

'I saw, think I saw, one of your pictures in town . . . It looked like your signature.' It seemed he was beginning to blush. ' I thought it was really good.'

'Thank you,' Ruth smiled, wondering what in the world that particular, excessively straight-looking man could possibly be doing in that particular place.

Andy, Marian's brother, arrived in the middle of December for his Christmas visit to inform his parents about his impending divorce. They were not totally naïve. The fact that Andy had come alone at such a time of year had already led them to infer that something was up.

Francis had only ever met Andy twice before and had forgotten what he looked like, so his appearance didn't come as a shock. For Liam, though, the fat, red-faced, balding man was like a stranger. He even talked differently, with the Australian twang so familiar from TV programmes.

'Liam, me old mate,' Andy said jovially. 'You don't change.'

He laughed heartily at the fact that Liam had never married.

'Quite right, mate, look at me up shit creek without a paddle.'

The three men went drinking – 'It's the least you can do,' hissed Marion when Francis was about to demur – and Andy got maudlin drunk to the embarrassment of the others. They had to carry him home, where to general dismay he fetched a full bottle of whiskey out of his case and insisted on opening it. Marion made hot punch, ensuring Andy's was nearly all water, cloves and lemon.

'I've missed out all these years,' Andy sobbed. 'The bosom of me family . . . ' He clutched at Marion's breasts as if forgetting she was his sister. Soon after he was poured into Valerie's bed – she had been sent to stay with a girl friend.

'I'm glad we aren't having him here after all,' Liam later told his mother, whose decision against her son's wishes it had been. 'He's changed, Mam. He's changed.'

'Of course he has, son,' his mother said, knowing when not to crow. 'They all do.'

Andy soon moved, in fact, to his parents' house and at some point told them that he and Terry had decided to split up. Both parents were conservative Catholics so his mother's long face became longer and his father shook the round bald head that Andy's now resembled so startlingly.

'Divorce!' his mother whispered, as though the very word were anathema.

'Everyone does it over there, ma. All me friends split up.'

'That doesn't sound like a good reason to me,' his father said sternly.

'We can't stand each other any more. On and on and on at me she is, all the bloody time.'

'With good reason, perhaps,' his mother said, an image of flimsily-clad girlfriends flitting across her mind.

'No, not at all . . . On and on at me she is to get more money. On and on at me about spending the money we got. Like, it's all right for her to spend it. But all wrong for me.'

'Well . . . ' his mother said, remembering that she had always thought Theresa a rather hard and grasping type.

'She's got a new boyfriend anyway,' Andy went on. 'Owns a marina. Terry likes that. Always on at me to get a yacht. Now she's got a whole bloody marina full of them.'

The parents were shocked, no doubt about it. Of course they knew that sort of life went on; they read about it; they saw it on TV. They had never associated it with their son, educated so well by the Brothers.

'And the children?' his mother asked. Not that she knew them except through photographs and a holiday video sent the previous year.

'They think Brian's the bee's knees. Just because he takes them out shark fishing.'

'Good heavens,' said his mother.

Liam, hearing the news of the break-up again from Andy, this time in a relatively sober state, found himself sympathising with his old pal. He was after all hard done by. The signs of degeneracy and over-indulgence he now attributed to the fact that Andy, unlike himself, lived in the fast lane.

'Why don't you come back, Andy?' he asked. 'Make a new life among old friends.'

'The old are the best,' Andy sighed, squeezing Liam's hand. Liam felt gratified. They reminisced about a boyhood that now seemed bathed in a rosy glow, talked of their school-days and laughed at the memories of teachers, of classmates.

'Remember old Doyle?' Liam said finally, 'Died last month.'

'No!' Andy tried to remember Doyle.

'Cancer of the colon,' Liam announced with the satisfaction of the healthy.

'No!' Andy said, giving up on Doyle.

'Remember that time we went swimming at the Forty-foot?'

'Jeez, yeah! That was cold enough to freeze the balls off a brass monkey.'

'Yes . . . Good fun, though.'

'Masochism . . . That's not my scene. No way. The opposite in fact.' Andy's small eyes glinted above his fat cheeks.

'Yes,' Liam said.

'Take women,' Andy went on. 'Take them. I always do, any chance I can get. But I like them to know who's boss. Know what I mean?'

'Sure.'

'Even if it means a bit of . . . chastisement. Get my drift?'

'Of course.' Liam giggled.

'It's you bachelors I envy. A free hand, eh. Two free hands . . . ' He laughed, showing brown teeth. 'Loads of hungry women after you, eh?'

'Well . . . '

'You got plenty of girlfriends then, Liam?'

'Ah sure. You know . . . '

'No one special?'

'No.'

'Not still carrying a torch for . . . me sister?'

'Oh no . . . no. Not at all.'

'A fine woman, Marion.'

'She is.'

'Still alone then, Liam, eh?'

'Alone, but not lonely,' Liam smiled. 'And I've always got mam.'

'True enough,' Andy replied, thinking in revulsion of the wizened old woman who had clutched his hand to her concave chest and grinned a reptilian grin, chuckling insanely while he told her how well she looked.

'So what about it?' Liam continued. 'Are you coming back or what?'

'Love to,' Andy replied. 'Love to . . . but I can't.'

'Surely in your line of work you could go anywhere.' Andy was a quantity surveyor.

'Yeah, but I got this chick see, Wendy.'

'Wendy?'

'You should see her Liam, beautiful girl, twenty-four years old, blonde, blue-eyed, the biggest bloody boobs you've seen in your life. She's like all me Christmasses came at once . . . I know what. You come to Sydney. I just remembered Wendy's got a sister.'

That night Liam went to bed thoughtfully. The prospect of Wendy's sister failed to excite him. And he no longer whistled.

Ruth liked Christmas, the preparations for it. She loved walking the wintry streets with Starveling, looking at the bright shop windows, one in particular catching her daughter's eye with its traditional display of moving puppets: giant teddies riding on a sledge in sparkling silver snow, teddies decorating their Christmas tree, hanging up their stockings, a teddy dressed as Santa coming down the chimney and going up it again to Starveling's endless delight – up and down, up and down. The child had to be pulled away; she would have stared forever. Then there were the street hawkers with their tinsel and their raucous cries; carol singers one group after another collecting for charity, some more tuneful than others, banging tambourines; red-cheeked, blue-lipped people dashing by or ambling like Ruth, many lugging huge plastic bags full of toys and other presents; garish lights fitfully illuminating random faces, strained, animated, expectant. There was an atmosphere of carnival, the festival of the winter solstice, a celebration of the death of the old year, much more appropriately pagan than Christian: eat, drink, be merry and spend, spend, spend. Forget that grey January bringing retribution will come all too soon.

They visited Santa in his grotto, although Starveling screamed and clung to Ruth's legs and took the proffered present only after much cajoling. It turned out to be a cheap Barbie-type doll in a red dress, with pointed breasts and curling long blonde hair that could be combed. Starveling looked at it with amazement – on principle Ruth had never given her such an object to play with – and fell in love. The doll's name was Mandy and henceforth she and Starveling were inseparable, the child speaking in awe of Santy, marvellous Santy who had given her this wonderful gift. Ruth stroked her child's silky head and felt the tears well up into her eyes.

In November she had made two puddings, Starveling helping her stir the glutinous mixture but unable to get the spoon to move at all. Ruth, laughing, had thrown in a small bottle of Guinness.

'Now we'll get drunk when we eat it,' she had said.

Starveling had frowned with the effort and carved a semi-circle through the mixture with the wooden spoon.

'Make a wish,' Ruth had told her, 'but don't tell me what it is or it won't come true.'

A cunning expression had spread over the child's face.

'Starling want Daddy,' she had said, stirring.

At a certain point, Francis noticed that the defacer of books had shifted slants. There was a possibility, of course, that it was a different person, with different obsessions, but a comparison of the handwriting, the technique of erasure – a neat box scored with criss-cross lines – led Francis Holmes-like to deduce it was the same. The name of Jesus Christ and God were still excised but no longer when used as expletives in detective novels. In fact, the defacer had changed his (or her) reading habits and had developed a taste for the heavier works of long-dead foreign writers, Thomas Mann, Balzac, Tolstoy and Dostoevsky, Franz Kafka.

The Brothers Karamazov came back with 'Rubbish!!!' inscribed next to the sayings of Father Zosima, 'Conjuring Tricks' where the elder dwells on the transformation of water to wine and a big tick in the margin when Ivan Karamazov states that if there is no God then everything is permitted.

Francis glanced round the library. An old man was dozing in an armchair. A student sitting at a table was taking furious notes from various large reference books. A middle-aged woman was hovering over the Patricia Scanlans.

He asked the assistant, Maureen, about the Dostoevsky.

'Did you see who brought it back?'

'Some young girl . . . Wait a minute.' She punched into the computer. 'Here we are. Rachel O'Reilly. I remember she took out *Bleak House*.'

After some thought, Francis decided to follow it up. It was, after all, an unacceptable level of vandalism. He called at Rachel O'Reilly's house on his way home. A stout woman in an apron – apparently she was preparing the evening meal – answered the door.

'She's upstairs studying,' she replied to his query and, without asking him in, stumped to the foot of the stairs yelling 'Rachel! Rachel! . . . It's some man from the library.'

Rock music blasted from an upstairs room as a door opened and a small dark-haired girl ran down.

She informed Francis that she was doing a module on great nineteenth-century novels at college and added that she hadn't actually read *The Brothers Karamazov*.

'It had a good introduction,' she said. Yes, she had noticed it had been defaced but that was quite usual, wasn't it. 'There are so many cranks about, aren't there?'

'Try and read *Bleak House*,' Francis told her, not unconscious of a certain hypocrisy on his part, 'It's very good.'

'But awfully long,' she smiled. 'Why do they always have to be so long? At least,' she continued, 'it's got a great introduction.'

So many cranks.

Miracle, mystery and authority, the guardian thought. The pillars of the church. Yes, they were cunning, yes. What was the word? A good word. Casuistry, that was it. They were casuists. But they couldn't fool him any longer with their magic tricks. He had seen through them. He knew how it was done. Not with mirrors, no. With fear. What was it he had read? Clever people believe nothing and stupid people believe everything. His wife, for instance, she'd believe anything they told her up at that church of hers. But he'd stared at the sky and seen nothing. Molecules, that was all. Dust making the sky blue. Light dazzling your eyes. A chance combination of elements stirring up life on one tiny planet among billions. It was absurd to think of a plan behind it all, bloody stupid sort of a plan it would have to be anyway.

Control, that was all this God thing was about. Because the logical corollary (another good word) of there being no God was moral anarchy.

Everything was permitted. Yes.

PART FOUR

NO RELIGION AT ALL

There had been noise and unrest in the city for days. Crowds roamed the streets looking for trouble, beating up foreigners, smashing and looting property. Old Joe, the Signor, stood at an upstairs window, looking down on the mob now encircling his own house. He could tell by their gestures they were debating whether to break in. He opened the window and bowed deeply.

'Genteelmen . . .' he started to say. Rotten fruit and vegetables were thrown up at him, some hitting the outside walls of the house, some reaching the grinning target — as Pantaloon he was well used to this sort of thing — some flying past him into the room where the mother of his children sat enfolding them in her arms. A cabbage rolled to a stop at her feet.

'No popery!' voices in the crowd called out.

The Signor leered even more broadly and spread out his arms. He bowed again and winked.

'But genteelmen,' he said, 'in dis hose be no religion at all.'

People in the crowd burst out laughing, some cheered. Gradually they moved away in search of other victims.

The mother of the Signor's children picked up the cabbage, scraped off the rotten part and cooked the rest with the stew for dinner.

The small, graceful tree stood in Ruth's tiny front room where she and Starveling were decorating it, Ruth tying homemade ornaments to the ends of the branches, Starveling flinging handfuls of tinsel in glittering streams up in the air.

'Careful, sweetheart, it's going all over the floor,' Ruth said.

Tom had bought them the tree, a Norwegian spruce, and delivered it to the house to appease a bad conscience, Ruth thought, since he was spending Christmas in Galway with his parents and no doubt his ex-wife and children. Ruth honestly didn't mind. Maeve had invited her and Starveling for Christmas dinner but the thought of Fionn leering at her over the port while Maeve slaved in the kitchen gave her the horrors. Other friends had invited her for St Stephen's Day and after. Christmas Day itself would be just for her and her daughter.

Starveling's face had been radiant with excitement for days, as they made streamers and hung them across all the ceilings, went to the market to buy tinsel and coloured glass balls, collected pine cones in St Anne's park and then sat by the turf fire painting them gold and silver, as Tom delivered the tree and now, as they adorned it.

'Stand back,' Ruth told her, 'and shut your eyes.'

Starveling obediently screwed her eyes up tight.

Ruth plunged the room in darkness, then switched on the fairy lights. The tree became phantasmagoric, flickering in the firelight.

'Open eyes!' Ruth said.

Starveling's tiny face was solemn, her eyes huge, filling with tears.

'What's wrong, sweetheart?'

But the child couldn't tell her. She pressed hard against her mother and sobbed and sobbed.

'My darling, my beloved, what's wrong? Don't you like it?'

Starveling nodded her head, looking away. Finally, she peeped again at the tree and started to smile.

Francis knocked on the door of the undistinguished terraced house. He thought that if he lived there himself, he would constantly be getting it wrong. Maybe in summer the flowerbeds, cleared now, would remind him with their brightness.

A small old man in a hand-knitted sweater opened the door. He had a sour and ratty face and looked hostile. He said nothing, waiting for Francis to speak.

'Mr Ryan? James Ryan?'

The man nodded grudgingly.

'I'm from the library . . . You borrowed this book.'

The man glanced at it and nodded again. So Maureen had been right. Not such a featherhead after all. Weird, she'd said he was. Creepy. She hadn't wanted to confront him herself.

Francis flipped the book open. On page after page, words were scored through, comments written in the margins.

'I'm afraid I have to ask. Did you do this?' Francis asked. Of course he had. Francis had known from the moment the man opened the door.

The man still said nothing.

'This isn't the first, is it? . . . Don't think it's gone unnoticed . . . Silence. 'It's very serious to deface library books, you know. We may have to ask you to replace the more badly damaged ones. This one, for example, it's barely readable.'

The man stared at him.

'Don't you understand? No one's interested in your comments. You're interfering with the rights of other members of the library . . . ' Not a flicker of response. The man was clearly a crackpot. 'I'm afraid a stop will have to be put on your tickets in all branches and I'd be grateful if you'd return to me any books you have out at present.'

The man shut the door abruptly. Francis stared at it. The dark brown paint was thick, an occasional globule dried hard. He was shaking, his hands were wet. He was about to ring the bell again when the door opened. The man stood with two books in his hands.

'Here,' he said.

Francis took them and hurried off.

'Who was that, dear?' the guardian's wife called from the kitchen where she was making mince pies.

'A man selling encyclopaedias,' he replied, putting on his coat.

Away from the house Francis paused to take a puff of his inhaler and to examine the returned books. One was a collection of short stories by the Russian writer Tolstoy. A cursory glance showed him the familiar system of notation on many of the pages.

The other book featuring Patricia Highsmith's amoral anti-hero, Ripley, was undefiled, probably as yet unread.

The old wife heard the door slam again. He's gone for one of his walks, she thought to herself with relief. A bit of peace and quiet at last. She switched on the radio and tuned in to that pleasant podgy fellow who played the old songs in the afternoons. She always used to listen to him when her husband was working. But not much in recent years. For some reason, the programme irritated her husband beyond endurance. They started playing 'Just the way you look tonight.' The old woman sang along.

Two hours later, her husband had still not returned. Four hours later. At nine o'clock in the evening she called the guards.

'He'll probably turn up,' the man said kindly. 'It's early yet.'

'You don't understand,' she insisted. 'He never misses the news.'

The guard made reassuring noises and took details.

'We'll keep our eyes open for him,' he told her. 'And ring me later if he doesn't come home.'

He didn't. Not then. Not ever. The moral guardian had disappeared as into a black hole, off the face of the earth.

How lovely the room looked, Marion thought. The white tree had been a great buy and six, seven years on it still looked as good as new. Apart from the lights, it was decorated only with red and green silk bows, an idea she had borrowed from a women's magazine, very elegant. Other bows were strategically pinned round the room, a red one to the corner of her painting of Ireland's Eye.

This year they had received more cards than ever. Well, not Francis so much. Marion had an enormous circle of acquaintances, an address book crammed full of the names of people she had met on holidays over the years – it was nice to keep in touch if only at Christmas – people she had been to various classes with, old school pals, friends from the time when she was working. She sent cards to all of them – charity cards, to justify the expense – and they reciprocated.

She felt relatively happy. Gerald was better and seemed to have learnt his lesson. He was no longer hanging around with the dubious crowd who had led him into trouble. She wished he had some nice friends, even a girl, but all in good time, all in good time. The counsellor had told her that these things couldn't be rushed. Valerie was grand, a little sullen perhaps but it was the age. Thank goodness she had finished with that awful Declan with the earring and was now going out with a much nicer boy called Stephen who was always very polite when he called to the house. She just hoped that Andy's domestic problems weren't going to sour things when everyone came round on Christmas Day. She said as much to her friend Bernie as they sat in the wedge-shaped living room drinking coffee. Bernie was on yet another diet and refused sweet cake or biscuits, even the home-made muesli ones that contained hardly any sugar.

'I'm saving myself for Christmas,' Bernie said. 'You can't diet at Christmas.'

There was no answer to that. Privately, Marion thought that no matter what diet Bernie went on she would continue to get fatter and fatter. But you can't actually say that to anyone, least of all your best friend.

'How's it going?' Bernie asked. She was *au fait* with Marion's domestic troubles, as indeed was Marion with Bernie's.

'Fine. Not a bother.'

'Weren't you hoping to get away? To sort things out.'

'It's not a good time of year, ' Marion replied. 'Maybe later. Maybe in the spring. Anyway, we don't really need to now. Gerald is better and as for Francis, he's as quiet as a lamb.'

'Father Sergius' is the story of a nobleman turned hermit, who cuts off his finger rather than defile his flesh by sleeping with a woman. Revered for his saintliness, his tiny cell becomes the focus of pilgrimages. Finally, however, he lets himself be seduced by a half-witted girl with breasts like pancakes. He runs away and roams the roads, breaking with organised religion to find redemption working on the land as a hired labourer.

In 'The Kreutzer Sonata' a man on a long train journey through Russia tells a fellow-traveller how he has murdered his wife because of her imagined adultery with a violinist. He rails against womankind, tight jumpers, bustles and copulation as well as the corrupting effect of music that inflames the senses and weakens moral judgement.

Ticks in tiny boxes dotted the margins. Where the man confesses to the murder of his wife the sentence 'Everything is permitted!!!!' was written in meticulously neat letters and underneath, in a separate box, 'There is no God but men. Women are devils and tear out the hearts of men to devour them. Exorcise! Exorcise!'

The man Ryan obviously needed help. He was evidently seriously disturbed. Francis wondered if he should inform someone, if he should return to the house – could he find it again? – and talk to the man himself, try to get him to see a doctor. Or should he talk to the wife if there was one? She might even be in danger. For a moment Francis was transported into one of those whodunnit novels he liked so much in which the amateur detective by means of intuition and accident solves the case that baffles Scotland Yard.

But this would be no joke. No lighthearted murder in the vicarage or sealed room mystery where the blood was so obviously paint. This would be Ruth Rendell or even Barbara Vine where the darkest recesses of the mind gave birth to unspeakable crimes and where the resolution was so often ambiguous.

He did nothing. In any case, by then it would have made no difference.

When it became obvious that the moral guardian was not coming back, when all the likely possibilities – heart attack, accident and so on – had been ruled out since there was no sign of him in hospital or morgue; when the tide had come in and gone out for weeks and his body had not been washed up; when officials at airports, ferries and stations, bus and rail, had been consulted to no avail, the old wife became resigned to his disappearance. People disappeared all the time. Hadn't the two of them seen that programme on TV about the man who walked out of the house one day whose car was found by the sea wall? In the end it turned out that he hadn't drowned himself at all as, following on the programme, he contacted the TV company to reveal that he had started a new life somewhere else.

She looked through her husband's things, thinking at first that it was strange he would leave everything behind. Then, inspecting it all, coming to the conclusion that not much of it was worth taking.

'Funnily enough,' she told her neighbour, the one whose cat had also mysteriously disappeared, 'though I feel hurt, I'm also relieved. Is that very wicked?'

The neighbour, who had loathed the moral guardian and who had actually briefly suspected him of having a hand in the disappearance of Monty, thought nothing could be more natural.

'Not at all,' she said.

Soon afterwards the old wife had a very private conversation with Father Byrne as a result of which he made a phone call on her behalf. Two days later, a woman turned up on her doorstep and fell into her arms.

'Mammy!' the woman said, weeping with emotion.

'It's my daughter, Lily,' the old woman later told her neighbour.

'I didn't know you had any children,' the neighbour said, astonished.

'No, well it all happened long before I met Jim and I never told him. It wasn't the sort of thing he'd understand. Then, a few years ago, I got a letter from her. She'd traced me, you see, don't ask me how. I wrote back and told her that I couldn't have anything to do with her for Jim's sake. He hated any immorality . . . Well you know that . . . ' The neighbour nodded vigorously.

'I can't help thinking,' the old woman went on, 'that I made a mistake. Not just for me and Lily – I was dying to see her and the grandchildren and her husband and I told her that but I'd never have gone behind Jim's back. Now I wonder if that was a mistake. If he'd had children, you know, it might have made all the difference. I think he'd have been a much happier person in himself.'

The neighbour thought nothing could have improved the moral guardian but nodded again.

'You may be right,' she said.

The old woman took herself and her knitting – a white matinee jacket for her first great grandchild, Lily's eldest daughter being pregnant – over to Lily's house in Skerries for Christmas. She left a note on the kitchen table for her husband, should he happen to return, and the neighbour promised to look out for him. In the event the neighbour herself went away for two days over the holiday to stay with another lonely widow, so that if anyone had come creeping around darkened windows at night looking for a sign of human warmth, looking for pity and forgiveness, there would have been no one at all to notice.

Santa brought Starveling a hand-made wooden jigsaw puzzle of two bright birds on a branch (from Sonya), a pastel pink plastic baby pony with a mane that could be combed (from Tom on the suggestion of his daughters who collected them), a big box of poster paints and brushes all of her own, a block of multi-coloured paper, denim dungarees and a canary yellow sweat-shirt with a picture of Alice and the White Rabbit on it (from Ruth). There were books, too, with colourful illustrations: *The Man whose Mother Was a Pirate*, *The Hill and the Rock*, *The Cat and the Devil*. Ruth had hung a thick wooden stocking at the foot of Starveling's bed and on Christmas morning it was mysteriously found to be full of chocolate coins covered in gold paper, mandarin oranges, a necklace of big wooden beads and a yo-yo that sparkled when you worked it up and down, only Starveling wasn't able to manage it and had to watch Ruth with her big round eyes.

They went for a walk along the sea-front at Clontarf, Starveling in her new clothes not wanting to wear her old coat on top of her finery, screaming with rage, then suddenly submitting, clutching Mandy, her over-developed and now nude doll. Ruth pushed the buggy expecting any minute that her daughter would be too exhausted to walk although in fact Starveling danced and skipped as far as the yacht club jetty, which she crept down in longing to see the sea between the gaps in the concrete and in terror at the little waves that splashed up at her.

Later Ruth lit candles at the kitchen table where they pulled crackers and put on the tissue paper crowns that fell out of them before eating their dinner of roast duck with cranberry sauce and rice. Then Ruth poured brandy over the pudding and set it alight with a magic flame that flickered blue for a few moments but did not consume.

In the evening by the fire Starveling played with her new toys, putting Mandy to ride on the little pony – her long blonde hair curling over her pointed breasts like a kitsch Lady Godiva – and splashing paint over several sheets of paper. Ruth curled up in an armchair and started to read a book that she'd bought herself as a present – a new novel by Ann Tyler. She sipped red wine and looked up from time to time at her child.

'Is Christmas nice?' she asked her.

And Starveling said nothing but smiled to herself.

Everyone was being very tight-lipped. Really, Marion thought, Christmas is the pits. Her mother wasn't talking to Andy because he'd brought some cheap tart back to the house on Christmas Eve for heaven's sake and even tried to smuggle her up to his bedroom while the parents were at Mass. Her father was still talking, endlessly in fact but bitterly, regretting the passing of the days when children respected their elders.

'Today's children are no good for anything,' he stated.

'That's a very generalised remark,' Marion replied.

'Look at your man,' her father went on. He'd been drinking heavily and purple veins dangerously decorated his cheeks and nose. 'Look at him.' He indicated Gerald, who was locked in a world of music, his eyes closed, the new tape Valerie had given him throbbing through his walkman.

'He's had problems,' Marion said frostily. She had no intention of discussing her children with her parents, who God knew had made plenty of mistakes themselves, even though they were unwilling to face up to them.

Valerie sprawled in an armchair, very overweight; Marion would have to take her in hand after Christmas. The girl ate chocolate after chocolate and flipped through a magazine, bored out of her skull. 'How to know when you've reached orgasm,' she read. That was more interesting. She cast a cautious look around the room to make sure she was unnoticed and started to study the article.

Francis was no use at all, sitting miserably tense and pre-occupied. Finally Marion snapped at him.

'Take father and Andy out for a walk, for Christ's sake.' Here her mother pursed her lips. 'And take Gerald and Valerie with you. I'm sick of the sight of you all.'

But if she wanted peace and quiet, she failed to find it. For the rest of the afternoon her mother went on and on about Andy.

'I don't know what we're going to do about him,' she kept saying until Marion exploded. It wasn't a good Christmas.

The rest of them ended up walking in a thin line over Howth

Head, the best Francis could think of. Not the lower cliff walk where he had met Sonya for the first time but the less strenuous, less picturesque high path from the summit. It was difficult to find a parking place, so many people were of the same mind, walking off their turkey and ham and pudding, sherry, wine and port. Andy stumbled a few times.

'Drunk,' said his father, who wasn't entirely sober himself.

It was terrible, Francis thought. This ugly pointless life they were all leading. And all the people walking with them or going in the opposite direction, was it any better for any of them despite their holiday smiles? Life grinding them on, grinding them down. Marion's father probably within five years of his own death, still full of obstinate opinions, his vision as limited as ever. None of them were even looking around over the rocks and heather or out over the sea to the Wicklow mountains beyond Dublin Bay. They were all looking down, staring at the stony path, to make sure they didn't lose their foothold. He couldn't bear it. He started to wheeze and felt panic-stricken around in his pockets. At last his hand closed over the familiar L-shaped inhaler.

'You all right?' his father-in-law asked.

'It's the cold air and the climbing,' Francis told him, getting relief instantly from the miracle drug. 'I'm better now.'

The old man shook his head. He was probably deploring again the degeneration of the race as epitomised in his son-in-law.

Valerie kicked a stone and thought of Steve. Probably he was at this minute as bored as she was. The last time they had met, he had sucked on her tit like a baby. The memory brought a smile to her face.

'She's my girl,' her grandfather said, putting his arm round her. 'The only one of the whole bunch worth bothering with. Amn't I right, Val?'

Bigger than he was, she giggled down into his purple face.

Over Christmas in Galway Tom slept with his wife. Never mind the separation, they were still married. And she was still pretty, devoted to him and available.

'Come back to us, Tom,' she whispered into his ear, making him tingle. 'We miss you.'

He could do worse, he thought to himself. There was a lot to be said for family life.

'My work's in Dublin,' he rubbed her belly.

'And your girlfriends.' She could afford to make light of it. Wasn't he now with her and not them.

'Girlfriends!' he said without conscience as his sperm flew into her unprotected womb (she had deceived him about that, though in a good cause) and fertilized the egg that was lying there patiently waiting.

After a wonderful few days in Skerries, the old wife, May, returned to her empty and objectively dismal house. Lily had asked her to stay on, maybe to move in with them but May had noticed that Lily's husband had looked less than enthusiastic and decided herself that it was rushing things a bit. Anyway, it was the first time in her life that she had a place all to herself, as she had married from home where she had shared a room with two of her sisters.

At first she was at a loss as to what to do. So much of her time had been spent running errands for others, her husband mostly. Suddenly she realised that from now on she could do whatever she liked.

'I can paint the walls black and the ceilings orange if I want,' she told her neighbour.

'You aren't going to though, are you?' her neighbour asked

anxiously. She hoped May wasn't turning peculiar.

'Not at all. I'll get a nice young man in to put up some paper with little pink flowers on it . . . I saw some lovely stuff at the hardware. You can get curtains to match only the flowers are that much bigger.'

She would surround herself with flowers, not only outside, which had always been her province, but inside too, on walls, on upholstery. She would sleep on sprigged sheets scented with roses, she would even buy flowers to put in vases – a waste, her husband, the moral guardian, had always said. She could have Lily and the children to visit, especially Barbara, who was having the baby without showing any signs of wanting to get married but who was determined to rear the child herself. And then she would be pleased to see the back of them again, close the door and sit down in front of some nice game show on TV with her knitting, a cup of tea and a plate of chocolate biscuits.

The only pang she felt for her husband was a conscience-ridden dread that he would return, something she couldn't bring herself to confess to Father Byrne with his solicitous face. She didn't think she could bear it if Jim came back and everything went on the way it had been before. Was it a terrible sin to think that way? Sometimes, in the most inappropriate places, she was overcome with guilt and started to weep.

'The poor woman,' people would say. 'Imagine him going off and leaving her like that.'

The kitten that Lily's youngest child had given her for Christmas started to play with her ball of wool. May looked at it indulgently.

'Naughty Fluff,' she said softly. She had always liked cats.

In the pub Andy was complaining of his lot to Liam.

'I thought they were taking it all right,' he said. 'Now they've gone all Catholic on me.'

Liam had been out with Andy on Christmas Eve when Andy picked up Nicki, a very common type of girl in Liam's view. He had virtually refused to speak to Nicki's friend though obviously the general idea had been that he should 'get off' with her. Luckily, she had spotted some of the gang and had abandoned him for them when her conversational efforts had met with monosyllabic replies.

'They hit the roof when they found old Nicki in the house after Mass. See,' Andy chuckled, 'she couldn't stop giggling. Real sense of humour, that one.'

Her top had been cut to her navel and her skirt clung to her thighs just below her knickers.

'She wasn't dressed for winter weather then,' Liam's mother had cackled.

'I don't know what he sees in women like that, Mam.'

'I don't know what women like that see in him,' his mother had returned drily. 'And he used to be such a nice-looking young fellow, too.'

He had. Andy. Never skinny, no. Well-covered but muscular. Wavy brown hair that fell in a lock over his eyes so that he kept having to toss it back. He would toss back his hair and laugh and his teeth were white and even in his mouth.

'He's changed,' Liam had said, not for the first time.

There in the pub he listened to his friend describing what his plans had been for Nicki. At last Liam could take no more.

'I'm going for a leak,' he said.

'Do one for me,' Andy laughed through brown teeth.

In the lavatory, Liam met a man he knew to say hello to, a neighbour from a few doors down. The man was unusually friendly.

It must be the season, Liam thought, but he felt so miserable that he gladly chatted on for a few minutes.

Returning to his seat he found it taken by a large woman in her forties, in earnest conversation with Andy.

'Remember Carmel?' Andy asked him. 'We all used to smoke cigarettes down behind the scout hall when we were fourteen.'

'Not me,' Liam said, motioning to the woman to keep her seat. 'I never smoked.'

'No other vices?' she grinned, widening bright orange lips. God above, where did Andy find them?

Liam bought a round of drinks and found another stool. He sat getting more and more depressed, while Andy and Carmel exchanged suggestive repartee. He looked round the pub aimlessly and found his neighbour from the lavatory staring at him quizzically from the end of the bar. The man winked. Liam excused himself, got up and joined him.

'I felt like a right gooseberry,' he explained.

The man, Mark, laughed. He had nice white even teeth.

'Your friend's a bit of a lady's man, isn't he. I've seen him here before.'

They talked on in a relaxed way. Mark happened to mention that he hadn't been able to get out much over the holiday because there was something wrong with his car.

'Happened Christmas Eve, would you believe. You can't get anyone to come out till after New Year.'

'I'll pop down and have a look at it for you if you like,' Liam said. 'I'm quite good with cars.'

Andy came over and joined them. It seemed that Carmel's husband had fetched her back to her own table at last.

'You don't remember her, do you Liam?' Andy asked. 'She was a lovely girl once you know. Lovely.'

On New Year's Eve, Ruth had been invited to a big party at Philip's friend's wine bar. She accepted for herself, hoping Tom wouldn't be back and hoping she could get a babysitter for Starveling. Her neighbour's kind daughter was going out but the neighbour said she would make up a bed for the child in her daughter's room if Ruth thought Starveling would stay with her. Of course Starveling would stay with her. Starveling would stay with anyone.

It was a loud and crowded party. The wonderful salads that were a speciality of the place were evident in abundance along with some Middle Eastern snacks and dips – falafel, hummus, taboulleh, taramasalata – Ari, the fat and jovial owner, Philip's partner, being Lebanese. Ruth actually found that she knew a number of people there, actors especially. Philip looked stunning in black silk trousers and a leather waistcoat over his naked torso, a long diamante ear-ring dangling from his left ear and an orange bandana round his head.

'I'm Long John Silver,' he announced, nudging her suggestively. In fact, a number of people were in fancy dress. 'But it's not *de rigueur*, darling,' he whispered in her ear. 'Not by any means. By the way, I advise against the rollmops. They taste like someone I know. Oh Paddy, love . . . ' he exclaimed and swept off.

Soon enough Ruth was talking to a woman director who had plans to do a one-woman play.

'*Strange Tongues*; it's by a new writer. Very intense. Very powerful. It just has to be done.'

She asked Ruth if she would be interested in designing the set.

'There's no money in it of course,' the woman added. 'Well, it'll be shares. If it takes off, we might make a fortune.' She laughed. Elephants might fly.

She told Ruth that she was looking for a certain type of actress and, as she described it, Ruth thought of Sonya. She mentioned her name but the woman hadn't heard of her.

'Certainly I'll audition her. Why not!'

She gave Ruth her number. When Sonya finally met the director weeks later, she was informed she was perfect for the part. She never heard any more about it and later found out the project had been abandoned.

On the other side of the room, Mark entered with Liam. To avoid another marathon drinking session with Andy, Liam had gladly accepted the invitation of his new friend. Mark told Liam that he had worked in the place for a few months when desperate. A washer-upper. A cockroach crusher (only joking!). A scrubber. Not his scene, though he'd been grateful at the time and the people were nice. Well, Ari – the small plump fellow in the turquoise tee-shirt – had been kind enough to invite him to the party. And wasn't it great? Liam wasn't sure. It certainly wasn't the kind of thing he was used to. Everyone was so excessive. Flamboyantly dressed, loud. He and Mark surely stood out in their sober suits but no one seemed to notice.

'Lots of theatrical people,' Mark whispered to him. That explained a lot. Liam even thought he recognised someone from the TV soap *Fair City*, drinking, eating and laughing like any ordinary person. That would be something to tell his mam.

'There's Ruth!' Mark exclaimed and pushed his way through the crowds. 'This is my art teacher. Ruth, this is Liam,' he said.

The woman smiled. She looked faintly familiar.

'And this is her wonderful picture,' Mark gestured towards the portrait of Philip and giggled. 'Isn't it marvellous?'

Liam stared at the picture. Surely not, he thought. That was the sort of thing for dirty magazines. He felt thoroughly disgusted but in the course of the evening his eyes kept going back to it.

Later after several glasses of a sparkling wine that was actually quite tasty, Liam found himself talking for a while to a man who turned out to be a woman. He mentioned it to Mark, who laughed, flashing his white teeth.

'Most of the women here are really men,' he said.

Fancy dress, Liam hoped. He didn't ask but looked around carefully, even at Ruth, who would have been amused rather than offended.

Midnight. The place turned silent for the chimes of Christ Church cathedral, audible in the distance. Everyone turned to everyone else and embraced.

'Definition of an optimist,' said Mark. 'A man who sets his alarm for midnight on New Year's Eve, wakes up, drinks a toast and goes back to sleep again.'

And he kissed Liam on the lips.

So that was that, at last.

Valerie pulled up her pants and her jeans. She wanted a shower more than anything else. Steve lolled against the garage wall – his parents' garage – moaning softly. The condom he had borrowed from his brother lay on the ground oozing liquid like a crushed snake.

'You OK?' she asked.

'Rapid!' he sighed.

It was that all right, she thought. Perhaps after all an older man was what she needed. She knew for sure that she had not experienced orgasm. It didn't need an article in a women's magazine to tell her that.

Marion, Francis and Gerald sat round the television waiting for midnight.

'It's nice when it's just us, isn't it,' Marion said, not needing a reply and knowing she wouldn't get it. Both her men were notoriously taciturn.

She had insisted on Gerald staying in, although where would he go. He had no friends. Valerie was out with the usual crowd and under strict instructions to be home before half past twelve. That nice Stephen had promised to see her to the door.

The programme they were watching was a sort of variety show. Francis looked at it blankly, everyone smiling insincerely, singing songs of love without feeling, telling poor jokes to predictable laughter.

'What do you call a Kerryman who hangs from the ceiling?'

'I don't know, what do you call a Kerryman who hangs from the ceiling?'

'Sean D'Olier.'

'Why do elephants have big ears?'

'I don't know, why do elephants have big ears?'

'Because Noddy wouldn't pay the ransom.'

Francis stood up.

'You can't go to bed yet,' Marion said. 'We have to see the New Year in. There's hot punch and I've made some savoury snacks.'

Francis sat down again. He wished he were dead. Gerald laughed like a maniac.

'This guy's really good,' he said.

'Yes, he is dear, isn't he,' Marion agreed, smiling across at Francis. He was hopeless, staring into space like that. She wasn't going to make a row now, not this time with the vol-au-vents warming in the microwave — she'd got it for Christmas at last. All she ever wanted.

She went out into the kitchen. When she came back, everyone

was singing 'Auld Lang Syne' except the two zombies on the couch.

'Did I miss it?' she asked.

Francis looked at her then.

'Yes,' he said. 'So did I.'

'Wake up then, dumbo.'

The bells rang out across the city. A few rockets burst open.

'Happy New Year,' Marion said, kissing them both.

She went outside and embraced her neighbours, even the ones with the terribly low-class cladding on the bottom half of their house.

Ruth walked home through the night city. Groups of kids swayed past, taking up the whole pavement, setting off firecrackers. Drunks lay in doorways surrounded by the litter of beer cans, cider bottles, fast food cartons.

Happy New Year!

No one bothered her. They never had, except to call out. Perhaps she looked sufficiently confident and aggressive to discourage attack. Perhaps she looked too poor. Her shoulder bag was under her coat, she swung her arms by her sides and strode on.

Her little street was darker, the amber lights falling in tiny frozen circles. Down at the end, there was her house. It was nearly three in the morning.

A large bulk hurled out of an alleyway and knocked her over. She banged her head on the pavement. The man, it was a man, started kicking her viciously. Frantic for self-preservation she grabbed his ankle and buried her teeth in it.

He shouted a curse and ran off.

She spat out all her saliva and any of the man that was in her mouth. Then she was blessedly sick.

Feeling the wet graze on her head she staggered to her front door, opened it and for some reason went straight to her living room.

Her blurred vision showed her another dark bulk hunched in her armchair by the fairy-lights of the tree.

'Damn,' she said, switching on the overhead lamp.

'Must have been a fucking good party,' Tom said.

Happy New Year.

'Had a good time, dear?'

Oh no, Liam thought. He had expected his mam to be asleep. Might have known better.

'Yes thanks,' he said, going into her room. She looked up at him expectantly, her teeth out. How could he tell her anything?

'There was that chap from *Fair City* there. The one who plays . . . ' He named the character. His mother perked up.

'Did you speak to him?'

'Not really. There was a crowd round him . . . He has a pony tail in real life.'

His mother made an expression of disapproval. How well he knew that face.

'It was a very theatrical type of a party,' he said. 'That's what . . . Mark said.'

'And Mark knows all about it, does he?' His mother was already prepared to put down his new friend.

'Yes, he does actually,' Liam almost snapped, kissing his mother briefly on the top of her thinning grey hair and putting out the light.

'Go to sleep now, mother. I'm tired.'

And his mother, snuggling down on top of the electric blanket that against all the warnings she kept on all night, thought to herself that for once in his life, her dear son was not telling her everything.

'Never mind,' she thought to herself. 'I can wait. I'll get it out of him in the end.'

Tom's irritation at finding Ruth out when he arrived back from Galway was tempered when he saw what a state she was in following the attack. He was all for taking her to hospital but she refused.

'There'll be hordes of people there. New Year. I'll be left sitting around till next New Year probably.'

All she wanted was bed but she let herself be put in a hot bath after he'd cleaned and dressed her head wound.

He woke her up after fifteen minutes in the bath, dried her carefully – she had the beginnings of several ugly bruises – laid her on the bed and rubbed aromatic oil into her skin. It was very sexy and of course they ended up making love, Tom for once gentle and tender. She was grateful to him for being there and it never occurred to her – fool that she considered herself in retrospect – that he might have a guilty conscience.

That night, however, she dreamed that she was dancing, dancing with Tom under a mirror ball that cast flickering multicoloured lights. He was smiling and laughing but she was fearful. He kept catching at the hand of another figure dancing near them, smiling alternately at Ruth and at the other figure and prancing higher and higher like a stallion and then like a winged horse or centaur (he still had hands and face) taking off into the sky, gripping on to her hand and to that of the other. Her hand was slippery with sweat and gradually she lost hold of him, falling into darkness . . .

She woke up, hot and sticky. The house was silent except for the nervy ticking of the alarm clock. Tom slept peacefully beside her. She curled up against his naked back. In the morning she had forgotten her dream.

'I shouldn't have done it, I'm sorry.' Mark stood hunched against the cold at the front door. Liam peered anxiously behind him at the dark shadows where his mother certainly lurked.

'Fancy a walk . . . and a talk?' Mark asked.

Liam put on his coat, gloves and scarf and told his mother he was going out.

'You're mad,' she grumbled. 'It's below freezing.'

Out they went into the steel light of the late morning, Liam and Mark, crunching over the grass verge. Mark at last broke the gloomy silence.

'You're very upset,' he said.

Yes, Liam was upset all right. He thought he had made a friend, a new friend. And then.

'I have to explain,' Mark went on. 'Just as we found each other . . . No, I don't mean that exactly. Shit.'

'You're married,' Liam said.

Mark laughed. 'Yes I am. Happily, in fact. Well, as happy as it's possible to be. I have three lovely children . . . '

Mark's wife was a nurse, a sister in a city hospital. Luckily for them. Mark had been made redundant almost a year previously and without her income they would have soon been in financial trouble. At first Mark had tried to get work – he was in computer software – at the same level as before. Then he had reluctantly decided he would have to settle for less but still no job emerged. Finally he took anything he could get – Ari's wine bar for example – before his wife had sat him down and talked to him. They would be better off if he stayed home and drew the dole. She was paying more to childminders than he was earning at his temporary work.

So Mark became a house husband and found to his surprise that he actually liked it. He had ideas for a little company of his own and was gradually – not too fast – doing a feasibility study. Meantime, he was attending classes in the mornings while the kids were at school.

'I'm reading a lot, too,' he had told Liam. 'I never had time before.'

They walked into a park, under trees. A few children shrieked in a playground where your bare hand stuck to the icy slide. They sat down on a bench.

'I could see you were disappointed about Andy,' Mark said. 'I wanted to give you comfort.'

Liam slammed his gloved hand against the bench.

'Why does everyone think that a man who lives with his mother is queer?' he almost shouted.

Mark looked round in amusement. Some mothers had looked up at the raised voice though probably they had not distinguished the words.

'Liam,' Mark said, 'can I explain something to you. Why I did what I did. It's got nothing to do with being queer. It's about putting men in touch with their feelings again. Women can comfort each other with hugs and kisses; they can show affection in a physical way without anyone reading anything into it; they can cry if they want to. Why can't men?'

'You mean you're not . . . one of them?'

'I don't consider myself homosexual. I don't consider myself heterosexual, particularly. I'm just sexual. I want to be totally in tune with myself . . . Listen, I've got this book . . . '

'I'm not much of a one for books.'

'No,' Mark said. 'It's a pity. It might help.'

'You think I need help.'

'I think you're lonely. Whatever you say, I think you had hopes of Andy that he would take away your loneliness. Didn't you, Liam? You had hopes and Andy failed you.'

To his horror, Liam found that he had tears in his eyes. Real tears, not from the cold. Not since he was a kid had he felt real tears.

'Go on if you want to,' Mark told him. 'It's all right.'

'Fuck you,' Liam said and strode off, briskly wiping his cheeks.

'Have you thought what you're doing to the children?' Marion was screaming as Francis packed a single suitcase.

He was sick inside, agonised, though he spoke with apparent calm.

'I can't do any more for them. I know I've failed as a father. They're better off with me gone . . . You'll be better off.'

'Oh yes. I'll be all right. God knows you've never been much use to me. Even the job . . . '

Marion had always hoped that Francis would rise in his profession. She would have liked a house in one of those new landscaped estates with fountains as you entered.

'I need time to myself.'

'You need time with her. Don't tell me that's not where you're going.'

He didn't know where he was going. He hadn't seen Sonya for two months. Probably the flat was no longer free.

'You're a selfish bastard like all men.'

As she screamed he began to feel strangely remote. He noticed how her hair stayed rigid no matter how much she tossed her head around. But her face blurred as her make-up ran, as if seen under water or through rain on his glasses.

He took a puff of his inhaler.

'You're using that damn thing too much,' she yelled, 'or do I bring on an attack?'

Francis floated higher. Partly it was the effect of the drug, partly the unreality of the row. Neither he nor Marion had ever believed it would come to this.

'I'll be in touch,' he told her and left.

In the event, the children hardly noticed his absence. And in Valerie's eyes his estimation actually rose.

'My dad's left home to live with a nineteen-year-old,' she boasted to her friends. This was the stuff of soap operas.

As for Gerald, he found it easier to watch the programmes he liked on TV, his mother and sister being out most of the time. He sat for hours in the evenings staring at the set and stubbing out one cigarette after another in the ceramic ashtrays that Marion had made at a long ago evening class. She chided him mildly for smoking but told people that it was way preferable to having him sniff aerosols – not that he ever did again, having had his fright. She also told Bernie and anyone else who would listen that she felt it helped him cope with being abandoned by his father and added that she had been on the verge of taking it up again, too.

Instead, she threw herself more intensely than ever into her activities, her classes. The other women she met were supportive and added their names to Marion's Christmas card list for the following year. Many of them had marriage problems which they all discussed after class over coffee and cakes or something stronger. She felt that men were looking at her differently but it might have been imagination. Or it could have been that she was looking at them in a different way. She set her hair and painted on her glittering mask. No one was going to say that she had gone to pieces.

And Francis? Francis crept off into the night to Sonya's house. He walked the four miles in the bitter January cold like a penance, having left Marion the car.

He knew he should have phoned first but he was afraid of a negative response. Wouldn't she find it harder to refuse him if he turned up in person?

The house was dark. Maybe she was out or away – it was still holiday for some, the twelfth night, women's Christmas. Maybe she had left for good. That was his dread.

He opened the door with his key and walked in. A light gleamed from down the passageway, the room where his piano stood. Without switching on the hall lamp, he walked lightly down the hall and into the room. The two women turned and looked at him, Sonya from beside the hearth where a fire flickered orange, setting her crest of hair ablaze, Charlotte Isabel from the piano stool, where she was fingering a book of music, her little feet hanging in air. A huge and gaudy tree loomed in the corner of the room in front of the french windows and gave off a scent of pine that didn't come from a spray can.

'Hello Francis,' Sonya said, her mouth drooping in a smile. 'Have you come for the room?'

Liam's mother was afraid that with Francis gone, Marion and her son would be flung together. Wasn't that what people had always said, though personally she had never believed it. It was true that since Andy had gone back to Australia – under a cloud, let it be said – Liam had spent less time with that family. He was wrapped up in his new friend and was even installing a ladder in the man's loft, would you believe. But she was still worried. If Liam left her what would she do? No wife would want her around. They'd try to put her in one of those homes.

With a sense of self-preservation in mind, she justified to herself the search of Liam's room. Usually she never went in there. He was very neat and saw to it himself. Indeed, he did most of the housework now that she couldn't get about so much. She still did the cooking. He always told her there was nothing like her dinners.

Liam's room was pristine. Rather soulless, in fact, like a cabin on a ship, though the resemblance didn't occur to his mother, even though two of the pictures on the walls were of schooners. Marion's still life, which his mother had refused to have downstairs, was hanging over the bed.

She looked at the thing and hissed. At least he couldn't see it as he lay down, only briefly, when he got up and dressed.

There wasn't much to look through. His underwear and socks lay neatly and soberly in one drawer, his sweaters and polo tops in the others. There was nothing else in the drawers, no billets-doux tied with ribbon if that was what she was expecting.

Shirts, suits and jackets hung in the wardrobe. She caught sight of her withered image in the long mirror and grinned at herself, hitching up the petticoat that hung below her skirt. At the bottom of the wardrobe was a neat pile of magazines, do-it-yourself yokes mostly. She looked through them, screwing up her eyes with difficulty. One was different from the rest, near the bottom of the pile. She looked at it then carried it over to the light to see better. She knew such magazines existed, of course she did. She wasn't born yesterday nor even the day before that. She turned the pages slowly and looked and looked. Then she replaced the magazine exactly where it had been and closed the wardrobe door.

What she felt was almost a kind of relief. It seemed to her now that there was no need to worry that Liam would go after Marion or any other woman for that matter. Her own position was unassailable. She left his room with a grim smile on her face.

PART FIVE

BUTTERFLIES

Dartford Blues, the pride of young Joe's collection of butterflies, were captured over three nights in a copse near the town in Kent from which they take their name. He would walk the fifteen miles from London after finishing the show at Drury Lane theatre, rest for a few hours at a friend's house, then, as dawn was breaking, set out on the hunt. The first morning he netted only one before returning to London for the evening performance, leaving again for Kent immediately afterwards. On this second day he managed to collect forty-eight specimens, which he immediately arranged in a special display case. So absorbed was he in the task that he lost track of time and had to race back to the theatre, where in his hurry he nearly collided with the famous actress, Mrs Jordan.

She asked him what he had in his box and he in confusion stammered out, 'Flies, ma'am.'

He opened the box for her to see and she stepped back, expected to be enveloped in a cloud of black houseflies. When she saw what it really contained, she was entranced. He promised to catch some for her too, and so again set out on the taxing journey after the show. The next day he was able to present her with two cases of Dartford Blues which her special friend, the Duke of Clarence — later King William IV — declared to be the best he had ever seen.

Many years later the house of young Joe was robbed and vandalised. The irreplaceable collection of butterflies among other things was smashed and scattered beyond repair.

Spring, and the old woman, May, was unravelling her husband's hand-knitted sweaters. The first, grey-green with a dark red fleck, had brought tears to her eyes as she worked. It was the newest she had made him, for his last birthday, and was hardly worn. It was lovely quality too, real wool, and would knit into a nice boy's sweater – she had in mind Lily's fifteen-year-old – but the style wouldn't have suited at all. It had been an old-fashioned design in moss-stitch and cabling with a collar. Boys wanted something simple, a crew-neck, plain.

After the first act of destruction, the job became simpler and she even hummed as she ripped apart the garments made with such diligence and care over the years. True, she paused at times and cocked her head as though straining to recall a conversation from happier days woven into the garment, a mood, a memory of time and place, but it was only a momentary glimpse. She would soon shake her head and unravel, unravel.

In Sonya's house Francis enjoyed a calm and contentment that he couldn't remember having experienced ever before. He now cycled to the library, his car abandoned to Marion, and felt fitter as a result as he took the back roads to avoid the worst of the exhaust fumes.

The room in the extension was a haven to him. No one bothered him there. It was entirely his own place even though the previous occupant had left a strong mark of personality which he was reluctant to dispel. Sitting surrounded by abstract wall-paintings, overlapping or broken circles of colour, blue and terracotta predominating, induced in Francis a sense of well-being and the feeling that an unseen, benevolent presence shared the room with him.

Although he had never shopped for furnishings before – Marion had appropriated that particular task to herself – he now took pleasure in rummaging around for Indian cotton weaves, hand-made rugs. He bought a mobile of thin white shells that tinkled in the least breeze.

He could sit for long periods of time in his room, pretending to read, listening to the tiny sounds of the mobile, the brushing of thin branches against his window, the hopping of light creatures upon his roof.

His appearance changed too, his hair curling over his collar, his clothes looser and lighter.

'Dad,' Valerie said when she visited him, 'you're turning into a hippie.'

Strangely enough, he seemed to see more of Valerie now than when they lived in the same house. She would often pop in with Steve on a Sunday because for some reason Steve and Francis hit it off. Perhaps it was the music. Francis was playing hard and had shown signs of improvement, particularly under the tutelage of Charlotte Isabel.

Steve had been taught classical piano and flute as a child and wanted to be a musician, even though his tastes now ran to traditional Irish music rocked up. He and some friends were trying to get a band together.

'Do you think Val could sing in it?' he asked Francis.

'Can you sing?' he inquired of his daughter.

'She has a lovely pure voice,' Steve said and stroked her arm. 'Only her taste in music's diabolical.'

Francis had no idea what Valerie's taste was in anything but at least she seemed to be developing into a pleasant girl, possibly as a result of this young man's influence. He wondered fleetingly if they slept together but put the notion from his mind.

He saw little of Gerald and worried about him from time to time. Valerie, however, told him that Liam had taken an interest in her brother so Francis stopped feeling anxious.

Ruth was making small cakes in Tom's immaculate kitchen helped by Joanne, his elder daughter. After a chaos of flying flour, an egg that fell to the floor and cooking chocolate that mysteriously diminished every time her back was turned, she had been forced to expel Starveling and Caroline, his other daughter, into the living room to watch television under strict instructions to touch nothing. Tom himself was out buying more goodies for tea. Ruth, though she said nothing, was appalled by the amount of sugar the girls consumed in the form of sweets, biscuits and fizzy drinks. Starveling of course was delighted. Whenever the girls were there, it was party time.

The child, Joanne, frowned as she mixed everything together. In a huge apron that protected her frilly dress, lace-edged white socks and patent leather shoes with a hint of a heel she resembled a midget adult from a fifties' film, while Ruth, in lime green silky pyjama bottoms worn as trousers, with a white and green striped jumper, purple socks and flat bar shoes, looked like an overgrown child. And this was even more evident in their expressions: the child knowing and tense, Ruth vulnerable and open.

Suddenly an uproar came from the living-room. Ruth rushed in. Starveling was screaming while Caroline, with her curled hair even more of an adult in miniature than her sister, looked on with satisfaction.

'What's wrong?' Ruth said, clutching her daughter. 'What's

happened?'

'Nothing,' Caroline answered.

'Something happened,' Ruth replied tartly, 'Hannah doesn't cry for nothing.'

The child smirked and remained obstinately silent.

Joanne watched her sister.

Starveling's sobs began to subside as she pressed against her mother.

'All right, love?' Ruth asked her. She nodded.

'I'll give you the wooden spoon to lick in a minute.'

'I want the bowl,' said Caroline.

'I want the bowl,' said Joanne.

'It's not fair,' said Caroline. She didn't get to make any cakes, she had to sit with the dope.

'You can share it,' Ruth told her, 'if you tell me why Hannah is crying.'

The child fought with her greed, which won.

'I only said she's got no daddy.'

Ruth felt Starveling tense against her.

'Of course she has a daddy,' she replied. 'Everyone in the world has a daddy. Hers doesn't live with her any more than yours lives with you.'

'But he's going to,' Joanne said.

'Going to what?' Ruth asked.

'He's going to live with us,' the child's eyes glinted with malice.

'Is he now?'

'Yes.'

'When the new baby comes,' Caroline said.

'The new baby?' Ruth started to feel sick.

'We're going to have a nice new house in Dublin and a new school with new friends and a new baby, and Daddy's going to live with us again.'

The two girls looked at Ruth in triumph.

'I see.'

'Can we finish making the cakes now?'

'Sure.'

Ruth took Starveling with her into the kitchen and sat her on the counter. What did she care if her daughter smeared grease all over the walls. What did she care.

Liam told his mother that he was worried about Gerald.

'His father heads off just when the lad needs him most . . . I mean, the business with the aerosol, that was a cry for help.'

'Why don't you help him then, son?' his mother said. She often encouraged him to go to Marion's now, almost as if she was throwing the two of them together. Liam wondered if she was coming to like Marion after all. Maybe she had developed a sudden urge for grandchildren. It was very strange.

But he didn't let the thought bother him for long.

'Do you think I should?' he asked. 'I don't want to intrude.'

'I'd say Marion would be grateful,' his mother replied.

So one day Liam brought part of his butterfly collection along to show Gerald. The creatures were neatly arranged in rows and labelled clearly with the name of each variety and the place and date on which it had been caught.

Brimstone. Back garden. 14. 6. 1963.

Small tortoiseshell. Back garden. 5. 4. 1963.

Silver-washed fritillary. Marley Park. 23. 8. 1963.

Small pearl-bordered fritillary. Botanic Gardens. 3. 6. 1963.

'When I was about your age, this was one of my hobbies,' Liam told Gerald. 'In fact your uncle Andy and I were both keen –' (he paused to take a breath for the word) – lepidopterists.'

'Isn't it a bit cruel?' Gerald asked Liam, eyeing the impaled insects warily.

'Not at all, not at all,' Liam replied. 'They don't feel a thing. And their lives are so short anyway.'

'1963,' Gerald remarked. 'That's a long time ago.'

'Yes. If anyone ever asks me if I remember what I was doing when JFK was assassinated, I tell them I was catching butterflies.'

Liam laughed. It was one of his regular jokes.

'Not in November,' Gerald said.

'What?'

'I saw a programme about it. Kennedy was killed in November. You weren't catching butterflies then.'

'No,' Liam said. 'That's true.'

There was a short silence.

'Well,' he said, ' what do you think?'

'Very nice,' Gerald replied.

'Will we go out one day with our nets and our jars?' Liam asked.

'What?'

'The killing jar puts them to sleep quickly and painlessly. It's filled with ether.'

'Oh.'

'See what we can catch. You never know what's going to turn up. How about it?'

'I don't think so,' Gerald shuddered slightly. 'It seems cruel to me.'

So Liam carried his butterflies back home, neatly stacking them with the others in the spare room that held all the carefully preserved relics of his boyhood when he and his pals – especially Andy – sported and played in an endless summer.

Then Liam went to his own room, sat on the edge of his bed and held his head in his hands.

The stage was bare except for a beribboned maypole, not designed by Ruth. The actors, each holding the loose end of a ribbon, stood around the maypole for the entire course of the play, intoning words in a kind of chant as they ducked and bobbed and wove the multi-coloured strips in and out to form, by the finale, a tight mesh.

It was an interesting idea, but the play was Chekhov's *The Seagull* and Francis doubted whether it lent itself to such an experimental interpretation.

Sonya, as the doomed Irina, clad in a shapeless white shift, clung to her pale green ribbon for dear life and chattered out her words like an automaton.

'It's to get away from the dusty old museum versions of the play we've had up to now,' she had told Francis in advance.

In the interval, Steve informed Francis, who had brought him and Valerie to see the show, that he thought it was wonderful, marvellous, 'so symbolic'. Valerie smiled secretively. She had almost dropped off to sleep but wasn't about to let on.

In the second half, Francis paid more attention but still could find little to recommend. Only when the ruined Irina confronts her seducer, the urbane writer Trigorin, he felt that Sonya had actually managed to rise above the constraints of the production. And when she relinquished her ribbon and departed forever in search of something never to be found, he was genuinely moved.

'Perhaps she can act after all,' he thought to himself.

One review was surprisingly positive and Sonya was singled out for special praise. Francis considered that it was probably her appropriately waif-like appearance that had impressed the critic more than anything else.

Steve's paeans after the show in the pub where he and Valerie each illegally drank a glass of lager were very gratifying to cast and production team. Francis was grateful too as it exempted him from expressing a judgement.

At the end of the evening, the director, a college boy with a terrible complexion, took Steve's phone number. Perhaps Steve and his band could provide the music for the next production.

'Sure,' said Steve. 'No sweat.'

Francis never ceased to be amazed at the self-confidence and assertiveness of others.

He and Sonya got a taxi home and she bubbled on uncharacteristically. At the house they went separately, she up to her room, he out to his.

He lay in bed for a long time in the dark, a dim light from the night sky causing thin shadows to wave across his walls from the wands of branches outside his window.

'You fucker, you bastard!' Ruth shouted at Tom, flinging his possessions at him.

Tom was genuinely surprised. Of course, it was unfortunate that Ruth had learned about Nuala's pregnancy so abruptly and crudely. He had intended slipping the news into her one night over a few glasses of wine, a joke against himself: look what happens when defences are down. All right, so he had a certain responsibility, but he'd had that before. One more child wouldn't make much of a difference. So they were coming to Dublin. He wasn't planning actually to move in with them, not immediately, or if he did he would insist on maintaining his independence. Quite frankly, he couldn't see that Ruth or his relationship with her would be in any way affected. He was fond of Nuala in the same way that he was fond of his parents, his children. There was no passion between them any more.

Ruth threw things at him and he felt only a slight remorse and gratification that she was jealous.

Only Ruth didn't consider it jealousy. She felt betrayed and cheated. Exasperated, looking at him standing in front of her so handsome with that sheepish expression on his face as if it didn't matter, as if things could go on as before while she was thinking never, never more.

He thought she would come round. He phoned her constantly, pleading, telling her she was petty bourgeois – one of his favourite expressions of abuse – he accused her of moral blackmail, he told her that she was his real wife but that he couldn't be expected to walk away from his children.

She stopped arguing with him and put the phone down. She unplugged it so that it rang and rang silently. And she started getting used to the silence again.

With Sonya's permission, Francis acquired a dog. In fact, she accompanied him to the Cats and Dogs home to pick out a discarded puppy. It was a mistake to take her. She became excessively upset at the sight of so many creatures facing imminent death and would have brought home half a dozen of the most pathetic. Francis was more circumspect and examined each of the livelier pups with care. Finally he chose a small friendly black dog with a rough coat and enormous paws. Sonya approved.

Cerberus she named him.

They had borrowed Charlotte Isabel's large and battered old car and Francis drove while Sonya held Cerberus and let him lick her face all the way home.

'That's unhygienic,' Francis said.

'I'm bonding with him,' Sonya replied.

So whose dog is it? Francis wondered.

As it turned out, the pup was friendly with everyone as if delightedly aware how lucky he was to be alive. He leapt on to Charlotte Isabel's lap, depositing muddy paw prints on her lilac dress. But he slept in Francis's room and received food mostly from Francis's hand. It was Francis who, after the three-week quarantine following injections against distemper, took him on dancing walks in the park or along the beach, where the creature dashed terrified from the waves or slid down the dunes. The dog, now called Russ for short, rewarded him with total adoration.

It was at Easter that Ruth's mother had a mild stroke. It was so mild in fact that the doctor was not sure that it was anything more than that old familiar, the nasty turn. She had gone to church on Easter Sunday and had felt so peculiar that she had had to sit down during the singing of 'There Is a Green Hill Far Away', one of her favourite hymns.

Ruth's sister, Linda, had come to fetch her mother as usual for Sunday roast but the old lady had not been up to it and had gone to bed, falling into an unarousable sleep. When she finally awoke, she was confused and numb down one side.

Linda had some difficulty in contacting Ruth, who generally still kept her phone unplugged. Finally she rang the old address and reached Sonya who immediately informed Ruth who in turn immediately and guiltily rang her sister. Linda, however, discouraged Ruth from coming over at once.

'Wait and see how she is,' she urged. 'She can stay with us for the time being until we find out whether she has become permanently incapacitated.'

Ruth agreed to come over if and when her mother was able to

return to her own home.

After that, she left the phone plugged in and listened to the silence when it never rang.

Marion was happy that Valerie regularly babysat for a man in the next street whose wife had died, leaving him with two small children. It gave the girl responsibility as well as a few pounds of her own to manage. Marion would have been less delighted to hear that one night the man had returned from the pub with a naggin of whiskey and had made hot punch for himself and her daughter. She would have been enraged to learn that this became a habit and that her fifteen-year-old child soon lapped up the diluted spirit like lemonade, that one night the man put his hand on her daughter's breast and was not slapped or name-called or kneed in the groin but was encouraged by a sleepy smile. That all too soon the two of them were lying naked on the man's bed engaged in vigorous and sweaty pairing until her daughter screamed 'Stop!' in a voice that almost awakened the sleeping babies. That this event occurred not once but on many occasions and that there were times when the man didn't go out at all but took Valerie straight up to his room for an entire evening of passion.

The man was careful but deft. He also insisted that Valerie take a shower before leaving his house. He too possessed an en suite bathroom, by coincidence the same colour and model as Marion's.

Valerie gave up Steve, that kid, and with him her only chance of a career as a singer. However, the boy continued to visit Francis without her. Sometimes the two of them would go for companionable walks with the dog. Her absence was barely felt at first and then not at all.

Marion had other interests. Remembering fondly the ballroom dances of her youth, she had taken up classes in Latin-American dancing and loved it. Soon she found that it was gradually encroaching on the rest of her life as she abandoned aerobics and weaving – though she kept up the Italian because you never knew – and spent her spare evenings in making elaborate costumes for herself. The men were smooth and slick and for a while she changed her partners weekly until she settled into a routine with Raymond, a tall man in his early thirties, a hotel manager.

Soon he was taking her dancing outside the class in a world of clubs she had never even known existed. Competitions were mentioned. Medals. Raymond was an excellent dancer and told her that she was the best partner he had ever had. A natural, he said, though she should lose weight for greater agility.

All he had to do was say the word. Marion was no Bernie. After only a few weeks she had shed a stone.

Charlotte Isabel and Francis had become the best of friends. Sometimes he even suspected the old lady of flirting with him. He gradually found out more about her past life which if she was to be believed had not been above reproach. The daughter of a wealthy lawyer, she had travelled abroad between the wars and had formed a liaison with a young Spaniard who had tragically died in the Civil War on the right side, she said. That is to say, on the left, the republican side.

Her next lover had been Jewish, a Frenchman, and though he himself had survived, many members of his family had disappeared to the camps, a circumstance which filled him with both inconsolable grief and guilt. He finally married a good Jewish girl and worked as a successful doctor in Boulogne for many years before his death in the eighties.

'I kept up with them, you see. A correspondence. I never saw him again although his daughter visited me once. Noémi. A lovely girl.'

She kept all her treasured letters in a small inlaid wooden chest, antique though battered, she said, like herself.

'One of the few possessions I value.'

There were other letters, mostly from her husband, an academic, a mathematician who wrote poems that he never showed to anyone but her. She had these, too, in the box. Thin sheets of yellowing paper covered in spidery writing.

'They'll die with me, I suppose. They'll all be thrown out.'

She looked at him oddly.

'I'm sure Sonya wouldn't throw them away,' he said.

'Oh, Mary!' she exclaimed throwing up her hands. 'She'll bury them under piles of her own rubbish.'

Francis suddenly guessed what she wanted.

'Would you like me to read them? To see if they could be published?'

'Francis!' She took his hand. It seemed absurdly large and clumsy in her tiny one. He kissed hers in a slightly awkward gesture that, however, seemed appropriate.

Witches. They burnt them in the middle ages. At Salem they hanged them. Not toothless hags on broomsticks with pointy black hats but wise women who delivered babies or made remedies from herbs or who lived alone or whom someone else simply didn't like and was jealous of.

Ruth remembered a school reading of Arthur Miller's play, *The Crucible*, in which the girl in the role of Abigail Williams had gradually become completely hysterical, almost possessed. The English teacher had slapped her and then told Ruth, reading the doomed John Proctor – Ruth always got men's parts because of her deep voice – to take her to the lavatory to wash her face. The girl, Edwina something, who was plain and mouselike and who had been given the part to try and bring her out, had been unable to explain why she had been so strongly affected. This part of Abigail Williams was the latest Sonya was auditioning for, more hopeful this time buoyed up by her recent good reviews. In the event, however, the part was was to go to another actor with hair down to her waist and and a good shrieking voice.

The two of them, Ruth and Sonya, were at the Museum of Modern Art at a visiting exhibition by an American woman artist. One room displayed storytelling chairs, painted and decorated with emblems of a particular moment in American history when native and colonial cultures collided.

The Chair of the Dead had feathered arrows for supports and was covered in a Hudson Bay blanket, the mainstay of trade between Indians and colonists. These gaily coloured weaves were said to carry the smallpox that, along with syphilis, measles and cholera, was imported from Europe and decimated the native population.

The Chair of History represented the clash between the Iroquois account of colonisation, carved in picture writing on the chair, and the white man's restricted view of the same events, symbolised by a pair of blind man's spectacles lying on a wooden book.

The museum corridor was lined with broomsticks and other emblems connected with the victims of the New England witchhunts – spikes, pitchforks, gnarled twigs, a wrought steel cross – all delicately draped in handmade white linen aprons, shifts, collars and other items of clothing, while the catalogue described the crimes of which each victim was found guilty: 'intending to make merry at Christmas', 'having an apparent teat in a secret part of the body', 'possessing mutilated poppets', 'confessing to having consorted with the devil', 'causing Henry Miles to discharge a pistol at Luther Banks'.

Accustomed over so many years to Marion's obsessive tidiness, Francis at first found it difficult to come to terms with the total disorder in which Sonya managed to live. Charlotte Isabel's tolerance of it had surprised him until he learnt of her Bohemian past. She picked her meticulous way through the squalor without seeming to notice it. Her own room, which he had only recently visited, was strewn with items of clothing, Persian rugs and Turkish cushions, Bedouin jewellery expressive of a lavish personality at odds with the impression caused by her appearance. Francis came to suspect that her lavender old lady image was something of a pose, something that amused her for the time being. Sonya's room he had still not visited and somewhat dreaded. It was certain to be topsy-turvy and probably filthy too.

He would walk through the garden followed by the ever-enthusiastic dog Russ, wondering vaguely if he should do something here at least. Now that spring was turning into summer, the violence of growth was even more evident. Huge leaves pushed at the windows of the house, darkening with greenish light the room where he sat playing his preludes and sonatinas. Bright grass grew high in the sun with daisies, buttercups and speedwell giving it the look of a meadow. One area of the garden was waist-high with nettles and covered in small brown butterflies, mostly tortoiseshells, and the occasional large-eyed peacocks. It was a charming sight but rapidly getting out of control. Only a portion at the very back, near a lane that constituted a short cut for pedestrians and cyclists, showed signs of attention, vegetables growing, trenches dug, the diligent work of the old man who had known Sonya's dead grandmother.

In something that might once have been a small orchard of pear and apples trees, he and Russ found a broken-down shed crammed with rusty implements. The dog sniffed around, turning up evidence of fairly recent habitation – sacks and newspaper on the floor, open and empty cans of food, milk cartons.

'You seem to have had a tramp living in your back shed,' he told Sonya.

She came to look, although he suspected she was barely aware of the existence of the shed, let alone of any tramp who might have been there. She glanced at the debris and shrugged.

'He should have called to the house. We've plenty of room and he'd have been warmer there . . . Maybe I'll leave a note in case he ever comes back.'

Francis found himself shocked at the idea of taking such a person into the house. Sonya's response might have been predicted, however. She was always handing pounds to beggars and even apologised to them for giving so little, although she had next to nothing herself.

Francis picked up a garment lying on the sacks.

'This would have kept him warm anyway,' he commented.

Sonya took the sweater and held it up against herself.

'It's quite nice and well-made,' she said. 'Hand-knitted . . . Maybe I'll wash it and wear it. Unless you want it, Francis.' He shook his head vigorously. 'I'll put that in the note too, that I've taken it, so that if the owner wants it back he can come and collect it.'

After washing, the sweater turned out to be an attractive shade of dark blue that looked extraordinarily well on Sonya with her crest of red hair. But despite the note that was to stay up through the next winter, becoming faded and stained and torn, the previous owner never turned up to claim it.

Francis took the mower and shears that he found in the shed and had them sharpened. While the dog, who grew bigger and hairier by the day, leapt and cavorted and barked around him, the blades cut through the leaves and stems of encroaching bushes, through grasses and wild flowers. Afterwards, when he paused and viewed the devastation, Francis began to regret his industry until he saw how soon everything sprang up to life again.

A group of Irishmen had lain in an English prison for many years convicted of a crime they hadn't committed. They had been beaten into confessing, their confessions had been doctored, alibis had been suppressed, the forensic evidence that pointed to their guilt had proved dubious, the scientist involved was discredited and given early retirement. A huge demonstration was being organised in Dublin to call world attention to the injustice, with floats and fireworks and a river pageant.

Many actors, street performers, artists and pressure groups were involved, among them Ruth and Sonya. The event would coincide with a street carnival and, as it was to turn out, an important football match for the Irish team in the World Cup.

Ruth was painting placards and helping Sonya with her costume which was simple enough, a plain black robe with a hood. She was to walk in a procession with a candle, chanting the names of the prisoners.

As they worked, Ruth could see that Sonya was distressed.

'What is it?' she asked her friend.

'My life,' Sonya replied. 'They've been in prison for almost all my life.'

She gripped Ruth's hand, tears running down her face.

'Since I was a baby. Before I could remember. All that's happened to me, all that time out of the sun. And all for nothing.'

141

To Lotte

Dark the night, my darling;
Dark your curling hair.
Your eyes like pools in moonlight,
Your skin so wondrous fair.

Come walk with me, my darling,
Through woodland tunnels green
Where branches bow before you
In worship of their queen.

Come lie with me, my darling,
Upon the forest floor.
We'll drown ourselves in kisses
Nor ever seek the shore.

Francis found himself touched at the simple verses if not impressed with their literary quality. He rather wondered, however, why Charlotte Isabel had shown them to him. Did she really imagine they had distinctive merit? Or was she more concerned to prove even to him that she had once been the recipient, the inspirer of deep passion? He tried to imagine the writer – to all outward appearances a somewhat dry individual, rather like himself perhaps. He, however, had never even considered writing verses to Marion. She wasn't the type. And he? Had he ever been sufficiently passionate about any woman?

Kindly he told Charlotte Isabel that while he thought the verses would not stand by themselves, they might be incorporated in a memoir, if she felt like writing it.

'You've led a very interesting life,' he told her. 'Why not try to set it down?'

'My goodness,' she laughed. 'I couldn't possibly do that . . . Could I?'

So Francis bought a ream of paper and lent her his battered Olympia. When he asked her how it was going, she said 'Fine' and let him look at the letters, real love letters almost sixty years old, written to a sparkling, dark-haired Irish girl in a literary Spanish or French that she had to translate for him into florid English.

The Irish football team were doing better in the World Cup than anyone could have predicted. They had reached the final stage and coachloads of fans tore around Southern Europe from match to match or flew down for just one and then stayed, intoxicated by excitement until nothing else mattered, not job, not family, certainly not expense.

Back home, people without any previous interest in the sport were suddenly familiar with the names of the entire team; children knew what position each man played in and re-enacted the matches on open spaces, clad in the green or yellow shirts of their heroes.

Liam and Mark went to the local pub whenever a match was on and watched it on a large screen installed for the purpose. Many pints were drunk and on the occasion of an Irish goal total strangers embraced, Mark winking slyly at Liam. Since New Year they had never discussed the nature of relationships among men but had slipped into what appeared to be an easy and relaxed mateyness, drinking together, going to matches, sometimes visiting each other's house for a game of cards. When this occurred at Liam's, his mother hovered hungrily, sometimes even agreeing to Mark's suggestion that she should join in. He was charming to her, as he was to everyone. She disliked him but no more than she disliked most other people. And when Liam brought home one of

Mark's paintings – he was still attending Ruth's classes – she agreed to let it hang in the living room, a group of magpies perched on bony winter branches so meticulously accurate in the detail of feather, beak and claw, the malice in beady eyes, as to be almost surrealistic.

'Four for a boy,' Liam's mother cackled, 'four for a boy.'

One day Ruth and Starveling went to see Maeve, who was once again pregnant and already huge although only in her fifth month. The women sat in the big untidy kitchen eating the cream cakes Ruth had bought and drinking coffee while Starveling explored the garden with Maeve's youngest, a boy of two.

'Nuala had a mis,' Maeve said and then, when Ruth looked blank, 'Tom's wife lost her baby.'

'Oh, I'm sorry . . . I suppose.' She didn't know whether she was or not. She felt cold.

'You should give Tom a ring. He's very down.'

'No, I shouldn't give him a ring and I'm glad he's down. I'm not sorry for him at all. For her maybe.'

'It was quite late. The fifth month. Her womb kind of collapsed.'

Motherly women, Ruth mused, always seemed to love to discuss grisly gynaecological details.

'The baby was perfectly formed. There was no reason it shouldn't have gone to full term.'

'What age is she?' Ruth didn't know why she was asking; she really couldn't care less.

'She's my age. Thirty-four. We were at university together in Galway.'

'I see.'

'All of us. Fionn and Tom too.'

'Cosy.'

'You shouldn't be bitter, Ruth. He's really fond of you, you know.'

'That's why he impregnated his wife, I suppose.'

'Ah, you know how easily these things happen. You know that.'

Below the belt, Ruth thought.

'I remember at college,' Maeve went on, 'Tom used to say he was capable of being faithful to eight women at the same time.'

'Good for him.'

'Some men are like that.'

Fionn, maybe.

'Not my man,' Ruth said. 'I'm not the jealous type but some things I'm not prepared to share. That's all. Anyway, Maeve, it's history. I'm not picking up with Tom again.'

'Someone else, is there?'

Trust Maeve to assume that. She would be the sort who only defined herself in relation to a man.

'No. I find that life's less stressful without anybody . . . Suddenly I have control of my time. I'm painting again. Proper stuff. For myself.'

'Good,' Maeve said taking a huge bite of meringue. 'Sod them all, anyway . . . '

She had a blob of cream on her nose, giving her a comical look.

'I said I'd say something and I have.'

'Tom put you up to this?'

'Only because he's an old friend. He's very down. But as you say, that's probably where he deserves to be. We'll leave the subject.'

And they did, Ruth conscious that she may have judged Maeve unjustly.

Later Ruth searched out her daughter in the garden and found her sitting on the ground with Ronan, each of them happily munching on a slug.

'Maeve,' she screamed, 'help!'

Getting Nuala pregnant had committed Tom to supporting her while leaving him free to continue his own lifestyle with a clear conscience. Her miscarriage changed things but not back to where they had been before. It was as if the dead baby's cord had bound him to her. Fleetingly, he hoped that Ruth would help him out, say the word and unbind him when she heard that he was again free. Only Ruth, it seemed, could release him from the reproachful image of his wife's drawn and despairing face as she lay in the hospital bed almost whiter than the sheets pulled around her. But Ruth turned away from him and he found himself returning to that gloomy bedside, squeezing his wife's poor hand and saying, 'We'll have another, if that's what you want,' and her squeezing back, suddenly strong, drawing blood from him, looping the cord about him like a lasso and pulling tight, tighter until there was no hope of breaking out ever again.

And because it was not what Nuala really wanted, the house in Dublin was never bought. Tom abandoned journalism and took up a well-paid post in an up-and-coming Galway public relations firm. He amused his new friends with the republican politics he espoused after a few jars and they bought him pints just to hear him rant. The Dublin flat was first let then sold along with all its japonaiserie. Among the few enough items Tom took with him was the little sketch Ruth had made of Fionn as a bacchanal. Nuala said it was rather good and asked who did it and to avoid trouble Tom told her it was by one of the cartoonists at the paper. So he was able to keep it by him and look at it from time to time to prove to himself that there was one small secret place of his own left to him.

And Ruth kept the portrait of Tom she had dashed off to show her clients: a lock of hair hanging over his forehead, his white teeth gleaming – teeth were hard to do convincingly and she was proud of their verisimilitude. She hung it in her bedroom and sometimes when she looked at it she cried with self-pity and sometimes she smiled wryly to herself.

On the pretext of having to discuss their financial affairs, Marion turned up one day at Sonya's house. She had phoned the library and found that it was Francis's day off.

Why not, she thought, getting his address off Valerie and hopping in the car. The house looked old and dilapidated, gloomy. She walked briskly up the gravel drive which had weeds growing out of it and rung a door bell which jangled like a real bell, not an electric shriek or chimes or the device which Marion had recently had installed (not by Liam) and which played at random the first notes of one of a selection of eight tunes and which drove Valerie and Gerald wild with mortification, especially when the tune was 'Dixie'. After a while the door was opened by an elderly woman who was dressed rather like a maid of bygone days in a black frock with a lace collar and a white linen apron.

'Francis?' she said in reply to Marion's query, 'Yes, he's playing the piano.'

And indeed the hesitant sounds of a piece of music could be heard in the distance.

As Charlotte Isabel led the way, Marion said, 'Excuse me, you aren't Sonya by any chance?'

At this stage she wouldn't have been surprised.

'No and I'm not Mary either,' the old lady replied cryptically.

Francis thought Marion looked older. She had lost a lot of weight, the effect of which was to make her age faster, slacker skin falling into wrinkles and pouches. Also she was undergoing sun-lamp treatment to give herself the permanent tan appropriate to a Latin-American dancer in flimsy dresses. It made her appear fit but it desiccated her skin. And this harder look was accentuated by a new short haircut and the cigarette she lit immediately on entering the room, a habit she had taken up again after twenty years to help her stay thin.

But if he thought her harder, she found him softer with his longer hair – it was longer than hers now – fuller face and looser clothes. Not that he was fat, not at all. It was as if he had relaxed and in doing so had spread out.

She didn't approve. Not of him, not of the murky room he sat in – despite his best efforts with the shears the bushes were already pushing up against the windows again – the heavy dusty furnishings.

'How your asthma?' she asked, exhaling smoke.

'Much better,' he replied.

'It can't be the dust mite you're allergic to, then,' she commented, a tight frown knotting her face.

Charlotte Isabel brought coffee and biscuits on a tray covered with a gleaming lace-edged cloth and served in tiny china cups. Francis smiled at her.

'You're amazing,' he said to Charlotte Isabel and Marion wondered at the warmth in his voice.

Francis was in fact relieved that he could keep his wife from entering the sordid kitchen or his own room. He particularly dreaded the speaking glance that would have contaminated his treasured refuge. Knowing her, she might even have started tidying up.

She spoke to him of money and he agreed to increase his payments to her even though it would leave him short. He wanted her to go as soon as possible but he couldn't resist raising his eyebrows at the sight of several items on the accounts she provided.

'£300 for costumes?' he queried. 'Seems steep.'

'And if I bought them instead of making them myself it would cost four times the amount,' she snapped. 'Latin dancing is my one and only pleasure these days. God, do you want me to stay in all the time like Cinderella?'

'Not at all,' he said. 'I'm glad you're having a ball.'

She gave him what she considered a withering look.

'At least it gives me something to do,' she said.

She had certainly never been short of that, he thought, but let it go.

He nearly didn't let go the installation of 'Dixie' but laughed instead.

'It must sound terrible.'

Suddenly Russ burst into the room, barking loudly and jumping up on Marion with muddy paws.

'My suede trousers!' she screamed.

'Naughty dog,' clucked Charlotte Isabel, entering after him. 'I opened the back door for a second to put out the rubbish and he just shot in . . . They know when strangers,' – and she emphasised the word ever so slightly – 'are about. Oh dear, your lovely outfit!'

She watched Marion rubbing the marks in.

'Never mind,' Francis said. 'You can send the cleaning bill to me.'

'I will,' Marion snapped. 'You can be sure of that.'

He caressed the dog and gave him a biscuit.

'You're rewarding it!' Marion exclaimed. 'It should be smacked.'

'But Russ didn't know he was doing wrong, did you, Russ. He was being friendly.'

Soon afterwards, Marion departed even though she had hoped

to hang on and see that bitch Sonya, described unsatisfactorily by Valerie as 'all right, I suppose.'

After the door shut behind her, Francis turned to Charlotte Isabel and said for the second time that day, 'You're amazing. You really are, you know.'

And she smiled very sweetly and collected the tray.

'You can wash up,' she said.

The city streets were crowded for the carnival. Ruth walked around with Starveling but they could see nothing. People pressed in on them on all sides and soon the child got agitated and started to gasp for breath. Ruth took her away from the main throng and, finding herself nearby, into Ari's wine bar.

The picture was gone, Philip was gone, other young men served. After a while, Ari came out to her. He looked less jolly than usual, less rotund.

'He left. I don't know where he go.'

Ruth looked at the space on the wall.

'He take it . . . I pay. He take it. Ha! It don't matter. I like to keep it but . . . I don't know where he go. I don't know who he's with.'

To her distress, the man's eyes filled with tears.

'Always laughing, that Philip, always joking. Friendly with everyone. I hope he's careful. I tell him so many times, be careful. He laughs. Such a funny man.'

Ari patted her hand, then the passing bum of one of the boys, who grinned at them.

'Ice-cream for miss, on the house.'

'A small one,' Ruth said. Starveling was often sick.

Ari winked and lumbered off to make it.

Outside, a group of clowns skipped up, pressed their faces against the window pane and grimaced in at Starveling, who stared back expressionlessly.

When the enormous ice-cream arrived, garnished with all sorts of fruit and jelly and cream and nuts she ate most of it and had no ill-effects at all.

The match was scheduled for early evening, Irish time. The pub was crowded and rowdy and already a large quantity of beer had been drunk. Liam had dashed back from work and was able only to make a sandwich before going out.

'You'll be late back, I suppose,' his mam said.

'I'd say so. Don't wait up,' he kissed the hair on the top of her head as usual and noticed how thin it was getting; he could see her pink scalp.

'There's a late film I want to watch, if I don't drop off in the chair.'

'Well, enjoy yourself, mam,' he told her.

'I will. I've seen it before. It's a good one.'

He knew most of the people in the pub and stopped to talk to them before working his way through to where Mark was saving a place for him.

'This is good,' he said, sitting down. 'A real ringside seat.'

'I got here early to make sure,' Mark told him.

'And the kids? Is your wife home?'

'No, she's on duty. I had to get a babysitter in. Your friend Marion's girl. She's reliable, isn't she?'

'I'd say so. She usually babysits for Mick.' They both looked over to where an undersized, fox-faced man sat downing a pint. 'I wonder who he's got in tonight.'

'She said she was free anyway.'

'You must have got in first.'

And they forgot about it in the excited build-up to the kick-off.

Back home, Liam's mam got a can of stout out of the fridge and fetched her special glass down off the shelf. Then she returned to the living-room where she tried to find something to watch that wasn't football while waiting for her film, *The Shining*, to start.

Valerie sat in Mark's front room staring at the television while the children played around her.

That bastard, she thought, having the cheek to expect her to turn up again after what had happened the last time. She hadn't believed it when he'd rolled in from the pub in a foul temper and started knocking her about because she wouldn't have sex with him. Well, her period had started and she didn't like doing it then. Not that she told him that. None of his business. So he'd tried to force her – she still had bruises on her arms and chest. She'd started yelling and even in the state he was in he must have realised he would have some explaining to do if anyone called the guards.

'I'm not your wife,' she'd said. 'You can't get away with that sort of thing with me.'

He'd got nasty then and she suspected she'd hit a large and ugly nail on the head.

He'd said he would tell everyone that they'd been having it off for months and she'd replied, 'Go ahead, I'll tell them you raped me. Who'll they believe?'

That had stopped him. He wasn't that stupid. And she was underage, too.

'I could go to the guards now with these bruises,' she'd said, 'only I don't want any hassle.'

She'd also said, 'Just how did your wife die anyway?' Then wished she hadn't because that nearly got him going again. He'd swung at her and caught her shoulder but she'd dashed out of the house.

He hadn't paid her for that night and when he'd rung to ask her to babysit again, he'd said she could collect the money owed her and a bonus as well. She'd told him he could stuff the bonus up his arse, which had caused Gerald, who was sitting in the same room at the time, to look at her in astonishment.

'Prick,' she'd said, slamming the phone down. Even now, she shook with anger when she thought of him. Little bastard.

One of Mark's children brought her over a book and she read *The Three Billy Goats Gruff* to them, putting on funny voices because, despite everything, Valerie was really very good with children.

The score was nil—all. It was all down to a penalty shoot-out. Tension was high in the smoky room. The place fell silent as the players got into position. One to Rumania. Groans. One to Ireland. Cheers. One to Rumania. Groans. Some people looked away or left the room, unable to bear it. One to Ireland. One to Rumania. One to Ireland. One to Rumania. How long could it go on?

One to Ireland. The players regrouped tightly. The Rumanian took aim; the Irish goalie stood trying to judge which way to jump. The Rumanian ran at the ball, kicked it; the Irish goalie, Packie Bonner, fell on it – a save. All over the country people erupted, in pubs and private house, hotels and clubs. One more risk. An Irish player had to win the next shot.

'The Rumanians are desperate men,' the commentator said.

They regrouped. O'Leary's kick shot into the net. Ireland had won.

The supporters at the ground, the supporters in the pub, leapt in the air, clapped each other on the back, embraced. Mark hugged Liam, who hugged him back tight, tight.

The man Mick tapped Mark on the shoulder and as he turned,

took a swing at him. Liam was faster and anyway had boxed in his youth. He blocked the blow, at the same time giving Mick a punch in the guts sufficient to wind him.

'What the fuck's up with you?' he asked the small man, who was coughing and gasping.

'Tell him to lay off my girl,' he muttered, stumbling off.

'What did he mean?' Liam asked.

'I haven't the slightest idea,' Mark answered, shocked. 'I don't even know who his girl is.'

'He's pissed out of his skull,' a man standing by commented. And they left it at that.

The thought of Valerie never even occurred to them. It would have seemed fantastic.

Night fell and the march was well-attended, an enormous crowd filling the street beside and behind the floats of caged men and women, the grotesque judge sitting on a heap of garbage, the procession of hooded mourners with their candles, chanting the names of the prisoners, fire dancers, acrobats, clowns. Gradually the throng, still in carnival mood, moved towards the river where six banners, each depicting the face of one of the prisoners, floated on the water behind six rafts.

Into this mass drifted football supporters from the pubs, buoyed up with euphoria. Already entrepreneurs were getting to work printing celebratory tee-shirts: 'Ireland 5 – Rumania 4' or cartoon pictures of the heroes of the match, O'Leary and Bonner.

Ruth was there with a crowd of people she knew and Francis too, on a different side of the river. Liam and Mark, the brief unpleasantness in the pub already forgotten, pushed through to the quayside. Marion, driving back from an Italian class got caught in the celebrations on O'Connell Street: people jumping on the roofs and bonnets of cars stopped at the lights or by the stream of bodies crossing the road. She was terrified. Cars around her were tooting a sort of tattoo – short short short long short long and people chanted 'Ire-land, Ire-land' or sang that irritating Olé! song. At last a guard waved her into Abbey Street and she swung round, a final joyrider still clinging to the back of her car until she stopped at the lights near the railway bridge, when he hopped off with a cheeky grin and a wave.

At the river, the rafts were being rowed towards the arched pedestrian bridge, the Ha'penny Bridge, where the banners were drawn up out of the water to hang in a row from the structure's ironwork. There were some emotional speeches, then music. And then the fireworks started.

Ruth loved fireworks. Magic. Her eyes sparkled with pleasure and tears of emotion. But everyone was caught up in it. The rockets burst open to gasps and then more gasps as they seemed to expand and bloom and swell and multiply, coruscating white turning to green turning to blue turning to crimson, each spark exploding in another riot of light, more and more and more and, before you could regret it was gone, another and another followed and then, when it seemed they were all finished, a clenched fist materialised from the black night, clutching a flaming scales of justice.

People were dancing in the streets, football supporters with freedom marchers. It seemed that everything was possible. It occurred to no one that this moment too was bursting in all its glory like a rocket and that in another instant the skies would darken again and that the darkness would be even more impenetrable after the light. For the moment, everyone danced. Ruth pausing, glanced across the river to where Francis stood staring at the crowd on the far bank, a smile in his eyes. They didn't notice each other. How could they among so many?

PART SIX

MIRACLES AND MAGIC

Since he was a toddler, thrust into animal skins and tossed around the stage for the amusement of the audience, young Joe's life had been the theatre. The harshness of the existence – the knocks and accidents, the long hours of energetic contorting, the meagre diet, the compensating quantities of cheap wine and gin – brought most of his calling to an early grave and young Joe was no exception. Ruined in body in his forties he still hoped that, as the custom was, his son would follow him on to the stage. But his son was a hopeless drunk whom no one found funny. He died even before his father.

There is a regular joke that when clowns get melancholic – as most of them seem to – they are advised by clueless doctors of an infallible remedy for it: go and see the clowns. This was said to have been prescribed to young Joe and to others as well. Perhaps the condition of having to inspire constant mirth is one of the saddest things in the world, for laughter is so often cruel.

And yet comedy is transcendent, too. Everyone knows how to sorrow since life is tragic and inevitably fatal. But to be able to laugh despite that, to find humour in the very facts of our mortality, the absurdity of our aspirations, imparts a kind of nobility after all to the miserable animals that we are, a kind of godhead.

And once, when a deaf and dumb sailor went to see young Joe perform, he laughed so much that those around him were astonished to hear him suddenly exclaim, 'I can hear!' and then realising what he had done, 'I can speak!'

Midsummer night.

Francis was lying on top of his bed reading a detective novel about a plausible villain who did away with anyone who blocked his path but so skilfully that murder was never suspected. Near the end of the novel it was touch and go as to whether he would be found out. He had taken one chance too many and eyebrows were being raised. Francis sipped his glass of Algerian red wine and looked out at the evening, the light still not completely gone even at ten thirty. The dog, Russ, was curled on the chair twitching in sleep, dreaming of chasing a squirrel perhaps. Francis felt good.

Later, when it was completely dark and the villain had convinced everyone of his innocence and a final hint pointed chillingly to his next victim, Francis decided to wander as he often did in the garden. The thinnest sliver of a waxing moon and a multitude of stars rare in a city sky set the stage for a dream.

Russ of course followed him out, sniffing in the lengthening grass. Francis went to the orchard where tiny fruits were already loading unpruned trees. He glanced at the shed; there was no light and all was quiet. And proving more conclusively than anything else that no one was there, Russ totally disregarded it and skipped off into the distance.

Branches framed the sky. What did the ancients think of the stars? That they were holes in a blanket covering heaven, that they were stuck to an invisible sphere rotating round the earth, that they were the children of the sky goddess clinging to the belly of their mother.

And what are they after all? Condensed globes of gas and dust shining more and more brightly as they heat up, fading as they slowly die or suicidally explode.

Francis was suddenly overcome with a yearning sadness there in the softly breathing night. He had never regretted leaving Marion. Of course not. But perhaps the wine had made him maudlin. He felt himself to be alone in the universe, with no close friends, without even the fiction of a family any more, the easily-won devotion of a dog all he could hope for. And he himself was without passion. He had never ached for any human being; he had never released himself enough to converge joyously with another. He had always been selfconscious to the exclusion of everyone else, myopic almost to blindness. Feeling his way through a benighted garden on overgrown paths just about summed up his life.

Yet the garden was sweet. A bush of orange blossom grew somewhere near and soaked the air with its scent. Francis discovered it by smell more than sight and tipped its delicate petals with his fingers. He picked just one sprig and carried it with him, gasping in the perfume.

The dog was moaning in the distance. Francis picked a darker path towards the sound without fear. There was no intruder or Russ would have barked frenziedly. Perhaps the dog was hurt.

He stung his hand on a nettle and cursed. The dog was still a way off, near the back of the garden. Francis rubbed at his burning hand. A twig scratched across his face.

He would have to be careful not to crush any of the old man's vegetable patches. Russ was still further off but suddenly ran up to him, dark out of darkness, and rubbed against his legs and whined. Francis followed the dog through the garden to where a pit had been recently dug. Something loomed there, pale and elongated. He crouched down to see by the thin moon and was filled with horror. A woman lay, naked and still, but what was even more horrible, she was covered in snails and the tracks of snails dimly gleaming silver by moonlight.

With the detective novel fresh in his mind, Francis immediately assumed her to be dead and violently so. He touched her face. It was ice cold but her eyes suddenly opened, causing him to cry and fall back.

'It's you,' Sonya said. Then, 'I wanted to know how it felt.'

He threw the snails from her body with disgust and lifted her out of the pit. She put an arm round his neck to let herself be carried but otherwise was disturbingly quiescent. She was light but seemed to become heavier with every step and he found himself staggering back towards the house. He had never known it to be so far away.

He put her in the nearest place, his own bed, having wrapped her in a towelling robe. He chafed her hands and feet, kissing them. He poured out some wine and held it for her to drink.

'You silly girl,' he babbled, 'what made you do such a thing?'

'There are so many dead,' she said in despair.

She was shivering so much he climbed in beside her and lay against her to make her warm. At last she curled up and slept against his chest as trustfully as a child, while he lay on his back staring out of the skylight at the thinnest sliver of a midsummer moon.

The year was over. The school year. Ruth was saying goodbye to her good class. In addition to the big glossy book on Frida Kahlo which they presented to her as a group, she received some small individual tokens from them: chocolates, a bottle of Rhine wine, a scarf, a couple of expensive brushes – deeply appreciated – a free pass for two to the greyhound track from one slightly embarrassed old man who had painted some extraordinarily messy abstracts during the course of the year, delighted to be allowed to do his own thing. Mark gave her a bunch of red roses.

He also suggested that they should all meet that evening for a few pints and several of them did, toasting art and Ruth and then ruder things as the drink took effect.

'Van Gogh's other ear!'

'Picasso's penis!"

They all laughed. Even the elderly maiden lady who went to Mass every day and who had painted three soppy-looking blessed virgins in what she called a 'trip-trick'.

'This is a lovely drink, you know,' she would say every time someone bought her another rum and blackcurrant.

Mark, ever the gentleman, drove her home. He watched the old lady make it safely into the house and then continued with Ruth, to whom he was also giving a lift. He started telling her how much the classes had meant to him.

'After losing my job, you know, I felt very unstable. This focussed me again. I'm going to keep it up.'

'Good,' she said.

'Can I come to your class next year?' he asked.

'Of course. Why not?'

'You might prefer new faces.'

'Not at all. The more the merrier. And this was a good group.'

They reached her house. She didn't feel inclined to ask him in. It was not that she disliked him but there was something disquieting about his relentlessly charming manner, his ever-smiling face. Burnished by the amber street light, it suddenly looked to her like a mask. There was a pause.

'Do you want to come in for some coffee?' she asked at last for something to say.

He was silent, smiling at her strangely. Then he took her hand, leaned across and kissed her cheek.

'Not tonight. Thanks.'

'Bye, Mark. Thanks for the lift. And the roses.'

'Bye, Ruth. See you.'

A funny fellow, she thought, and forgot him.

She paid off the baby-sitter, turned off the television which was showing a Barbra Streisand comedy the babysitter said was 'brilliant' and listened to the slow ticking of the inaccurate old clock on the mantelpiece.

It used to drive Tom wild.

'What's the point of a clock that's always wrong?' he would say.

She told him that she bought it because she liked the look of it, that he had a watch if he wanted to know the right time.

She looked past the clock to Mark's roses in the large kitschy jug she used as a vase. They had an uncannily artificial look but she knew they were real because she had pricked her finger on a thorn while trimming the ends. She thumbed through the Frida Kahlo book, staring into the searching eyes of the artist in one self-portrait after another. Ruth had never painted a self-portrait. The only mirror in the house was a small one in the bathroom for she found the unexpected sight of her face depressing. Suddenly she wondered if she really knew what she looked like. She felt her face, like a blind person might and considered whether it would be easy with practice to recognise someone by touch.

Then she went into Starveling's room and stood over the sleeping child and ran her fingers over her face and felt that she would always recognise her. The child rolled over in sleep, stretched out thin arms as though trying to catch hold of some elusive thing. Then sighed and was still again.

'You don't know what happened to Mary's parents?' Charlotte Isabel asked Francis in her lavish room where he had sought her out the morning after midsummer, leaving Sonya sleeping in his bed.

'No. Is it relevant?'

He had told Charlotte Isabel what had happened, where he had found the girl, what she had said.

'They committed suicide together when she was very small. She found them dead.'

'My God.'

'No one knows why they did it. They were young, healthy, with a family. No money problems.'

'It was definitely suicide?'

'They took strong barbiturates dissolved in sweet wine.'

'One could have flipped, killed the other, then committed suicide.'

'There was a note which said "Sorry, we can't go on." Both of them signed it.'

Francis shook his head.

'Mind you,' Charlotte Isabel went on, 'I always found him too nice, too controlled, like someone playing a part. My daughter, Mary's mother, was totally bound up in him.'

'You must feel bitter.'

'Not now. But I don't know how she could have left her child like that. Or let her find them afterwards. It was a thoughtless, selfish cruelty.'

'What was your daughter's name?'

'You know it.'

'No, I don't.'

'Her name was . . . Sonya, of course.'

So that was it.

'His mother, Mary's other grandmother, owned this house. She left it to Mary because the poor child had nothing else.'

'Did she rear her?'

'Yes. Mary loved her and she loved Mary. When the old woman died – a few years ago now – Mary didn't tell anyone for two whole days. She tucked her up in bed like she was sleeping. You see, she couldn't bring herself to admit the fact that her gran had left her, too.'

So many dead.

'It broke her little heart.'

'She had you.'

'Me? I'm a poor substitute. But then, she doesn't need me any more.'

'She must still be very disturbed . . . Last night . . . '

'She's all right. She's grieving. Her gran's death stirred up terrible memories. But it's passing. It's healing.'

'You don't think we need to call in a doctor?'

'Is she sick?'

'I don't think so. Not physically. It was a warm night.'

'Just love her. That's what she needs.'

Francis looked at her in amazement.

'Me? No, no . . . I didn't touch her. There's nothing like that.'

'Oh,' said Charlotte Isabel.

Francis had been required to dip into his not-very-deep pocket yet again in order to pay for his two children to go to the *gaeltacht* for three weeks in the summer to improve their Irish and get out of Marion's now very short hair.

'You don't know what it's like,' Marion had said reproachfully, 'having them under your feet for all those weeks – Gerald especially mooning about the place.'

And Francis, who had hoped to get a week off himself somewhere abroad, had to change his ideas.

Valerie was delighted to get away. The man Mick seemed to know when she was going out or coming home and would lie in wait for her, grabbing her arm and asking her in front of her friends when she was coming round to 'babysit' again or, when she was by herself, pressing her up against a wall, rubbing up against her and trying to kiss her with his wet, beery mouth. But he couldn't follow her to the west of Ireland and three weeks was a long time. Maybe he would find someone else.

Gerald was apprehensive. He feared his peers and the pathways down which he might be forced to follow them. But it was something to do. The summer stretched ahead with only the same old computer games to play or Liam knocking hopefully at the door, a tennis racket or swimming gear in his hands.

While they were away, Marion planned to go to a sun spot with Bernie – Spain or Majorca or Greece – though she didn't mention this to Francis. Well, it was none of his damn business.

Ruth's mother had insisted on returning home from Linda's house, where she had been staying since Easter, despite not being fully recovered. Ruth decided to go over to her, if possible making arrangements for Starveling to be left with someone for a short time.

She thought first of Maeve but decided that she couldn't inflict another child, and such a child, on a pregnant woman even though Maeve would probably be willing. Linda had offered to take her but Ruth refused on the grounds that Starveling would be disturbed among strangers in a strange place. Secretly she feared putting her in a position where her mother might see her. Ruth was vulnerable enough to dread what her mother might say – the unanswerable questions she would ask – or what she wouldn't say, her mouth pursed in an I-told-you-so expression.

She was explaining her predicament to Sonya, who immediately said, 'No problem!' She would mind Starveling.

A week had elapsed since the incident in the garden and Sonya was fine again as if nothing had happened, clowning around St Stephen's Green with a white face, tiny red mouth and red cheeks, zig-zag scar exaggerated with green paint, and wearing hugely baggy trousers. She was accompanied by another actor who could juggle well but who made a comic point of almost dropping everything. They were collecting an impressive amount of money from the generous summer crowd.

Ruth thanked Sonya for her offer.

'But you're out so much. I don't know how long I'll be away. It would be too much of a tie for you.'

'Me and Charlotte Isabel,' said Sonya. 'And Francis.'

'Who's Frances?'

'The man who plays the piano.'

'Oh. Well, I don't know . . . '

'But Charlotte Isabel is home all the time. She's good with children . . . Starveling'll be grand. Honestly, Ruth.'

Starveling was well used to Sonya and had met Charlotte Isabel on several occasions.

'But the garden . . . '

'It's safer now. Francis has cleared it up a lot. Anyway, Starveling is older.'

'But no more sensible.'

'Oh Ruth. She's a lovely child.' Sonya's mouth drooped right down in a large smile. 'A special child.'

So it was arranged that Starveling should go to Sonya with Maeve standing by as a fall-back in case anything went wrong.

Starveling was very excited at the prospect of returning to the old house and it caused Ruth a rueful qualm to see the absence of sorrow on her daughter's part at the prospect of being separated from her mother.

May, the old woman, had employed two of her grandchildren – the seventeen-year-old girl and the fifteen-year-old boy – to do up her house. They had stayed with her for a week in June, during the school holidays and had enjoyed being so near the city centre as well as earning money.

May was glad and sad to see them go.

'They livened the place up,' she told her neighbour who thought 'too much' having endured late-night heavy metal through the bedroom walls, slamming doors, thumping up and down stairs at all hours. Not to mention the bang bang banging of the hammer day in day out.

'Let's see how it looks then,' the neighbour said. She had been dying of curiosity.

The house was like an arbour. The front door had been painted deep pink and pink was evidently a favoured colour of the owner. Pink flowers grew up the wallpaper from the skirting boards (painted pale green in the hall, along with the doors), looping and twining and turning mauve and blue in the living-room, pale orange and yellow in the dining room, poppies bursting all over the kitchen. A carpet of flowers lay underfoot everywhere except in the kitchen where the floor tiles were green as grass. Pictures of flowers hung on the walls, vases stood around the house filled with the real thing or paper or silk imitations.

'My gracious,' the neighbour said. 'Jim would never recognise the old place.'

'I personally wouldn't like it,' she later told her next neighbour on the other side. 'Even the chair coverings, even the curtains have flowers on. It's too much if you know what I mean. But whatever else it is, it's certainly cheerful.'

The front garden too was changed, no longer confining the flowers and shrubs in neat beds but letting them overrun the whole of the small patch. Small stone cherubs were entwined with sweet peas or peered out from under rose bushes, *Joseph's Coat* and *Albertine*.

'This must have cost you an arm and a leg,' the neighbour said to May.

'I had a bit put by,' she smiled, looking up at the cloudless sky, 'for a rainy day.'

'I hope she hasn't gone off her rocker,' the neighbour commented to her next neighbour, adding as often before, 'though it wouldn't be surprising after what she's been through. I nearly went to pieces after Monty disappeared.'

May shut the door. Now the noise was all gone, the loud clatter of the teenagers, the clack clack clack of the neighbour's mouth. Only herself and her cat Fluff left to enjoy the enchanted garden.

Ruth's mother was sadly changed, much reduced. Ruth was amazed that Linda had given in to her wish to return home. Evidently she couldn't cope. The house was filthy. It took her ages to pull herself up the stairs to the lavatory and she must have been caught short a few times for the remnants of inadequately cleared up messes formed discoloured patches on the carpet. Her right arm was weak and as a result she couldn't open tins or prepare food properly and sucked on crackers and biscuits instead of eating meals.

But she was more stubborn and cranky than ever which probably accounted for Linda finally giving in and bringing her home. They had been robbing her things, she told Ruth. He, Linda's husband, took her underwear so she had none to put on.

'Dirty, dirty,' she said, though it was unclear whether this referred to her underwear or to Linda's husband.

Ruth cleaned up the house and her mother. She established herself in her old bedroom, still full of her books and early paintings. Among them she found a teenage self-portrait she had forgotten about, atrociously daubed, with sepia skin, long heavy hair like wholewheat spaghetti and the lightest, most penetrating of blue eyes, striking but totally unlike the soft grey ones that looked out at Ruth's world.

My diaries are probably still there, too, she thought to herself, in among the copybooks and files of notes for English A-level, beloved *Anthony and Cleopatra*, loathed *Jude the Obscure*. She would look them out some day and see whether she recognised herself any better in them than she recognised the face in the self-portrait.

After a few days she had the terrible feeling that her mother had given up. Of course, she had to be looked after, no doubt about it. But she stopped making any effort for herself, ringing at the slightest thing the little brass bell Ruth had found for her.

She would sit for hours dozing. She seemed to have forgotten about the Judgement, at least she never mentioned Starveling or enquired about her. Her old favourite Linda and family were the object of her complaints now. She seemed to take Ruth's presence for granted as if she had never gone away. As if she had stayed like a dutiful daughter when her parents wanted her to and had subsequently lived out a totally different life.

A pal from the Mother's Union visited her occasionally, full of virulent gossip, especially concerning the vicar's independent wife. Ruth, overhearing, was amused. To hear them take the woman apart, you would almost think they were jealous.

Ruth soon realised that her notion of a flying visit would have to be rethought. Impossible to consider leaving her mother alone again and, both sisters baulking at the idea of a nursing home or hospital, she decided to prolong her stay. And though Ruth was missing her daughter badly, it was equally inconceivable that Starveling should be brought over to this house of sickness. In any case, the child was reportedly content.

But Ruth was frustrated by inactivity. There were of course plenty of menial tasks to be done. Her mother was demandingly houseproud and, although herself forced through weakness to let the place go, kept thinking of jobs for Ruth to do over and above the necessary washing and cooking. The venetian blinds needed cleaning – a hand-shredding task. She wanted the outsides as well as the insides of her saucepans to gleam. Endless ornaments and knick-knacks required constant washing or dusting. Brass handles and knockers, silver cutlery, had to be polished. She even started hinting that the windows could do with a coat of paint. Ruth largely ignored her. Her own attitude was that you could spend your life bothering with such things and then wonder what had happened to it. In any case the old lady was beyond doing an inspection and soon forgot what new task she had laid on her daughter.

In a press in her room, Ruth found a bag full of old but largely unused bottles of ink, a pad of cartridge paper with embarrassingly bad drawings on several pages – these she ripped out and up – but also many blank pages full of possibilities. There was in addition a roll of wallpaper, the back of which would do very well as a Japanese type of scroll. She took out the good brushes presented to her by one of her students and in the long silences of the day started working more intensely than ever before.

'Well, what do you think?' Charlotte Isabel asked anxiously, with a quizzical look in her eyes at the same time, that gave Francis the uncomfortable feeling that he was being sent up.

'This isn't a memoir,' he commented, patting the handwritten pages on the table. 'Is it?'

If what he had read were true, the first years of Charlotte Isabel's life were even more amazing and off the wall than he had suspected. She had also enjoyed an extraordinarily raunchy sex life.

'I couldn't do it. It didn't work. I found it completely tedious and kept wanting to add little bits to jizz it up. Then I thought, why bother with my real life. Why not write about the life I would like to have lived instead?'

'You'd like to have lived like this?'

'Only in fantasy perhaps. When my heroine gets old I'm going to give her a passionate affair with a much younger man.'

She was sending him up for certain.

'Well, what do you think?' she asked.

'It'll be a best seller if it isn't banned.'

'The nice thing about fiction is that you can make it up,' the old lady said. 'And if you want to throw in a bit of fact, you can jizz it up and no one can complain that you're telling lies because it's all just a story anyway.'

'I see you decided to write it out by hand in the end.'

'Yes, I can't get the hang of that old typewriter of yours. The letters fly up in the air or disappear completely or get all mixed up . . . I was wondering, Francis . . . would you ever have the time to type it up for me and maybe correct my spellings and grammar and things like that.'

'Oh God,' he groaned.

'I'm so good to you,' she winked flirtatiously, 'And I'll dedicate it to you and give you a percentage if it ever is a best seller.'

What could he say?

Between that and work and minding the strange little child that one of Sonya's friends had loaned her for some peculiar reason for the summer his days were full.

And Charlotte Isabel's book was very entertaining.

The Irish school attended by Valerie and Gerald was in the wild west of Ireland on the side of a mountain in a village the name of which wasn't to be found on ordinary maps, only on those on the scale of half an inch to a mile or less. Valerie's accomodation, her *teach*, was over the other side of the mountain and though a minibus was provided to bring them to and from their classes, she and the others in the small cluster of houses often had to walk up or down the steep lane between dry stone walls. Gerald's lodging was at the very bottom of the mountain, near a long sandy beach they were forbidden to visit unchaperoned in case of accident. Most things were in fact forbidden them unchaperoned though plenty was organised for them to do in the form of Irish classes in the mornings, sports in the afternoons and céilí dancing in the evenings. Valerie at first tolerated it and then enjoyed it because she soon made close friends with the other girls in her house. Close in more ways than one. With six to every available room in triple bunk beds, the annual influx of students no doubt provided a necessary bonus to the income of struggling folk in a depressed part of the country but this charitable explanation didn't improve tempers when you couldn't even brush your hair without sticking an elbow in someone's eye.

Gerald, in similarly squashed circumstances, hated it. He was bad at Irish, disliked sport and loathed céilí dancing. On top of everything else the youth leader, the *ceannaire*, in his house was some sort of warped sadist. He lorded it over the boys, making them clean his runners with spit, deliberately dropping the contents of ashtrays on the floor for them to clear up before the woman of the house, the *bean a' tí*, discovered them. He confiscated their letters from home before they had a chance to read them and made them pay him to get them back, having first read what was written and using the information, the warm expressions of loving parents, the pet names, to mock and jeer. The reason no one reported him was the one usually relied on by bullies: no one will believe you and worse will happen to you if you tell. The *bean a' tí*, a harassed woman with troubles of her own, noticed nothing, only thanked the lord that the boys in her house were quieter than usual.

One night as they were preparing for bed the *ceannaire* came into the room Gerald was sharing with five others – at least he didn't sleep in the same room, Gerald often thought, grateful for this small mercy – and asked them if they had said their prayers. They looked at him blankly. It wasn't cool to pray and anyone who did prayed silently and in bed. The *ceannaire* got them all to kneel down and then grabbed their hair and forced them to say one after another in Irish, '*Is pit mo mháthair* – My mother is a cunt.'

One little eleven-year-old, who for his small size and immaturity had been the bully's particular butt, refused at first until the youth said to him in threatening tones, 'It'll be worse for you and for your mammy, if you don't.'

That night, the little boy woke the whole house with his nightmare screams. The *bean a' tí*, grumbling that she needed her sleep, brought him a hot chocolate drink and wondered aloud why they let them away from home so young.

It so happened that the following weekend the little chap's mother and father visited him to find out how he was getting on and became very worried when he burst into tears, clung to them and begged them not to leave him. Already guilt-ridden at having sent him away in the first place, they decided to take him home immediately. For some weeks thereafter he would wake up screaming from nightmares. They never got to the bottom of what was troubling him and never sent him to Irish school again. His departure left a spare bed in Gerald's room and the bully took to sleeping there on alternate nights, to the partial relief of his usual roommates and the dismay of the others.

Starveling had been reported content and indeed seemed so. Charlotte Isabel's only worry, expressed to Sonya, was that she was too good, doing what she was told immediately, sitting still for hours in the dim rooms and bothering no one if she was left.

Of course they made an effort to divert her. She was taken out. Children were brought to the house but after eyeing her and sniggering at each other, they tended to avoid the oddball. Not Maeve's children for they were used to her. Others. The children of Sonya's friends left exploring the wilderness while their parents sipped white wine among the buttercups and speedwell. On one of these occasions, when the garden seemed full of the voices of children, Charlotte Isabel suddenly missed Starveling's silences and went in search of her. At last she found her, up in the dim bathroom, staring intently at the drip drip drip of the tap on to the fishy tail of the mermaid painted on the tub by Ruth.

'Do you miss your mammy, Hannah?' she asked, putting her arm round the rigid shoulders.

The child stared at the water. Drip drip drip.

Valerie, noticing one day that Gerald was looking depressed and withdrawn and remembering what had happened the last time, asked him what was the matter. After swearing her to secrecy, he told him everything.

'You shouldn't take that shit,' she said. 'You should all gang up on him. Make his life a misery for a change.'

'We can't,' Gerald said, totally demoralised.

That night at the céilí the same bully found himself partnered by a large girl with enormous thighs which she displayed generously and tits that wobbled as she danced. She kept smiling at him in a come-on way and at first he couldn't believe his luck.

After a few turns, she fanned open the top of her tee-shirt.

'Jesus, I'm sweating,' she said, looking at him in a meaning way.

He decided to chance his arm and ask her to step outside for a minute for some air. She agreed at once. Dublin girls!

'Let's go down to the beach,' he suggested.

'We aren't allowed.'

'I am. I'm one of the bosses.'

'All right, so.'

It wasn't quite dark. They went down on to the wide sandy beach. A cold wind that had howled across the Atlantic caused them to take shelter among the dunes. He pushed his hand up under her tee-shirt and encountered a redoubtable brassiere.

'I'll do it. You take off your jeans,' she whispered huskily. 'And don't forget your jocks . . . And shut your eyes and don't open them till I say.'

He never suspected a thing. What a wally! Clumsy with excitement, fumbling at his clothes with his stupid eyes screwed shut.

'Ready?' he whispered. 'Are you ready yet?'

By the time he looked she was far across the dunes with his jeans and underpants.

'Hey, come back here, you bitch,' he shouted when he realised he had been tricked.

Bare-assed he started after her but suddenly eight or nine more bitches rose up in the dunes and started cackling and cat-calling. He attempted to run away, but they formed a closing semi-circle round him, pushing him towards the sea, him trying to hide his privates with his hands as his shirt flapped in the wind.

When the waves started lapping his feet he charged them but they were ready and closed in. Valerie pushed him and he sat down abruptly in the icy water. She stood over him her hands on her hips.

'Why?' he asked pathetically.

'Just to teach you not to mess with my brother.'

'What?'

'He's in your *teach*, see, and me and my friends don't like what he's been saying about you.'

'It was only a bit of fun,' the *ceannaire* said.

'Giving little kids nightmares.'

'I never . . . '

'Say, it, go on, say it,' another harpy screeched in his face.

'Say what?' he asked. He'd say anything.

'Tell us what your mother is. In Irish.'

'My mother? . . . Oh, that was a joke.'

'Say it. We can all have a laugh.'

'Then you'll let me go?'

'Maybe.'

'*Is pit mo mháthair.*'

'Now promise to leave the boys alone.'

'Yeah, OK.'

'Promise to be nice to them.'

'Right.'

'Now get lost.'

'My jeans . . . '

'Oh dear, they're all wet,' Valerie said, dunking them in the sea.

'Bitch!'

'Come on, it's only a bit of fun.'

'He's no sense of humour, has he?'

'Go on, prick. Get lost.'

'Listen, girls, I can't go back like this.'

'You should have thought of that before you took them off.'

'They're Levis. Cost a fortune. Please.'

'No way,' said Valerie, 'Bugger off before we think of something else to do with you.'

She meant what she said. He dashed up the beach. Looking back across the dunes he saw the girls dancing wildly around, shrieking in the wind, throwing his underpants in the air and tearing his jeans into several pieces so that each girl could keep a bit as a souvenir.

He tried to creep unnoticed into the house, hoping everyone was still at the céilí. But tipped off by Valerie, the boys were all waiting for him – smirking or mocking or exultant. It was his only stroke of luck that the woman of the house and her husband were stuck in front of the television watching an engrossing chat show.

Sometimes Linda would relieve Ruth so that she could have a few hours off. Not that their mother couldn't be left at all. Occasionally Ruth had to go to get supplies but she confined her outings to the little corner shop and was away no more than half-an-hour. Once a week, she phoned a list of necessities to Linda, who drove to the supermarket and then delivered the order round. Desperate to see people, Ruth sometimes took a short bus journey or walked to a café where she would sit for twenty minutes over a weak coffee and custard slice or some other barely edible horror, just to remind herself that life went on.

After one of these outings she came back to find her mother

prostrate on the floor, unable to get up, lying in a pool of urine. Ruth felt very guilty, even more so because her mother only blamed herself and kept saying, 'Sorry' as if Ruth were going to tell her off.

She had deteriorated considerably since Ruth had arrived and would do nothing but lie on the couch in the living room, vacantly staring at the television or dozing. She talked of the past, her early married life when the girls were small, the way she was courted by Dad who preferred her to her livelier, prettier friend, the one all the other boys were after; her girlhood when she won a prize for an essay and had her picture in the local paper. She described great-aunts and uncles that Ruth had never known existed, the same incomprehensible anecdotes over and over. Finally she was quiet as if she had gone back to a time before memory.

So Ruth's days off were very welcome. She would take the train to central London and wander round the streets or galleries and sit in anonymous cafés eating wholefood salads or salt beef on rye or chicken satay and look at black and brown and yellow people. It was so different from Dublin, she had forgotten how exhilarating it could be. She was very taken with an exhibition of mechanical creations, part-art part-toys, made from found objects and household rubbish, cardboard boxes, tin cans, metal coat hangers, plastic containers, bits of broken chairs, polystyrene, papier mâché. A pressed button set everything in motion: a mountaineer climbed nearly to the top of a mountain but kept sliding back down again; a door opened to show an eighteenth-century couple in a stately dance – there was even squeaky music, a minuet; a house turned out to be haunted, skeleton in the clock, chain-rattling ghost in the wardrobe, bats under the eaves. All was charmingly stiff and jerky, crudely painted, primitive. Ruth's favourite was one of the simplest, a solemn faced stripper who jerked her arm to bare her breasts, twirled round and repeated the process with the other arm.

Another time she went to an exhibition of ancient Mexican art, horrified by the cruelty of the culture that called for constant blood sacrifice but impressed by the power of the inscrutable carved stones statues. The imagery was undeniably beautiful. The rain god, Tlaloc with his goggle eyes and fanged lips, was depicted with waterlilies falling from his mouth. From his open hand, water and precious objects emerged. Special worship was given to women who died in childbirth in the same way that soldiers who fell in battle were revered. Ruth took a particular fancy to the goddess Tlazolteotl, the goddess of fertility and also of dirt and carnality, with a leer on her face, so unlike the meek and mild madonnas of the Christian church. And, before going home once more to her irrecoverable mother, she copied down a little poem from the fifteenth century by Nezahualcogotl, king of Texcoco:

Not forever on earth, only a little while here.

If jade and gold fall apart and wear away

Then faces and hearts, more fragile

Will have to die and be erased like paintings.

Later, supporting the dead weight of her mother to the lavatory, helping her wipe her bottom, washing her with a warm flannel, feeding her the little mouthfuls that were all she could take, Ruth watched the face that she could only ever remember as tight and tense, relax and blur and fade.

Francis had become shy of Sonya since midsummer night and the subsequent revelations of Charlotte Isabel regarding Sonya's parents. He couldn't admit to himself that as she lay next to him in bed, he had fought with desire not to kiss that poor down-turned mouth, that strange zig-zag scar, that thin, flat body, traced with the silvery secretions of snails, as she hugged up to him for warmth and protection.

She was the same to him as ever, vague and gentle, the way she was with most people and never referred to that night as if she had put it from her mind.

With Starveling, however, she was loving and tender, playing with her, reading her stories, taking her out with her when she was clowning, the child wanting nothing better than to sit on a bench watching the antics: the juggler so nearly losing control and dropping everything, Sonya frantically running here and there to try and help catch the coloured balls that rained out of the sky, always missing, always getting in the way. Sometimes Francis would join them and after a while, take the child to a playground or a café. She was totally trusting and Francis was worried that one day when Sonya wasn't looking she would go off with a stranger.

'You wouldn't, sure you wouldn't,' Sonya asked her, stroking the child's face.

'Wouldn't,' Starveling replied, not understanding but ready to please.

It was Charlotte Isabel's idea to go down the country for a week, renting a cottage, after Ruth had phoned to say that her mother was worse, that she wouldn't be able to come back for a while.

So one day they crammed themselves into Charlotte Isabel's old car – Sonya and Francis, Starveling and Russ the dog, and Charlotte Isabel herself – and took off for Connemara to a cottage right on a coral strand. There you could peer down through clear water to glistening green rocks where tiny fishes darted among swaying weeds and sometimes, barely visible, moving through the water transparent jellyfish waved their tentacles.

Starveling would scream with terror and delight when Francis took her into the sea, kicking and splashing, followed by Russ, who now loved the water and endlessly fetched back sticks thrown for him. Starveling roared with pleasure at this and at the way Russ would shake his huge hairy self on emerging from the sea, shooting spray over all of them.

Charlotte Isabel would bathe in a stiff, elderly swim suit, doing a nifty breaststroke, her head held high out of the water. Only Sonya refused to go in further than the edge. While the rest of them swam, she would stay fully dressed on the strand, running coral through her fingers and collecting some of the more extraordinary shapes and colours.

Sometimes there were horses on the beach. Russ would bark at them and run round their legs if he wasn't held back. The horses would race riderless into the sea and walk in it up to their bellies, enjoying the lapping coolness. One evening at sunset when Francis was wandering by himself around the small bay, he caught sight of a horse outlined against the red sky, its mane and tail lifted slightly by the breeze, like something out of one of the old myths.

In the evenings they would stay in and read or listen to a crackly radio or walk to the pub, Starveling too. She would sit sipping her lemonade, watching large-eyed the big country men with their red faces and loud laughter. One time they drove into Clifden for a fancy meal, with cloth napkins and lots of knives and forks and spoons and a lighted candle stuck in a bottle. Starveling stared at the flickering flame, as Francis's long finger fearlessly passed through it. She wanted to do it too; she tried it and laughed at the sensation of nearly burning. She wanted to do everything Francis did, eat and drink like him, and pestered him until he gave her a taste of red wine and everyone laughed when she screwed up her face at the tartness of it.

Francis, looking round the table at the shining faces, tried to fix the moment on his memory. Again he felt undeservedly happy. Fear touched him for a moment but was soon lost in laughter. He exulted in the magical journey home to the little cottage on a winding road that dipped into night mists rising from the bog, in the child dozing on his chest, her goodnight kiss that was a privilege granted only to him as generally she disliked being touched, raising a solemnly puckered face to his.

Later that night, he asked Sonya to walk with him on the beach. The mist had lifted and it was clear and warm.

'I've never seen so many stars,' she said.

They sat down on the strand, slightly apart.

'I'd like to swim now,' she said after a silence.

'I thought you were afraid of the sea.'

'Well, sometimes. But not tonight. It looks friendly.'

They stripped down, modestly leaving on their underwear. Sonya cried out at the coldness of the water while Francis decided all or nothing and splashed in fast.

'It's lovely,' he called back to her.

'Liar,' she cried.

'When you're used to it.'

'People always say that.' But in she went, up to her skinny thighs, visibly shivering, then suddenly plunging under a wave so that Francis could no longer see her. Just as he was starting to get anxious, she emerged from the sea further out, her crest of hair flattened sleekly on to her small round head. Suddenly he remembered the seal he had seen off Howth Head the first time he met her, that a short-sighted sailor might have taken for a mermaid.

'You're right,' she said. 'It's wonderful.'

'And you're a fraud. You're not frightened at all. You're a good swimmer.'

She laughed and in the starlight he could see her mouth turned down as far as it could go. He swam out to her and held her, their limbs entwining. He kissed her zig-zag scar, her eyelids, her ears. She rose out of the water and he kissed her tiny breasts through her white shirt. They swam back to shore and at the edge of the sea, wavelets breaking over them, pulled off each other's clothes and made noisy love, Sonya screaming into the night so that an old man stumbling home the worse for six pints, swore blind the next day and for the rest of his life that he had heard the banshee.

Though not exactly enjoying himself, Gerald had become reconciled to the Irish school since the *ceannaire* had started behaving and falling over himself to be nice to everyone, especially to Gerald once he had established that he was the brother in question.

'Your sister,' the *ceannaire* chuckled, having decided to try and make a joke of it, 'she's something else, heh?'

One of the boys not in Gerald's house was the son of a hypnotist and claimed he knew how to send people into trances. This boast attracted a small crowd, including Gerald, to the hall one evening when they were supposed to be walking on the beach with the others The first volunteer giggled and smirked and refused to succumb, the second likewise. The audience were starting to get restless and one girl denounced the would-be hypnotist as a fraud. Stung, he demanded complete silence and picked a young boy out of the group instead of asking for a volunteer. He sat the lad with his back to the audience and stared into his eyes. Then he started speaking quietly, swinging a small ball on a chain in front of the subject's eyes.

'He's out,' he said at last, in triumph. Everyone crowded around. The boy was certainly rigid and glazed.

'Make him do something,' someone demanded.

'I can't,' the hypnotist admitted.

'Is that it, then?' people muttered. 'That's not much.' They had hoped to see the subject make a fool of himself, quack like a duck, bark like a dog, take all his clothes off. Wasn't that what people were supposed to do under hypnosis?

'I don't think he's hypnotised at all,' someone said.

'Oh no? Anyone got a pin?' A safety pin was produced which the hypnotist jabbed into the subject's finger. There was no flicker from him, even though a bead of blood appeared to the fascination of the watchers, growing larger and finally running down on to his trousers. Someone else pinched him hard. His hair was pulled. No response. A hand was passed in front of his eyes and he didn't react, staring fixedly ahead.

'He's out all right. Pity you can't get him to do something.'

They considered the boy for a while, then someone said, 'We'll tell him he took his clothes off. He won't know whether or which.'

'Yeah, that's a good idea.'

'OK, now bring him out.'

The hypnotist clapped his hands. Nothing. He clicked his fingers. Nothing. He ordered the subject to wake up. Nothing. The boy just sat there, rigid, a trickle of blood drying on his hand.

'Can't you wake him up?' someone asked anxiously.

'I thought I could,' the hypnotist was looking worried.

'Count to three.'

'One two three . . . four five . . . six seven eight nine ten.'

They stared at the boy again. Not a flicker. He barely seemed to be breathing.

'I hope he's all right.'

'Why don't you phone your dad?'

'I can't. He's away in France.'

'Oh Jesus!'

There was nothing for it. The principal had to be informed.

He arrived soon after and looked gravely at the situation. This was no time to make his charges grapple with the intricacies of the Irish language.

'Where precisely is your father?' he asked in English.

'I don't know. France. Provence, I think. Or Paris. Something with a P.'

The principal sighed.

'Who would know?'

'The clinic might.' The father was a doctor. He used hypnotism to cure smoking, overeating, bed-wetting.

When the clinic was phoned it was the night porter who answered. Everyone had gone home, he told the principal but at last, impressed that it was urgent, gave him an emergency number. The man who answered, having put his feet up for the night was annoyed at being disturbed. No, he didn't know where the father was and no he was not qualified to give any advice being an orthopaedic specialist himself. Then, relenting, he provided the name and number of another person who might be able to assist.

'And tell that young hypnotist of yours he's a bloody fool,' he shouted.

'I've done that already,' the principal replied.

At last they got hold of someone who knew what she was talking about. The boy would eventually come out of it by himself, she said. It was merely necessary to keep him warm, quiet and comfortable.

'Plenty of TLC,' the doctor said. 'It's often the best remedy.'

In the unlikely event of complications, she was willing to be contacted again at any time. The principal took the boy to his own home. The sore finger was sterilised and bandaged and he was put to bed. He woke in the night, confused and weepy, so was given a hot drink and soothed and comforted by the principal's wife who was good at that sort of thing. The next day he displayed no ill effects but the would-be hypnotist was grounded for the rest of the week and grounded again after the course by his furious parents on their return from Perigord.

The incident caused many parents, hearing about it afterwards, to raise eyebrows very high and wonder just what else might have been going on in the wild west among their little chicks.

As for Gerald, he found it difficult to forget the strange otherness of the hypnotised boy. Shut off from feeling and awareness, without dreams, blank.

Marion was appalled at the incident but at least her own children weren't involved, Valerie not even having been present, to the girl's total disgust. Marion never knew of the other matter, with the *ceannaire*. Fit and browner than ever after two weeks under the Mediterranean sun, flattered by the masculine attention she had aroused, not only from the waiters who saw it as part of the job to flirt with and if possible bed the female tourists, but also from a man on the same tour, legally separated, a businessman from the midlands. He had wined and dined her to the neglect of poor Bernie who was finally reduced to going out with the man who supplied the fish to the hotel, who had been pestering her for days. He was half her age and half her size as well, and they made a strange couple. As it turned out, they got on very well. He took her to low dives off the tourist track, where rough wine accompanied gorgeous seafood served in wooden bowls. He called her his goddess and bonked her continuously, revelling in the plentiful flesh that remained determinedly white. Bernie never sunbathed; any exposure immediately turned her bright pink.

Marion's gentleman was more restrained. He was considerably older than she was and no oil painting. But he was courteous, witty and rich. They slept together twice, more because it seemed the thing to do than because either was driven by uncontrollable lust. She put his address in her book and even met him in Dublin once when he was there on business. On that occasion he took her for a fancy meal at the expensive hotel where he was staying but did not invite her to his room, for which she was grateful. They parted the best of pals and he subsequently wrote her two long letters on lined yellow paper to which she conscientiously replied. Then silence, except for the inevitable Christmas card. Marion's heart, however, was not broken.

It was different with Bernie. She actually fell in love, menopausal and all as she was. The fisherman himself wept as they parted and loaded her with souvenirs and trinkets and a bottle of the harsh local spirit.

'It was all so Shirley Valentine,' Marion told a mutual friend on their return. 'Almost embarrassing, really.'

The following spring Bernie returned to visit her fisherman, who welcomed her warmly and gave her a great time, not telling her until the night she was leaving that he was engaged to be married.

'To raise the children,' he told her. 'It is important for me.'

By then in any case she had realised the spark had died.

'We will always be friends,' they agreed and never saw nor heard from one another again.

The Hill and the Rock was one of Starveling's favourite stories, with its bright, intricate illustrations. She never got tired of it. Mr and Mrs Quest lived in a house on top of a hill with a view out over the whole countryside, only Mrs Quest couldn't see it from the window of the kitchen where she, as a housewife, spent most of her time, because a great rock blocked most of it. When Mr

Quest, to please his wife, dislodged the rock and sent it rolling down the hillside, it released the air keeping the hill in place. Gradually the hill went down and down until the house was on a level plain but it didn't stop there. Down and down it went until the house was in a deep valley. Then the rock rolled back into place, in the hole behind the kitchen window of the house. Gradually the hill rose up again until everything was as before or worse, since the rock now blocked the whole window. Then Mr Quest had a brainwave. He painted a beautiful view on the rock that Mrs Quest could look at all the time: mountains and lakes stretching into the blue distance beneath a sunny sky, the best view for miles around.

Another one Starveling liked to hear over and over again was entitled *The Man Whose Mother was a Pirate*. And Francis would read how the little man threw off his boring and secure job, fear and convention to follow his wild and extravagant mother to the coast where they joined the disreputable crew of a pirate ship bound for the south seas.

The child would run her fingers over the picture of the large and brightly clad mother, 'Ruth,' she would say. 'Starling mammy.' Then she almost looked at Francis as she tipped his hand and added, 'Starling daddy.'

Like Charlotte Isabel, Francis found disconcerting and unchildlike Starveling's aptitude for sitting very still for long periods of time. He wondered whether it was a vacancy, that Starveling was somehow 'out,' or whether she was daydreaming, although she never chatted to herself or fidgeted the way children do but just sat staring. One day soon after their return from Connemara, a rainy afternoon, she was doing just that, sitting gazing apparently vacantly at him while he was playing the piano.

'Would you like to try?' he said, suddenly aware that unlike most other small children she had never indicated any desire to bash at the instrument.

He lifted her up and she turned her luminous eyes from him to the piano. She touched the ivory keys carefully, not pressing them down.

'I'll show you,' he said and picked out 'Pop goes the Weasel' with his right hand.

Starveling immediately copied him faultlessly.

'Very good,' he said amazed.

Then she played, from start to finish, with hesitations and mistakes but nevertheless with both hands, the piece he had previously been playing.

Francis was aghast. The child had neither been vacant nor daydreaming. She must have been concentrating to a superhuman extent on what he was doing.

'That's wonderful, Hannah,' he told her. 'Let's try and do it again for Charlotte Isabel, will we?' And he called the old lady down.

'It's incredible,' he said to her. 'Of course she makes mistakes.'

The old lady listened as the child played the piece through again.

'She makes your mistakes,' she commented.

'What?'

'She has exactly reproduced your last playing of it,' Charlotte Isabel explained. 'Do you think that child knows what Bach intended? What music is supposed to sound like? . . . Get up, angel.'

She lifted Starveling from the stool.

'I'll play for you.'

She dashed through a lively reel while Starveling stared at her hands.

'Now you try.'

Obediently the little girl sat on the stool and gave a totally accurate rendition of 'The Wind That Shakes the Barley'.

'I can't believe this,' Francis exclaimed. 'You clever little clogs.' He kissed Starveling on the top of her shiny head. 'Let's try something else.'

Charlotte Isabel took another prelude, complicated enough, and played.

Starveling's tiny fingers couldn't cope with the chords. She looked puzzled, then compensated with a lightning glide along the notes. Her performance was otherwise faultless.

'Bravo, bravo!' Francis cried catching her up in his arms. 'You'll be famous! You'll be rich! . . . What will we do next?'

'Just a minute,' Charlotte Isabel said firmly. 'I think that's enough for today . . . Go and get some biscuits from my bedroom, Hannah; you know, in the green tin by the bed. You can have two yourself and give one to Russ.'

The child bounded off instantly, calling the dog to follow.

Francis looked inquiringly at Charlotte Isabel.

'You think we should hold back?' he asked.

'I think her mother should be told before anyone else.'

'Of course. But isn't it great?'

'The poor wee thing can do something after all? It's a gift, Francis. Something precious and strange. Something sensational, nevertheless. There are people who would look upon it as freakish.'

'Not at all.'

'Starveling doesn't need that sort of attention, not now . . . Francis, you know I'm right.'

The little old woman looked at him with an agitation which he found excessive. Still he acceded.

'I won't tell anyone,' he promised.

The vicar would come every week to give communion to Ruth's mother. She had become totally bedridden, incontinent: relying on a catheter for her urine and a nappy for faeces. Luckily she was seldom aware of the indignity. Indeed, she had slipped into a naughty and flirtatious way of talking, a girlishness she had probably never displayed before in her life, even as a girl. Her voice had lost all its stridency and turned into a whisper. She beckoned Ruth over and said to her, 'You should put raspberry jam on your nipples.'

'What!' Ruth exclaimed, startled.

'The vicar would like that.'

She told anyone who would listen that there was honey in her knickers. Ruth thanked heaven that she had few visitors and that those who came usually couldn't make out what she was saying. The pal from the Mother's Union still turned up the odd time but Ruth's mother no longer took any interest in malicious gossip because she couldn't call to mind any more the people being talked about.

'Mrs Bates, dear, you remember. The one in charge of the flowers for the altar. Remember you and me smelt a rat. Seems she has a cousin in the trade. That's what Dolly told me and I've no cause to doubt her truthfulness, despite the business of the margarine in the butter shortcakes. I said to Dolly, I did, if that Bates person wasn't ripping off the petty cash, why didn't she come out straight and tell us she was getting them at cost.'

Ruth's mother looked at her blankly.

The pal, deprived of a gratifying response to her latest barbs, didn't stay long, shaking her head at Ruth and whispering audibly, 'When the time comes, dear, I'll take the clothes off your hands. She's got some nice things, your mum, and there's many a poor person would be glad of them.'

'Who was that?' Ruth's mother said loudly and clearly for once as the pal was leaving. 'She looks like meals on wheels.'

For some reason, her imagery usually combined food, which had always been very important to her, and sex which had not, or so it had always seemed.

'My bum's a bun,' she whispered, 'inviting a bite.'

The vicar smiled blandly. He probably made a point of not hearing, Ruth thought.

'Who are you?' her mother asked him one day in ringing tones. 'Are you the man?'

'I am a man, yes.'

'Are you the man with the long stick with the hook on the end of it?'

'What? Oh . . . A fisherman? Yes. I like to think I follow my lord as a fisher of men.'

'And a fisher of women?' Ruth's mother broke into a harsh and lewd cackle. The vicar looked taken aback.

Ruth smiled at him brightly.

'She's cheerful today, thank God,' he said to her.

'Yes.'

Her mother pointed at Ruth.

'She's got raspberry jam . . . '

'Has she? That's nice.'

'That's enough now, mother . . . I think she's tired.' Ruth hastily pushed the vicar out before he could hear her mother add 'up her cunt.' A word Ruth didn't think her mother knew.

Downstairs the vicar pressed her hand and looked meaningfully into her eyes.

'I hope you're ready, my dear,' he said.

She wondered what could possibly be coming next. Perhaps he had been less deaf than he made out, perhaps he had been turned on by the dirty talk. He was a middle-aged man with a rakish beard and possibly a libido to go with it. And he had an independent wife. He only commented however, 'I don't think it'll be long now.' Adding with the embarrassing sincerity of the morally superior, 'Our prayers are with you.'

'Thank you,' she said.

When Valerie returned from Irish college she found that indeed the man Mick had got himself a new babysitter, a skinny girl improbably called Shree with a brace on her goofy teeth. By the following spring, after so many other terrible things had happened, Valerie noticed that the girl was pregnant. Her family bore the scandal for a while – though what scandal in this day and age? – but nearly crumbled when Shree moved in with Mick, three times her age.

'How disgusting!' Marion commented. 'I hope he never tried anything like that with you, Valerie.'

It wasn't really a question but Valerie said 'No' anyway. Her mother had, after all, suffered enough.

It was in August, finally, that Ruth's mother died. In the night, when the bell didn't ring.

Ruth had left the small brass bell in the form of a lady wearing a crinoline by the side of her mother's bed, so that her mother could attract her attention in the night if necessary. Her mother rang the bell continuously at first, night and day, not making the distinction and for the slightest reason which she had often forgotten by the time Ruth staggered in to her. Then she became incapable of reaching out and lifting it but somehow was still able to knock it to the floor, the tiny sound enough to stir Ruth's hypersensitive nerves.

'What do you want, mother?' Ruth would ask, gazing into the

clouded eyes.

'Drink?' There might be a small nod.

'Tea? Hot milk?'

'Gin.'

And because it didn't seem to matter, never mind what the district nurse said, Ruth would bring up a minute quantity of spirit diluted with warm water, with a little sugar stirred into it. She would hold it to her mother's lips as she sipped. At four in the morning, she would sometimes have one herself, sitting on the side of her mother's bed, stroking the hair which still held its colour.

On one such night, her mother roused herself, gripped Ruth's hand with a return of strength and asked clearly, 'Did I let you down?'

'No,' Ruth hushed, lying. 'Not at all.' And kissed the old face.

The night her mother died, Ruth woke up suddenly, hearing the silence. She rushed into the room, already convinced of what she would find. The old woman didn't look asleep any more. She looked empty, like a vacant house, no longer lived in. Ruth didn't even have to touch her to know.

PART SEVEN

FOUND AND LOST

One night, when young Joe had just finished a performance, he heard that someone was asking for him at the stage door. Two men in sailors' gear were shown in and at first young Joe failed to recognise either of them. Then he discovered to his great joy and amazement that one of the men was his long lost brother John, who had run away to sea as a lad and had never been heard of since. The brothers embraced with emotion and young Joe told John to wait for him: he would be down directly after removing his costume and make-up. Young Joe hurried as best he could but when he returned to the stage door he found no sign either of John or of his companion. He tracked his brother through the dark city streets to old haunts, always missing him by an instant, then finally losing him altogether. John had disappeared without trace and was never seen nor heard of again and his fate could only ever be guessed at.

At last Francis had been admitted to Sonya's room. Not that she had ever locked the door against him. She had always been there if he had wanted to visit. That's what she told him: You only had to knock. The room was not as he had expected. No mess, no dirt, big and spare and bare, a mattress on the floorboards, a rack for clothes, a small press, a plain table and chair. The little wooden figure he had bought her in Brittany hung solitary on an expanse of blank wall. Recently she had tacked up a couple of Starveling's scribbles but otherwise the room contained no personal touches. It was as if it had been deliberately denuded of individuality like a whitened face waiting for an identity to be painted on to it. Impossible to make love there: it wrenched his heart too much; it was such a desolate place. So he always engineered it that they stayed in his cosy, colourful and cluttered room instead, where the shell mobile tinkled companionably through the night in the breeze from his window.

They weren't a couple. Sonya's behaviour made this clear. She didn't like to hear him say that he loved her and put her finger over his lips when he did. She never said it back to him and sometimes he wondered if she regretted getting so close. Then she would come to him laughing and pagan, their lovemaking would be wild and noisy and beyond his dreams and he would forget his doubts and fall deep asleep on her flat body.

Liam and Mark were planning to spend a few days in the Wicklow mountains at the end of August and had invited Gerald to join them. Marion was surprised when the boy accepted, as he wasn't much of a walker, certainly not an outdoor type.

Actually he was bored stiff. The weeks after his return from Irish school had been empty and endless. He found Liam a pain in the neck but the friend, Mark, was amusing enough and had promised the trip wouldn't be too strenuous.

'Camping!' Mark had exclaimed. 'The great outdoors. Communing with nature. If you haven't pissed on top of a mountain with the wind behind you, you haven't lived.'

In fact, Mark himself had never slept in the open before either.

Marion was delighted, especially as she wanted to get away for a few days herself. Her dancing partner, Raymond the hotel manager, had been offered and had accepted a post in a new hotel in Cork. He had suggested to her that she might consider working there as a receptionist. After all, she needed a job too.

'In Cork?'

'It's a nice city. You need a change.'

There was nothing between them. In fact, more than once Marion had fancied that Raymond – tall, blonde and delicate – was a bit of a pansy. But they were good friends and a brilliant dancing partnership. They had already won several medals for their *paso doble*.

'I'd like to make ballroom dancing a feature of the place,' Raymond said. 'It's got a good-sized function room. We could hold competitions there. One way of attracting custom.'

It sounded exciting. Raymond was positive and go-ahead, so unlike Francis. He had invited Marion down to look at the place, check it out, explore Cork city. She had been attracted by the prospect but discouraged by the practicalities. Under no circumstances would she consider leaving her children unsupervised in the house; you heard so many things. But if Gerald was away with Liam, Valerie could easily stay with a friend for the few days.

A new life. A new start. I'm not dead yet, thought Marion.

How dingy the house looked with the life gone out of it. In the days before the funeral Linda and Ruth sorted their mother's possessions to see what was worth keeping. The clothes all went to the pal from the Mothers' Union, who passed it on to the poor of the parish after removing certain items she'd had her eye on for some time. Similarly, furniture, delph, kitchenware were picked over by the ladies of the church for forthcoming bazaars, the remainder to be cleared by a dealer. One press was stuffed with some good china, silver cutlery, crystal glasses – the sort of things given to a young couple starting out – that had been put away for best and rarely used. The sisters shared this out, along with the more striking ornaments, the better books.

They knew the terms of the will. Everything split strictly down the middle. However disapproving their mother might have been of each of them in turn, she was nothing if not fair. There was the house to sell and as it turned out, considerable savings.

'We'll be almost rich at the end of all this,' Linda commented. 'Who'd have thought mother had so much stashed away.'

'What a shame she did nothing with it herself!' Ruth said. 'She could have gone out and had a good time.'

'She was always threatening to sell up and go on a world cruise.'

'Well, she should have done.'

'She never meant it. You know mum. She hated parting with her cash. She only said it because she thought we'd get worried at the prospect of our inheritance being cast to the four winds . . . In any case, she was afraid one day she'd have to go into a home. You know how expensive they are. Especially the ones that are any way decent.'

Ruth looked through her own things. She'd need a van to take everything back to Ireland. Suddenly she realised that soon she'd be able to afford to buy one, a decent banger anyway.

'You can leave your stuff here for the time being,' Linda said. 'It'll be a while before the will goes through.'

Still Ruth sorted her papers, throwing out all her school copy books, notes from college, carefully stored by her mother as if they were valuable manuscripts. Reading an old diary, written in her early teens, was a scary experience. She didn't recognise the handwriting, let alone the girl who had put down all these intimate things. She couldn't remember the events described, the places she was supposed to have visited, the people who had once briefly meant so much to her. Who was that girl? What had become of her? Seeking answers she looked into the ice-blue eyes of the self-portrait, a fourteen-year-old bundle of potential. The eyes looked back at her appraisingly but gave nothing away. After some consideration, she packed up her diaries and the self-portrait to bring with her, not yet ready to discard the past. Not yet.

Starveling was fascinated by it all. She had been brought over by Charlotte Isabel when it seemed that Ruth could bear the parting no longer. The experience of flying had amazed the child, seeing the ground fall away, the cars, streets and houses become tiny, people shrinking till they disappeared. They had cut through a bank of cloud and flew above it in brilliant sunshine. It looked as though you could get out of the plane and roll in it, though Sonya's granny said no, you couldn't. You'd fall right through and be dead.

She greeted her mother as if they'd been parted only a few hours, not weeks and weeks, and looked wonderingly at Ruth's wet face, letting herself be hugged.

'This was your granny's house,' Ruth told her and Starveling touched the furnishings, the beds, the chairs, shaped to her granny's body. She looked at the photos of granny as a young girl and as an old woman; at long-dead granddad, smiling as an old man, looking purposeful as a soldier off to North Africa in the Second World War, at Ruth and Linda as babies, children, young women, at Linda's wedding photograph.

There was no picture of her own daddy, although she looked for it. Now that she knew what he looked like.

'Was I wrong not to bring her before?' Ruth asked Linda.

'I don't know. Who can say?'

Charlotte Isabel had come to London specifically to visit an old friend, an old flame, a man in his seventies recently widowed.

Francis would have been amused to see her. She had cast off her dear little old lady image in favour of that of a bluestocking, suits of shot silk or crushed velvet in rich, dark colours artily combined: puce and purple, black and green, brown and orange. Her hair no longer curled but was bobbed short, cut into a straight fringe. She even wore spectacles with round gold frames.

For now she was a writer. She had brought her completed manuscript, *Blushing Hippocrene*, to show another friend in publishing, having kept Francis up night after night to have it typed in time for her, feeding him coffee with a dash of brandy for stamina.

'Five weeks to write a book. It must be a record,' he had grumbled.

'It was all there in my head,' she had replied. 'All I did was put it down on paper.'

Not great literature, no. But a rattling good read, he had to admit, sighing at her inconsistent misspellings, crossing out all the hyphens she inexplicably had a penchant for, breaking up her long rambling sentences into pithier units.

Sonya told Francis about the course one light evening when they were walking Russ the dog along Portmarnock strand.

Francis stopped still.

'Italy!' he said.

'I was really lucky to get a place.'

She skipped ahead of him and threw a stick far into the waves for the dog to fetch.

'He never minds, even if it's freezing,' she commented, looking at the sturdy creature bounding through the water.

'Italy!'

'It's only for ten months. And I'll be back in the meantime for visits.'

'You didn't even tell me you were auditioning for it.'

'I didn't tell anyone. Out of superstition. I always think if I say a thing, it won't come true. Like telling your wishes.'

'Sonya!'

He was crying. It was stupid but he couldn't stop. None of it had meant anything to her; sand running through her fingers.

'I want to be a clown, Francis. A proper clown.'

She did a perfect cartwheel on the beach, her shirt falling as she turned upside down, baring her thin white body. Then she walked on her hands and Russ dashed up to her, barking and excited, licking her face.

Despite himself, Francis laughed, it was such a comical sight. Sonya jumped upright again.

'Maybe I should use Russ in my act,' she said, coming up to Francis and hugging him.

'I'll miss you so much,' he whispered.

'Don't say that. You'll make me feel guilty.'

'Of course you have to go. It's a wonderful chance.'

'I'm very fond of you, Francis. You know I always will be.'

It sounded like a dismissal. And after all how could it have lasted? The summer dream of a middleaged man. He watched as she dashed off again where his age and his asthma prevented him following, chased by the black dog and silhouetted for an instant against a rose pink sky before disappearing behind the darkening dunes.

Francis shivered. Autumn was in the air.

They had studied the map, the guide book of the Wicklow Way before planning a route which took them into the wilderness.

'We'll avoid all civilisation for three days,' said Mark. 'Get in tune with nature and with ourselves.'

Liam didn't know about that. He just wanted a good hearty tramp across country. For himself but also to bring some colour to the boy's pallid cheeks.

The weather looked as if it would hold for the trip, though they packed wet gear as a precaution. Liam drew the line at trainers and suggested that Gerald buy a proper pair of walking boots. They finally compromised on Doc Martens. It was a Friday morning when they set off, loading the three enormous rucksacks into Liam's car which would be parked at a convenient point on the large circle they had mapped out for their route.

'You'll give me a ring tonight?' Liam's mother asked petulantly. She was against the whole idea. Grown men sleeping under the stars in this day and age.

'How can I, Mam? We're going to the mountains. No phones there.'

His mother, reared in the Liberties, muttered curses on nature and uncivilised rural life.

'I'll try,' he said, 'but I can't promise.'

He kissed her selfconsciously in front of the others.

'Mrs next door will keep an eye on you,' he told her. And before she could damn and blast Mrs next door too audibly he climbed into the car and drove off. For some time she stood watching them, Mark's arm stuck out of the window waving merrily.

The first stage of the walk was wonderfully enjoyable. They were all in a good mood, energetic, the sun was shining, the path a gentle slope. Only later, after they had stopped for a lunch of sandwiches and fruit and Liam wanted to press on, the other two lingered, paddling with bare feet in a mountain stream.

'It's twelve more miles to camp,' Liam said.

'We can camp anywhere,' Mark smiled.

'But we agreed. It was the plan.'

'The best laid plans of mice and men . . .' Mark replied. Gerald giggled: it was clear whose side he was on and Liam felt irritated.

'All right then,' relented Mark. 'Come on, Gerald, if we must. Onward and upward.' Mark gave an exaggerated sigh, clambering out of the stream, followed obediently by the boy. Drying his feet, Mark winked across at Liam who nodded back amicably enough. For the first time, however, he started to wonder if three would prove to be a crowd.

There was an upright piano in Ruth's mother's house. The vicar had his eye on it for the church hall. The present instrument was in a terrible state from the cubs and brownies who consistently thumped it, stood on it and put sticky drinks and fingers on it and from the pianist who came in once a week for the old folks' sing-song, leaving her dreadful cigarettes burning down on the walnut frame while she played 'My old man said "Follow the van"' or 'Lily of Laguna'.

When approached, Ruth for her part would immediately have said he could take it but told him she would have to consult Linda. In the meantime, she had a telephone conversation with Charlotte Isabel, who informed her of Starveling's extraordinary gift.

Ruth went and looked at the dark old instrument. It was locked, had been for as long as she could remember, so that children couldn't damage it. It came to her that the key hung on a hook inside the hinged top and there indeed it was. Ruth took it and unlocked the lid. The keys were ivory – palest yellow – and dull ebony. Had anyone ever played on them? An uncle had, she thought, one Christmas, accompanying carols that two little girls and their cousins sang with more enthusiasm than melody to a group of adoring parents. She and Linda had played, too, when very small until their mother got migraine from the racket they made practising. It was really a status symbol, an emblem of middle-class pretensions, like the classics of English literature which stood with tooled bindings in the glass-fronted bookcase in the living room and remained unopened in case a would-be reader had greasy fingers or the execrable habit of turning down the corner of a page to mark the place.

She called her daughter.

'What about a tune?' she said. 'I hear you can play. Come on,' she patted the stool. 'Sit up here.'

Starveling looked at her solemnly, then climbed on to the stool. She made no effort to play, however, but stared at the keys as if puzzled.

'Come on, love. Charlotte Isabel says you're great.'

The child still gazed blankly.

Ruth stretched her memory. Hadn't she once been able to fly through 'Für Elise'? She played the first few bars with the right hand, then stalled.

Starveling smiled. She copied her mother precisely.

'Lovely,' said Ruth, frozen with fear.

She would have liked to chop the piano, all pianos, into firewood immediately but instead, because she sensed that it was what her daughter would like to hear, she said, 'Will we see if we can take the piano home with us?'

The child nodded and submitted yet again to a big bear hug and more of those tears.

Linda had no objection and the vicar could make none. It was not as if the piano had been promised to the church in so many words. He tried not to feel disgruntled; it was unchristian, he knew. But he complained to his independent wife – used to acting as a safety valve on such occasions – that God knew he had dropped enough hints and surely they might have expected some gesture of recompense for all those visits to that nasty, foul-mouthed old woman.

'Typical,' Sonya commented, pouring over the book on the *Commedia del Arte* Francis had borrowed from the library for her. 'No good parts for women.'

'Columbine?' Francis asked.

'No. Too wet,' she said. 'It was the church, you see. Forbade women to go on the stage for sixteen centuries. Sixteen centuries! Typical.'

'I see you as a Pierrot, all in white. Like in that French film, what is it, *Les Enfants du Paradis*. The tragic clown.'

She didn't know which film he meant and anyway she disliked the notion. Clowns should make people laugh.

'That's a cliché,' she told him. 'Anyway, it says here that it was only in the nineteenth century that Piero became like that. He was a comic character before, like all the rest . . . You see, it all depended on the actor who took on the part. He made it his own.'

She looked so serious and knowledgeable, telling him about it. He wanted to kiss her.

'This guy now, Scapino,' she went on, 'I like the sound of him. He's a valet, an adventurer but basically an awful coward. He falls in love for sheer joy, every day with someone new.' She rolled over and stared out of the skylight at the clouds scudding past.

'Yes, it's Scapino for me,' she said.

Marion liked the look of the hotel, though the setting was rather more rural than she had anticipated and she had never lived in the country. Raymond said it only took half-an-hour to drive to Cork city, no more than from one side of Dublin to the other, less probably. The main hotel building was surrounded by a cluster of chalets, still under construction.

'Self-catering is the thing,' Raymond said, 'especially for families.' They could use all the facilities of the hotel, swimming-pool, jacuzzi and sauna, games room, disco, coffee shop and restaurant.

The function room was a dream. Very tasteful, Marion thought – all pine and Laura Ashley – with a view out across the bay. Moreover, it would be totally suitable for dancing, with its large expanse of wooden floor. Raymond took her for a spin across it, humming a Latin tune. She closed her eyes. She could see it all so clearly, how it would be under the chandelier, the flushed faces of the patrons, smiling from their candlelit side tables, applauding the slick footwork, the dramatic twists and twirls.

'Of course there'd be a live band,' Raymond said.

Naturally she adored the whole idea. And what an opportunity. She'd have agreed immediately if it wasn't for the children.

'They can't live here in the middle of nowhere. What about their schooling?' she asked Raymond.

'Can't their father take responsibility for a change?'

She looked uncertain. Was that what she wanted?

'There are some excellent boarding schools, I understand. Not at all expensive.' Raymond went on. 'Then they could visit at weekends.'

'They'd like that.'

And she promised him she would think about it. Although in her heart she had already decided.

Francis still occasionally met the young man, Steve, who had once gone out with Valerie and who had wanted to start a rock band. Steve had found the going harder than anticipated; the musicians had all had different ideas of where the band should be going, what they should be doing. Promoters were unsympathetic and payment often failed to cover expenses. For a while after they broke up, Steve played by himself or sometimes with a girl who sang in husky, bluesy tones totally unlike the clear bell-like voice of Valerie. He had never yet got together with the play director he had met through Sonya.

His disappointment affected Francis. Already the boy was considering giving up, giving in to his parents' desire that he should get a proper job instead of the part-time efforts he made to get a few pounds together to buy better and better equipment.

'I know if I give up the music now I'll never go back to it,' he told Francis. 'I'll get stuck in a rut. I'll be trapped like my parents: marriage and mortgage and kids and bills. What kind of a life is that?'

'Never say never,' Francis smiled.

'Oh you, you're all right, you're different. But what you did took a lot of courage. I don't know if I'd be able to do it. Break out, like.'

Francis was taken aback. He had always considered what he had done to be cowardice, shirking responsibilities, almost a crime. Now here was this child telling him it was an act of bravery.

'That sort of life – settling down, a family – suits most people you know. You might be very lonely without it. Your parents are probably happy. No regrets.' Why did he say that? What did he know?

'They're zombies,' Steve remarked. 'I don't think they've ever really lived. I know they're not living now.'

'Say you went to college,' Francis suggested. 'Then you could keep up your music.'

'They can't afford to send me, even if they wanted to.'

Steve's father was a driver. There were five children in the family.

'Sometimes I feel like running away to sea,' Steve said.

The funeral service was well-attended, mostly by elderly ladies of the parish. The vicar, his resentment damped down by his reasonable wife, gave a laudatory oration, speaking of a life of good works, piety, of a woman who would be sadly missed. He mentioned Linda and her children and Ruth but not Starveling, who was not present but out for the day with Charlotte Isabel and her beau. Though tempted, Ruth had finally decided it would be uncharitable for her to turn up with the Judgement on her mother's final journey. It would certainly have given all the old dears something very tangible to sink their false teeth into, even meatier than the fact that Linda was wearing flamboyant red, known to be her mother's least favourite colour and anyway hardly appropriate, while the black worn by Ruth was in the untraditional form of jeans and a large baggy sweat shirt that she often used while painting, slightly spattered, a comfort garment.

Only a few came along to the actual cremation which was less horrible than Ruth had expected. Certainly the coffin wasn't trundled along a conveyor belt like checked-in luggage at an airport disappearing behind a curtain of plastic strips, a preconceived image Ruth had acquired from somewhere. Instead, surrounded by flowers, it sank down into the floor as canned music played, a tasteful piece from Handel's *Messiah*: 'Comfort ye, my people'. Ruth even found herself moved to weep. The poor old soul, she thought, remembering how she had visited her mother for the last time at the undertaker's.

An elegant woman in an Oxford blue suit, speaking in hushed tones dripping with sympathy, had first asked her to wait, ' . . . while I see if mum's ready,' and then brought her through to the room where her mother lay, obviously fresh out of a fridge, icy cold and all in white with a sly smile on her face that made Ruth think she was about to open her eyes and say, 'Ha, fooled you!'

Of course she didn't. And Ruth looking closely had even momentarily doubted that the body was her mother's at all. It looked like a rather inadequate waxwork, not quite true to the original. The flesh felt nothing like flesh and when she kissed her mother's forehead the skin seemed to leave a coating of something on her lips.

'Are you happy with the way she looks?' the elegant lady undertaker had whispered as she made her way out.

'Yes, thank you,' Ruth had said, lying. Why was her mother dressed in a silky white garment like an elderly angel in a nativity play? Why not in her best suit of soft-toned Harris tweed (now, if Ruth but knew it, hanging in the old pal's wardrobe) or in the blue woollen dress she habitually wore around the house? Why make her up to look as if she is sleeping when she is dead dead dead?

Then she had walked in a park that she had always loved as a small child when brought to feed the ducks or walk the dinky little paths round the lake and across a toy bridge where a contrived waterfall splashed down and you could see the murky depths of the pool through the cracks under your feet, clinging to your daddy's hand. As she grew up, she would go there by herself and sit for hours pretending to sketch, enjoying the almost natural world of the gardens set amid spreading streets of suburban houses.

This last time, she had taken solace in its darker corners, under pines or chestnut trees with late summer leaves on the point of turning, pressing her lips to a rough trunk to get rid of that terrible coating on her mouth, gathering petals from a fallen rose and crushing them against her face.

It was designated a three-man tent. A three-midget tent more like, Mark quipped. He lay in the middle, the most squashed but, as he said, the warmest. That first night, Gerald had barely slept at all, the ground so incredibly hard and him missing the two pillows he was used to, only a rolled-up sweater under his head. Strange night noises cut through the silence, the cracking of branches, rustlings in the bracken, the cry of an unidentified creature far away or sometimes so near that Gerald felt it was hovering over him, just beyond the thin membrane of the tent. He was warm in his sleeping bag although his feet stayed icy for hours and he couldn't rub them for fear of disturbing his companions who both seemed sound asleep. In fact, just as Gerald was dozing off, Liam started to snore, gently enough but enough to disturb him awake again.

The next day he walked in the unreal state you get into when short of sleep. His feet were slightly blistered but, padded with plasters, caused him little discomfort. The bright morning glared at him, making his head spin, a leafy branch seemed unnaturally green. He drank a large quantity of strong sweet instant coffee which succeeded only in making him tremble. How he was going to manage to walk twenty miles he had no idea.

His companions were almost as sombre as himself. Liam claimed not to have slept at all, Mark then informing him that he had snored loudly most of the night, which Liam rattily denied. Gerald was too exhausted to join in the incipient argument, especially as he sensed Liam resented it when he took sides with Mark as he usually did. There was a tension between the two men which showed signs of getting ugly and here, at the back of beyond, Gerald had no intention of adding to it.

Liam had never been so aware of another person's body as he had been the previous night, through the silky and yielding fabric of the sleeping bag. To his shame, he had got an erection which he had been unable to relieve. How could you wank with people rubbing up against you? People? Mark of all people. The man who had once kissed him on the lips. He hated him for what he was stirring up. So he snapped at him and strode off ahead, leaving the others to stagger along behind him.

Tempers improved as the day progressed. It was hot and heavy, they were all dripping with sweat and had a swim in an icy mountain lake to cool down, laughing and splashing each other, slipping on weed-covered rocks. Liam swum strongly across the deep, peaty water while Mark lay floating, totally relaxed, staring at the sky, the black clouds swirling towards the sun.

'Storms ahead,' he said.

Liam squinted up.

'We'd better start moving. We don't want to get caught in a downpour before we've made camp.'

They leapt out of the lake, towelling themselves down roughly, Gerald self-consciously ogling the nudity of the older men, Liam's profuse body hair, the smoother skin of the other.

In the event, they made camp early. A wind was blowing up. Across the valley they could see a grey veil of rain moving towards them fast and decided to sacrifice the plan to expediency. The spot they chose was not ideal, on a rocky incline, but the experienced Liam decided it would do.

That night they listened to rain lashing down. It was some storm. Branches of overhanging trees cracked above them in a mighty wind that seemed to be trying to lift the tent into the air and send it spinning across the valley. Each of them felt uneasy. Then Mark produced a half-bottle of whiskey from his rucksack.

'Emergency rations,' he said. They mixed it with rain water and drank it down gratefully, even Gerald despite Liam's feeble enough expressions of disapproval.

'He's a man now, aren't you Gerald,' laughed Mark, slapping him on the back. 'You have put aside childish things.'

And that blurry night, as the rain continued to hammer the tent, as Liam snored, Gerald felt Mark unzip his sleeping bag, put his hand in and take Gerald's own hand. He rubbed his thumb softly on the boy's palm, up and down and round and round. The boy's breathing grew deeper. He felt a low tingling. Then after a while Mark drew Gerald's hand down inside his own bag against his smooth, naked body, down down to where his penis thrust up hard and erect. It was oddly comforting to hold, like clinging to a still point in the midst of flux. The boy fell asleep still gripping the penis and in the very early morning was woken by a harsh kiss.

The roundabout went round and round and up and down. Starveling clung on to the horse's neck, half delighted, half terrified. There was no need to fear. The speed was geared to the safety of the very young and Charlotte Isabel smiled reassuringly every time the child passed her even though the child's eyes were fixed in a stare that saw only the whirling world. Charlotte Isabel was standing arm in arm with an elderly man, John, her old flame who had flared into life again at the sight of her.

He had been miserably and childlessly married for more than forty years to the wife who had recently died, who had been threatening to die for nearly thirty years from one or more of a variety of dire complaints and who only now, when it was almost too late for him, had fulfilled her promise.

'Why did you stay with her?' Charlotte Isabel had asked with the insouciance of one who had been happy and who had never been faced with the problem.

'I don't know. Habit, duty, a lingering affection for what we once both were, fear of loneliness. Despite the statistics, most people do still stay together, you know.'

He smiled at her affectionately. How game she still looked in the funny blue velvet hat with the floppy brim, bought in a street market, designed for someone much younger, but suiting her in a strange way. They had stayed friends for years, seldom meeting except at marriages and more lately at funerals but exchanging long letters every six months or so. On seeing her again at last, he had warmed to her instantly, though the young woman had dried up like a flower pressed in a book, only a token of what had been.

The roundabout slowed down and stopped. Starveling staggered off, failed to see the waving hand in its grey glove and stood waiting until the two old people found her again.

'More,' the child said, 'more.'

'Not right now,' the old lady said firmly. 'John and I have been standing here while you've had at least six goes and now we want to sit down and have a drink and a bun.'

John owned a house in Hampstead where Charlotte Isabel was staying. Developers were always on at him to sell, for it was far too large for one person and would convert, as had most of the other properties on the street, most satisfactorily into several self-contained flats.

He held out. Where would he go? Why would he go? He was used to the area. He was known by old inhabitants like himself, corner shopkeepers, the Turkish proprietors of the café where you could play chess for hours over one coffee. Occasionally he would drink at the pub at the bottom of his street, outside of which a woman had once shot her lover dead, a crime for which she had been hanged. He walked on the heath with his arthritic golden retriever, Silk, and had never seen any of the crime that was supposed to be rife there nowadays, although admittedly his walks were confined to daytime and to frequented paths.

After their sustaining tea, he took Charlotte Isabel and Starveling up there, where kites swooped on the windy heights and where you could see halfway across London, the post office tower, Centre Point, houses and flats and offices and shops and palaces and theatres and galleries.

'How can I give up all of this?' he asked. Then turned to Charlotte Isabel and said, 'You can have it too if you want.'

'Get thee behind me, Satan,' she replied. But she was laughing.

His whole body shuddered. The girl's back arched as she pushed towards him and he came into her. As they relaxed back, he laid his head on her flat breast and she caressed his thinning hair.

'Don't cry, Francis,' she said. 'I can't bear it.'

'Let me come with you,' he whispered. 'I don't think I can live without you.'

They lay in silence. He knew how foolish he sounded, how abject.

'Come if you like,' she said after a while.

'What?'

'Come with me if you like. I don't mind.'

He laughed softly and kissed her.

'You don't mind?' he asked.

'If that's what you want.'

'Because I wept?'

She said nothing.

'You don't really want me.'

'It's not that. But what would you do?'

'I'd be an old fool chasing after a young one.'

She kissed his eyes.

'I'm very fond of you, Francis.'

He believed her but in two weeks she would be gone and the seas and mountains and plains, the cities between them would push them further apart as the crowd separated Deburau forever from his beloved Garance in *Les Enfants du Paradis*. Only it was Sonya who was supposed to be the clown and she wasn't in love with him at all. Then it seemed to Francis that it was he himself who was the figure of absurdity and fun, not sweet Pierrot at all but the vain and ugly Pantaloon.

Liam woke out of a heavy sleep to find the tent empty. Maybe the others were washing themselves or boiling water on the gas for tea or frying rashers. He lay there for a while, listening for voices. Then he got up and looked outside. The wind had slackened, the rain had stopped and the ground gleamed soft and wet. He pulled on his clothes and shoes and walked out into the morning. Where were they? He stood still, listening. Nothing. Not a sound.

He called out, 'Mark! Gerald!'

Silence.

A black bird flew across the sky and he followed it with his eyes as though it might lead him to them, up the ridge. And as if indeed it had, his eye caught a red streak, Mark's sweater perhaps.

He slipped on the mud, cursing, then continued in the direction where he had glimpsed the splash of carmine, not seeing it any longer.

Why did he take care to be as quiet as possible, avoiding the crunch of twigs or swish of bracken, digging his feet into the soft earth for a foothold? Why did he move so slowly and warily? If only he had blasted his way through the bushes and branches like that infamous bull in the china shop. If only.

Charlotte Isabel woke in the big old bed and looked across at John, lying on his back still asleep, breathing through his open mouth. Out of habit he had removed his teeth and now his lips sank on to shrunken gums, his nose and cheekbones standing out sharply. Deep pity filled her, for him and for herself and for all mortality. Then she rolled towards him and slapped his belly.

'Wake up, you big ugly geriatric,' she said. 'And give me a kiss.'

Ruth and Starveling made their way across London in the early morning, as the rush hour was beginning. They were taking the train from Euston for the ferry. Ruth, down to her last few pounds, couldn't afford the plane because she would have had to have paid for Starveling's seat as well. She knew anyway that she would enjoy the train and the boat well enough once she was on them, the real feel of travelling, the miles chugging under her. But in the long corridors of the underground station she lamented her lot, weighed down with her rucksack and the cumbersome folder that held the precious pictures she had painted at her mother's house. And fearful of losing her daughter among the crowding people, she needed to hold on to her, too.

The child had also wanted to know why they couldn't bring the piano with them as Ruth had promised.

'If you can carry it we will,' Ruth had said and regretted her sharpness instantly as Starveling tried to lift it, her eyes filling with tears of effort and dismay.

'Don't worry, sweetheart,' Ruth had told her. 'We'll get a man with a van to bring it over for us.'

'A man with a van,' Starveling had liked that. She had said it over and over and kept pointing to passing vehicles from the bus they had started their journey in, 'A man with a van. A man with a van.'

The solicitor had said it would be a few weeks before the will could be proved and the ready money released. After that, in a sluggish market, Linda and Ruth would try and sell the house valued at about ninety thousand pounds. But there would be almost twenty thousand each before that from the savings. Ruth had never possessed that sort of money. It would mean security for herself and her daughter and if eventually they could buy a house, then 'we'll be on the pig's back,' Ruth had told Starveling, laughing. And the child had listened and imagined riding a pig would be like clinging to the roundabout horse, dizzy and sick and thrilled.

They made it to Euston in good time and settled into window seats with a table. The train started, the dingy inner city gave way to miles of suburban houses and finally to meadows with cows, a canal carrying bright barges looping under the railway line, holiday makers sitting outside country pubs momentarily distracted by the passing train, fields piled with square bales of hay or flaming where stubble was burning.

Mark was standing up against a tree, his head thrown back, his eyes closed. Gerald was kneeling in front of him. The older man's trousers were round his ankles and his rigid penis was in the boy's mouth. The boy choked as the man thrust towards the back of his throat. The thing seemed to have an inexorable life of its own. Who would have thought it could become so monstrously big? But as Mark caressed Gerald's hair, the boy's own body responded. Pleasure and pain. Pleasure and pain. There was nothing else.

Liam howled, a hair-raising sound. The boy leapt up and ran. Mark gazed at Liam for a pleading moment then took off after Gerald, pulling up his trousers as he ran, calling him. Liam raced after them both, yelling too, yelling for them to stop. The boy was fast, careless of the branches that whipped at his face and body. It was as if he had suddenly woken or as if he were still in a dream, running, running from his demons.

The path led along the steep and rocky ridge. Mark, behind the boy, croaking, 'Gerald, wait, wait!' suddenly slipped on the mud, his trousers still hanging loose. Down he slipped and rolled, down over rocks, stubby bushes, slipping and screaming. Gerald stopped in confusion. For a second he couldn't understand what had happened. Then he looked back at Liam, still running towards him, arms outstretched, face taut. With a final despairing glance up through the net of trees to the white sky, the boy spun giddily down after the other.

After the crashing, after the screaming, the mountainside was silent. Liam, dizzy, waited then again called the names of his companions.

'Gerald! Gerald! . . . Mark!'

Not a sound.

He peered over the ridge. The foliage concealed everything. Watching carefully for footholds, he climbed down. It took him forty minutes that seemed like forty hours. Even then he had trouble finding them until he caught sight of the red sweater, glowing like a beacon and redder now with blood. The boy lay nearby, his mouth open in the soft wet soil.

'The train says "tra-tra-tra",' Starveling said as they sped through the midlands, through north Wales, past Snowdonia with its seductive valleys that led into the secret vastnesses of the misty mountains. Anglesea was flatter and duller with little lakes and a village with an enormously long and unpronounceable name.

Starveling had stayed good as gold for the long ride, listening to the train talking, watching the flickering towns and fields and grey sea.

Ruth had got into conversation with an American who boarded the train at Chester. He wore his blonde hair in a long pony tail and had a gingery Zapata moustache. He told Ruth he had been to Liverpool to visit the Beatles museum, being a big Beatles fan.

'"Abbey Road", that's the greatest ever,' he said. '"Come Together". Wow!'

She offered him a sandwich which he accepted when he found it was cheese on wholemeal bread.

'I used to eat junk food,' he told her. 'Wow, did I eat junk food! You name it, I ate it. I snorted. I smoked. Now I cherish my body.'

He brought out an array of little jars that made Starveling's eyes pop. Vitamins and mineral compounds, essences of this and that, tablets like jewels, clear gleaming pellets.

His name was Otto but he pronounced it Oddo and he had a long and very Germanic last name displayed on the label on his rucksack.

'I used to live in Minneapolis but now I live in Santa Barbara.'

He was full of information about himself, asking for none in return, his eyes gliding over Starveling as though she wasn't there.

Later he settled down and listened to a tape, closing his eyes and moving his lips.

He stayed latched on to them on the boat.

'Perhaps you'd like to listen to this,' he said to Ruth, offering her his walkman. 'I feel that you are a person not happy with your life. This may help.'

One of the tapes consisted of a man speaking American English with a Spanish accent, exhorting the listener to stare at a mirror for a period of time every day, repeating the incantation 'I like myself. I am the person I most want to be. I like myself.'

The other was a tape of meditation, a velvet voice describing an idyllic scene and exhorting the listener to enter in, sink down and rest, caressed by soft warm waves, sated by the sweet juices. Ruth listened obediently for a while then was seized with an irresistible desire to go up on deck and clear her head. Starveling was asleep and Ruth deliberately asked Otto to keep an eye on her, to tie him down. She went to the back of the ship where the foam trailed behind them and a tattered Irish flag danced in the sky. It was soothing just to stare. Soon, however, she discovered that Otto had followed her up.

'That woman knitting, she said she'd watch the kid.'

He glanced around brightly.

'Gee, this is nice and fresh,' he commented. Evidently he was the sort of person who had to keep talking and smiling at all costs.

'I hope you're not a sad person, Ruth,' he said after she had continued to stare silently at the sea for a while. 'It seems to me you are.'

'Not particularly,' she said and added, conscious of some hypocrisy, 'My mother just died.'

'Gee, that's tough.' He looked downcast for an instant. 'But she was old, right?'

'I suppose so.'

'And sick maybe? In pain?'

'Yes.'

He smiled triumphantly. 'So the best thing happened to her, right?'

'Well . . . '

He touched her shoulder. 'Listen Ruth, the problem is you, not her. Death, well, I guess it's heavy, but for the old and sick it's natural, too. Right?'

She nodded. 'Maybe.'

'Think about it. Everything's just fine.'

She stared away from him, stupidly wanting to cry.

'You know, I used to hate myself, Ruth,' Otto went on. 'Can you believe that? I thought I was worthless, not a valuable person. I was a defeatist. Then I discovered this Del Oro method. Now I am an optimist. I believe that everything happens in the world for a good reason.'

'Even bad things?'

'Everything.'

'Even . . . I don't know, Hiroshima, the holocaust, the murder of children?'

'I knew you'd find it hard to believe. People do, first time round. But you see Ruth, there's a plan.'

He looked earnestly into her eyes, his own pale as water, emptier than Starveling's.

In a minute, she thought, he'll try and sell me a set of tapes.

'I was like you once. A doubter. But you see, positive thoughts come from within. If everyone starts thinking positive, the world will start to clean up its act. Good vibrations.'

He started to sing the song 'Goo-oo-ood good vibrations' smiling at the people around him.

She looked down at the surf, the boat making lace out of the grey sea. A light drizzle started to fall. She'd have to get back to Starveling.

'There's going to be a meeting in Dublin next Thursday. Why don't you come along, Ruth? Hear what the man himself has to say. I know you'd find it helpful.'

She could have replied sharply, to the effect that he had a bloody cheek making assumptions when he knew nothing of the way she thought about things, not having even bothered to find out. But he was childish and enthusiastic, a proselytiser, smiling into her face. And anyway she was tired and her shoulders ached.

'Maybe I will,' she smiled back.

It was a lot later that day when a group of hikers passed the abandoned tent, its flap waving open, the sleeping bags soaked in the steady rain that had resumed mid-morning. A search was mounted. The spot where the men had fallen was at last identified and two of the party descended to take a look.

They found one man hunched and dazed but apparently unhurt beside the bodies of two others, a teenage boy and another man, both cold and stiff.

When they gave a sip of brandy to the man, he started shuddering uncontrollably and remained in shock. Evidently it would be impossible to get him up the side of the ridge in the state he was in without assistance. So others went off to get help, first lowering a flask of tea and a blanket and two sleeping bags from the tent to cover the bodies.

The man reacted briefly then, shouting violently, 'That's wrong. You've got the bags wrong,' and only went quiet when they switched them around.

Help didn't arrive for two long hours. By that time evening had started to crawl over the mountainside, covering everything with its velvety trail.

Identification was found on Liam. As she later claimed, his mother's heart nearly stopped beating when the guards called to the house that night. But on learning that her son was safe in hospital, she was able to relax and even to take macabre pleasure in the accident.

'I told them it was crazy but they wouldn't listen,' she told the guards, the doctors, the nurses, the receptionist, Mrs next door.

She gave the guards Mark's address and Gerald's too, adding that the mother was away and the father lived somewhere else, as though those very facts had in some way contributed to what had happened.

When they finally tracked Francis down via Valerie, his first thought was also that he was responsible. That if he had been a better father it might never have happened.

'So many funerals,' Ruth said to Sonya, sitting in the garden as the leaves turned about them and the wind started to swirl. It was the first week of September and Sonya was telling her friend what had been happening while she was away.

'It was me who was to have left,' Sonya commented. 'Of course, I'm still going. But Francis was to have stayed on here. And now he's disappeared, I don't know where. Just headed off.'

He had departed immediately after the huge double funeral when it seemed the whole of the parish in which Gerald and Mark had lived had turned out in sympathy at the terrible tragedy. The boy would have been astonished, maybe even gratified at the attendance even though most of those present would have had no idea what he, or Mark for that matter, looked like. And even though they would have had no time for the youth had he survived.

Francis and Marion had walked together heading a procession that included Mark's wife and children and Valerie. Sonya had held back discreetly in the crowd.

'He couldn't bear it,' she told Ruth. 'He thinks God took his son because of him not loving enough. Because of him leaving home and being with me.'

'Oh Lord!' exclaimed Ruth, 'The Catholic guilt complex. What a terribly destructive thing it is. I mean, the boy died, didn't he, because he was fooling around on a slippery slope.'

'I never knew Francis was so religious. He never said.'

'It's ingrained. Even when they turn against it, it's still there, controlling them.' Tom and his self-immolation. 'Do you miss him?' she asked her friend.

'I'm so sorry for him. His heart is broken.'

But her eyes couldn't help sparkling at the thought of Italy, Scapino, the ineffable future.

'Who'll be here?' Ruth asked, watching the whipping wind.

'Charlotte Isabel is staying in London for the time being . . . Some friend of Francis's daughter is living in his room, your old room, looking after Cerberus.'

'Who?'

'The dog.'

'Of course . . . Listen Sonya, do you want me to keep an eye on the place?'

'Great. You can live here if you like.'

'No, thank you. I've come to appreciate my own little refuge. But I'll certainly look in from time to time.'

Starveling trotted up to them munching on a poxy apple. She had been exploring.

'Francis gone,' she said. And tears spilled down her dry cheeks.

Marion shouldn't have blamed her husband. It was after all she who had okayed the trip to the mountains because it suited her own plans. She shouldn't have blamed him but she did. Screaming with grief, spitting with resentment, tearing at her short hair until it stood on end, her make-up cracked across her face while he stood there taking it, that was the worst, taking it all, his head bent in speechless grief.

As for Liam, she cursed him, smashed at the improvements he had made over the years, never wanting to see him ever again, the bastard, the bloody fucking bastard.

Francis had visited the old family friend in hospital. The man was a pathetic sight, suddenly wizened, suddenly starting to look disconcertingly like his mother. He too was consumed with guilt.

'They asked me how it happened,' he said to Francis, gripping his hand. 'I couldn't tell them, I couldn't.'

Francis understood that Liam hadn't been with the others, that he had found them later.

'I couldn't tell them.'

'No, no. It's all right. It wasn't your fault. These things happen. A tragic accident.'

'But it was my fault. It was the devil, you see. I consorted with the devil.' And Liam stared at Francis with his haunted eyes.

The peculiar circumstances of the accident – the distance from the tent, the fact that the older man's trousers were undone, evidence of a chase along the side of the ridge – none of this was known to Francis. No one in fact had paid any attention to it. It all seemed perfectly straightforward to the investigators. The two inexperienced climbers had gone exploring while the other one, who knew better, still slept. It was very slippery after the storm. One fell, the other tried to save him and lost his balance, too. Such things happen, unfortunately. No need to dwell on it. If people stayed at home they might get burnt to death from a cigarette left alight, a spark from an unguarded fire; they might get run over crossing the street. Such things happen.

Liam had burbled on to the police but so disjointedly that they had made nothing of it. The man knew nothing. He was in shock. He was leader of the group and felt he should have prevented the accident. And maybe he was right, maybe he had indeed been neglectful, but they weren't going to tell him that now. It was an accident. Such things happen.

'It shouldn't have been Gerald,' Liam insisted to Francis, gripping his hand. 'It should have been me. It should have been me.'

He started to sob, to shudder uncontrollably the way he had been doing for days. The nurse came in with a tranquilliser. She shook her head sadly.

Because Liam had got so agitated at the sight of Francis, the doctor said it would be better if he didn't come and visit for a while.

'Give him time to mend. It's been a terrible experience.'

Then he shook Francis by the hand and, being a countryman bred, said courteously that he was sorry for his trouble.

Francis had also called on Mark's wife, a woman he had never met before though she told him that Valerie occasionally babysat for them. She was small, plump and neat and seemed to be taking it well, although every so often she choked and shivered.

'He was a good husband, a good father,' she told him. Unlike me, thought Francis, lacerating himself. 'We'll all miss him.' And she gathered her babies around her.

Valerie sobbed at her brother's funeral but found it impossible to relate him to the box they put in the ground. For several days whenever she came unthinkingly into the house or sat in the kitchen eating her tea and reading a magazine, she would expect to hear electronic noises coming from the computer, the heavy metal music Gerald liked playing in his room, him coming home and slamming the door in that heedless way of his. Then after a while his image started to fade, she got used to not hearing him.

Marion too began to mend but more slowly. She smoked more and more heavily, she ate less and less. She covered her yellow pallor and the heavy rings under her eyes with makeup that gave her a mummified look. But Marion was resilient. She was no runaway. She ruthlessly cleared Gerald's room of everything, passing anything decent to the St Vincent de Paul. Even Valerie was dismayed. All that remained of her brother were a few snapshots. And even those would have gone if she herself hadn't objected. The boy's room stood anonymous and empty and at last Marion was satisfied. Only the sight of Liam shuffling through the street could agitate her. Once, after meeting him face to face, she came home and vomited. In her own hands lay the cure for that final affliction. She told Raymond that she would certainly take him up on his offer if it still stood. That in the spring she and Valerie would move down to Cork.

PART EIGHT

GRIMALDI'S GARDEN

What good is a garden without flowers? Old Joe, the Signor, became very sad when he realised that he would have to wait until the spring for plants to start to grow on his little plot of land. He could not wait, he would not wait. From the theatre he took bouquets of all manner of artificial flowers — silk and paper — basketfuls of wax fruits, papier mâché or wooden fruits — all painted in luminous colours: crimson and saffron and peacock blue, terracotta and cerulean and flame-red and aquamarine — and carried them off to his grey garden where he set them in the hummocky ground or tied them to the bare branches of the trees with bright green ribbons. The lush abundance delighted him. He had turned January into July.

At the library where Francis worked, they had been sympathetic to his wish for immediate sabbatical leave, though he would have left anyway even if they had refused him permission. Exactly where he had gone was, however, a mystery. He just disappeared one day, not even saying goodbye. Only the boy Steve had known anything of his plans, though not where he was going. Francis had offered him free accommodation and a lump sum in exchange for staying in the room and minding Russ, the dog. He also left a cheque for Steve to give Sonya, three months rent in advance, even though she wasn't looking for it.

Steve's theory was that his friend had taken off to the foothills of the Himalayas. It was a place Francis spoke of, somewhere he would one day like to explore, land of the yeti, the red panda and blue sheep, the rare and mystical snow leopard, the Crystal Mountain. Books stacked in his room attested to the fact that he had dipped widely into the subject, explorers' tales, pilgrims' tales, accounts of attempts on Annapurna and K2, books on Tibetan art and philosophy and even Zen Buddhism, though markers suggested he had not finished any of the books yet. Steve hoped Francis had gone there. It was the sort of place he himself would like to go to, to get away.

Sonya believed that if Francis went anywhere exotic it would be to Mexico, for the Day of Dead when children ate candy skulls, skeletons rode on bicycles through the city and La Chatrina twirled her parasol flirtatiously round her ghastly, fleshless head.

'Why there?' asked Ruth.

'Because he talked about it. The Mexican death obsession fascinated him, the way it showed itself in the art. He liked Spanish American writing and the pictures of Frida Kahlo.'

'Did he indeed?' commented Ruth. 'How interesting.'

'And if he wanted to come to terms with his son's death, what place would be more appropriate?'

Sonya longed to go there herself, where shrines of whatever material came to hand, net curtains, garish strips of plastic, tin cans beaten flat and silver, noisily commemorated the lost beloved in jinglings and tinklings and rustlings, where on this one day of the year the dead rose up and walked easily through the streets beside the living, instead of staying locked silently and surely away in the dank earth without hope of resurrection.

But to go like that would have taken money and Marion knew

that Francis was very hard up, especially following the funeral. Her notion, after Valerie had spoken to Steve, was that he had gone to London with that old woman he liked so much. Maybe he was her toy-boy, she giggled, slightly hysterically, near-hysteria being her habitual condition these days. Valerie refused to see the joke. She was sulking. She was sick at the thought of having to go to boarding-school in Cork and had hoped, before his disappearance, that she might be allowed to stay on in Dublin with her dad. 'To avoid disruption in my education' was the phrase she had thought up.

Now it seemed that her fate was sealed. It wasn't fair.

Then Sonya left too, for Italy, shining with expectations. The year declined. The clocks were put forward and suddenly it was dark by five o'clock. The smell of smoke again filled the night air.

Most of Ruth's mail had been forwarded to her mother's house by Sonya, and Charlotte Isabel had brought over a bundle with Starveling but there was still a small pile awaiting her on the mat from the intervening period. One of these letters was from Philip, in elaborate arty handwriting, full of misspellings. The gist was that his latest special friend had another friend who owned a gallery and who was absolutely wild about Ruth's portrait of Philip. This friend was really keen to see more of her pictures with a view, maybe, to holding an exhibition. Ruth herself was very excited about the work she had done in London. She was sure it was good. Moreover, it was almost the first time she could really say that it was distinctively her own, work in which she expressed herself wholly, without selfconsciously nodding to other artists or influences.

She phoned Philip and agreed to meet his friend although she was worried that he might only be interested in the kind of slightly expressionistic representationalism she had employed for the portrait or else, even worse, in the titillating subject matter.

She needn't have worried. Aonghus was delighted with what she showed him.

'I call the series *Glimpses*,' she told him diffidently. Did it sound stupid? 'What I had in mind was kind of glimpsing behind things for an instant, beyond the outer skin of things.'

'Yes, I see, I see,' he exclaimed, thumbing through the sheets and pausing occasionally over a particular piece.

They were delicately abstract but suggestive of natural forms, perhaps a vivid flame suddenly bursting through grey ashes, a plant deprived of the sun turned albino under a stone, the liver-spotted skin of an old hand striated with thin white bones. As yet they were unframed but he could arrange all that if she said what she wanted. Raw white wood, how would that be? Narrow black for some of them. An austere effect. Ruth said that would be fine.

Did she have any more, any oils for example, larger works, anything at all? And Ruth found how regenerating it was to be wanted, to be appreciated fully at last.

Aonghus spoke of the New Year for the exhibition. Maybe February.

'Once I get rid of this rubbish,' he smiled looking round at the thickly daubed, crudely coloured acrylics that decorated his walls at that moment. 'Quite popular, though. I suppose it's the vulgar cheerfulness of them that attracts, although they're supposed to be heavily symbolic and all that.'

Afterwards Ruth met Philip who had been hovering, almost as nervous as she.

'I didn't want him to doubt my bona fides,' Philip said. 'He's gorgeous, isn't he?'

'Don't tell me you set this up just to get off with him?' laughed Ruth.

'Heaven forfend!' Philip exclaimed. 'I'm deliriously happy with Brendan, darling. Or rather Breandán. He's from the Aran Islands, silent and so butch.'

Ruth's mind boggled. It hardly sounded like a match made in heaven though she knew that through all the camp glitz, Philip was kind and considerate and no doubt lovable. It reminded her to mention to him that she had seen Ari.

'He was worried about you,' she said.

'Not at all, not at all. We're the best of chums again. Well, I never quarrel with anyone for long.'

They took their leave of each other. Afterwards Philip remembered he had been meaning to say how awful to Ruth about Mark, whom he knew 'in passing, darling, only in passing' from the time Mark had worked for Ari. Because he forgot, Ruth never heard about the fate of her erstwhile student for she had no reason to connect him with the accident to Sonya's friend's son. She only noted, even with a little subconscious relief, that Mark did not after all attend her new class and assumed that he was developing other interests.

Never a sight, never a sound of her lost husband. May, the old woman, had got well used to her solitary life that was, however, broken too frequently to become lonely with visits to her daughter and family. She didn't even much regret the passing of summer for now she had summer all year round in her floral arbour.

The kitten, Fluffy, had grown up and had four kittens of her own that May was half-heartedly trying to place in good homes. One would go to her neighbour, who had never before had the heart to replace poor Monty but who found the tiny tiger-striped creatures irresistible. One would go to that nice nurse whose husband had so tragically died. May knew her from way back, from the time when she went into hospital to have her veins done and, chatting to the nurses as you do, discovered the friendly little staff – as she was then – lived only a few streets away from herself. After that they noticed each other from time to time at the shops or in the park when May paused to watch the children playing and found the nurse there with her own brood. They always passed the time of day for a while and so learnt something about each other's lives. May was able to congratulate her on her promotion to sister; she knew when the nurse's husband had lost his job and after that always asked how he was getting on, remembering how demoralised and difficult her own husband had become in the enforced idleness of retirement. It was on a recent chance meeting of this sort that the nurse had told May of the fatal accident and May had suggested that a new kitten might distract the kiddies from missing their dad too much.

The other two May thought she might keep. Why not? It was a big enough house, plenty of space. The only thing that troubled her was what would happen to them when she died. But Lily had said God willing that was a long time off and that anyway she would make sure they were all right.

The kittens played with the old woman's ball of wool.

'Naughty!' she said indulgently, stretching out her toes to the fire in utter contentment.

It was typically inconsiderate of Francis to disappear, Marion thought. Just when she wanted to think about putting the house on the market. She only hoped he would return soon, that he wouldn't be one of those people you heard about who walked out of the house one day to buy a paper or cigarettes or something and never came back. That would make the legal side very complicated. In fact, her solicitor had told her that that under no circumstances would she be able to do anything by herself without her husband's consent for at least seven years.

'Well,' he had added with a fat smile, 'let's hope it never comes to that.'

The worst of it was she could no longer bear the estate where she was living. The houses looked mean to her, even her own with all its improvements. Admittedly, she felt less strongly about Liam these days. It was rather pathetic the way the man couldn't pull himself together. She might have expected that of Francis but not of Liam who had been so supportive at the time of Gerald's first accident.

Marion shivered. At the back of her mind she had a superstitious notion that death, having failed to take Gerald once, had marked him down. That after all it was only a matter of time before the grim reaper succeeded in bringing the harvest home.

She never mentioned this to anyone. It was fanciful, possibly even blasphemous, and when her own mother said something very similar, Marion flared up in anger.

'He was such a strange boy,' her mother remarked. 'I never thought he was quite normal, never meeting your eye, never answering a simple question. It was somehow difficult to think of him ever growing up.'

'What the hell do you mean?'

'Language, Marion!'

'What do you mean exactly?'

'Oh, nothing. Don't get on your high horse. Only after that first time, well, it was almost as if he was certain to come to a bad end, one way or another.'

Marion's explosion of anger and grief astonished her mother. It had never struck her that her daughter was particularly devoted to her children. She herself had always had the attitude regarding her own offspring that they were there and that was that. You did the necessary and heaved a sigh of relief, albeit privately, when they were gone and you could wash your hands of them. Her shock over Andy was essentially that he had failed to toe the line. The collapse of his marriage and now of Marion's, was certainly not something she connected with a lack in herself. The plain truth – and here she agreed for once with her husband – was that children these days were after all not up to much. Standards had slipped. With regard to her grandchildren, Valerie she judged all right though gross but the boy had always seemed to be wandering around in a world of his own. The fact that he had lately left this one irrevocably to roam through who knew what great computer game in the sky seemed to make very little difference to anything.

Now it turned out that her daughter was imbued with traditional maternal feelings after all. Marion's mother held her daughter to her breast and comforted her.

'I didn't mean anything. God help the poor wee fellow. He's happy now, anyway.'

Liam was back at work but his mates noticed that the spark had died in him. He was only going through very perfunctory motions. It seemed to most of them that he was overreacting. Of course, no one denied it was a terrible thing, but still accidents happen all the time, don't they.

It was muttered that he had once carried a torch for the mother. Maybe he was even the boy's natural father. That would account for the excessive grieving that so often caused him to retreat weeping to the men's. And time didn't seem to heal in his case. The weeks passed and he was as bad as ever.

It began to get on his mother's nerves.

'Pull yourself together, son, for God almighty's sake.'

Then he would look at her with those bloodshot eyes of his and say, 'Sorry, Mam.' And soon after leave the room to go upstairs and cry some more.

'A grown man blubbing,' his mother would grumble. 'It's unnatural. It's unmanly.'

He went for long walks, God knew where, through the streets for hours on end, leaving her all alone in the evenings when everyone knew only too well how many muggers preyed on isolated old folk these days. She told him over and over, but would he listen?

At least he wasn't drinking. Not excessively. That was what she feared above all else. That he would take after his dad, who had drunk himself into an early grave. At the time, of course, she had praised God for it, for releasing her from the heavy, sweaty, piss-stinking monster that wanted sex off her night after exhausted night and wasn't above slapping her around in front of the boy either. A coronary at the age of forty-two from drink and smokes and overeating and she had almost skipped to the funeral. And even though still nice-looking at the time and even though she could have if she wanted, she never let another man near her. Except her son. Her own and only son.

Where he went he probably would have been unable to say. He walked compulsively through streets that wound and crossed and looped and linked, all with names that were confusingly similar – Walks and Views and Roads and Groves and Avenues and Crescents and Greens – on and on past houses with curtained windows where sometimes the fluorescent gleam of a television screen flickered through thin fabric, till it seemed to him that everyone was safe and secure indoors except himself, the one wanderer that could find no peace.

Ruth was unsure what to do about Starveling's strange musical gift. Certainly it was the only thing the child was good at. She spoke about it to Maeve, now enormous in her eighth month and Maeve, who thought Ruth had to be exaggerating, suggested a good teacher.

'I'm not sure that's what she needs,' Ruth said, 'though I'll try it . . . You appreciate I want to keep this a secret for the time being.'

Meaning, don't tell Fionn with his big mouth. Maeve smiled her agreement though she asked her husband to recommend a good piano teacher to Ruth, which he did.

At the last moment, Ruth chickened out. The day of the first lesson, she rang to cancel. The night before she'd had a nightmare in which people in blue coats and masks that covered their whole faces came poking at Starveling who sat at the bottom of a deep pit. Then the pit turned into a boat made of sand on a beach. Starveling was sitting in hers in a long row of similar boats full of silent people shaking their heads. Ruth was looking on but could neither speak nor move. Suddenly the tide came in and the sand boats sailed out to sea. Starveling was clapping her hands and laughing but then the boat she was in started disintegrating and she was screaming. Everyone was screaming. Ruth ran towards her but the water was warm and brown with swirling sand and pulled her down too.

She woke abruptly to find the duvet wound around her. She threw it off and let the early morning air sooth her sweating body with chill fingers.

Francis was floating. He seemed to have achieved a degree of peace of mind in the weeks that had passed since he left home but suspected that it might be illusory. That it might be based only on the rarified existence he was living.

At first he had been in total despair. The burden of life seemed too heavy. He had thrown off the responsibilities that had been laid on him and now found himself a hollow man, unneeded, unlovable, without virtue. Death would have seemed the answer but cowardice pulled him from the brink as he contemplated water swirling under the bridges that had always filled him with dread.

He remembered some graffiti once spotted on a lavatory wall:

'I'd like to hang up my hat and hang myself beside it.'

'Why don't you?'

'I don't have a hat.'

Francis didn't have a hat and despite himself, the realisation made him smile.

So now he was in a monastery, not so far after all from home. Marion had been right in assuming he couldn't afford to travel very far.

The monks were tolerant and left him alone. He could take part in services if he wished or keep to himself. After the initial conversation with the father abbot who told him he was always there if needed, Francis stayed mostly solitary, merely nodding greetings to the monks who silently crossed his path or speaking the odd word to them at shared mealtimes.

Francis had been bred a Catholic but had come to realise that like so many things in his life, his adherence was mechanical. His Massgoing had lapsed long before although he would not, not until recently, have questioned his creed.

Of course he had doubted the existence of God in his time but the dreadful concept of an empty universe always sent him back. And hadn't he always felt the power of something beyond, in his prayers, something listening, comforting, telling him that after all he was not alone?

Increasingly, however, this sense had not matched what the

orthodoxy of organised religion said to him. Whatever the doctrine, it seemed to him tight and closed and exclusive and intolerant. The evils of the world traceable to the abominable interference of the masters with the spiritual dimension and their subsequent attempt to impose one perceived and circumscribed truth on all. At times, the horror of what people did to each other or to the precious earth on which they trod so heavily, pressed in on him almost unbearably. He felt like an open wound walking. Only here in this silent place of strict ritual, he was salved.

For, despite turning from the religion of his tradition, he did not avoid the services in the monastery. In fact he was a very regular attender although he never took the sacrament. If God was anywhere it was surely here, where the male voices of the choir soared in glorious praise of creation. Or else along the paths Francis walked alone, avoiding people and places where people might be, the changing sky above him, the still uncorrupted ground beneath.

Sometimes he talked to Gerald, asking forgiveness and, fancifully perhaps, thought he found it in the blessings on the road, in bright berries on a bush, a bird that stopped and cocked its eye at him and flew off, a plate of ice on a puddle or crepitating frost in grass.

Time passed. He knew he couldn't stop in this charmed place forever. But just a little longer.

A publisher had accepted Charlotte Isabel's novel and had offered her a contract to write another, which she signed. In the meantime, John had asked her to stay on with him and why not? Pleasant though the company of the young might be, it always put you in your place, a fossil, a has-been. With John she could relive her youth in shared memories, they could recall old acquaintances long forgotten, many now dead, some still struggling on like themselves. Furthermore she enjoyed big-city life, the cafés full of varicoloured people, the good restaurants where they would go and eat once or twice every week, exotic and relatively cheap compared to Dublin.

She loved the shops too and managed to be quite vain about her appearance, particularly, as she informed John, now that she was about to become 'a celebrity'. Her publisher told her there would no doubt be great interest in someone, so let's say senior, starting a career as a romantic novelist. It was the sort of thing the media loved. She would have to be prepared for interviews, photographs, the works. And she was. She could hardly wait the eight months until the launch and bored John stiff with her talk of it so that he made sure to have a newspaper and his pipe to hand if the subject loomed. She showed no interest, however, in starting her new novel.

'I'll think of something one of these days,' she said airily and hopped on a bus or tube to Knightsbridge or John Lewis in Oxford Street, never returning without some small but expensive item, gloves or panties for herself or a silk tie for John. Her estranged son and his stuck-up wife would have been horrified at her prodigality. The very thought caused her to smile all the more and reach again for her purse. Money passed through her hands like there was no tomorrow.

She smiled at the phrase and of course, she mused, maybe there wasn't . . .

Nothing from Sonya except scribbled postcards that gave no indication of anything except that she was happy. That she would be home for Christmas bringing with her a friend.

Ruth worked at her exhibition, scheduled now for the early Spring. Whether it was the encouragement she had received or whether it was just that she had struck gold in herself, she was working as never before, unable to stop. Teaching, doing the necessary chores, fetching and taking Starveling here and there, she was always thinking about her painting, getting new ideas. Now she was working in oils, colours and forms bursting off the canvasses like great flowers blooming, volcanos erupting, waves smashing on rocks – none of these things exactly, only herself full of energy and power.

It seemed as if her vision were sharper and clearer than ever before. She could feel colour physically. Walking in the park with Starveling one autumn day she saw black ducks gliding through the white sparks of light that struck off the surface of the pond, she saw yew berries on the ground like beads of blood, she saw conkers gleaming against the dead leaves; when you lifted a conker up, looked at its whorled surface and felt its smooth hardness, it seemed you held the secret of life itself in your hand.

'Take it,' she pressed it into the child's little fist. 'You're holding a tree like that.' And she pointed up to the huge horse chestnuts that loomed over them.

Starveling looked with her big eyes.

'We'll take it home and see if it will grow in a pot.'

They filled their pockets with conkers, not by flinging sticks at the branches as others did, but by carefully looking and turning over brown and yellow leaves and sometimes prising open a spiky green case to find the treasure within. And as they walked back along the path under the trees, a wind rose up, stirring the leaves and sending them scudding forwards and upwards and downwards from the branches. A shiver of expectation ran through Ruth.

One wet night there was a knock at the door. Grumbling because she disliked being disturbed, Liam's mother made slow progress to answer it. She put the chain on before opening it a crack.

There was a woman standing outside.

'I wonder if I might speak to Liam,' she said.

'He's not here,' the old woman replied with hostility but also with curiosity.

'Oh . . . never mind.' The woman made to go back down the path.

'Who will I say called?'

'I'm Mark's wife. Widow. But it doesn't matter.'

The nurse. Liam's mother attempted to smile, baring crooked, yellow teeth. 'Come in and wait if you like. I don't suppose he'll be long.'

Running rapidly through her head was the thought that she might get some good gossip out of this. And also that the nurse might be able to advise her on some chest pains she'd been having. But the woman thanked her and refused.

Liam came back late that night, dripping wet, soaked to the skin.

'You'll catch your death,' his mother muttered.

'Good,' he replied.

'Good is it. Then who'll look after me? Eh? Eh?'

'Sorry, Mother,' he said, kissing her head. 'I'm a selfish bastard.'

'You are.'

She forgot to tell him about the visitor until several days later. Forgot or omitted for whatever reason. When he finally heard, he was uneasy. Did the wife, the widow, know something? What could she have to say to him? It had to be unpleasant. She must blame him, too.

When his mother saw that he was in no hurry to repay the visit, she started nagging him.

'Go and see her,' she said. 'What harm can it do?'

Then on another occasion, 'What are you afraid of?'

He looked at her sharply, the squashed old face with a failed attempt at innocence, malice glinting in her rimmed eyes. Or were they just watering?

So he went. The nurse was called Sarah, a nice woman, plump and pink. Liam had encountered her a few times before, at the house in passing, but had never really spoken to her. Not when Mark was there. Now she brought him into the comfortable little kitchen and gave him a cup of tea with a slice of homemade sweet cake. She told him that she had heard how depressed he was, that she hoped he didn't think he was in any way to blame.

'I know what Mark's like,' she said. 'What Mark was like. He never listened. You couldn't tell him anything. If you said don't do it, then at the first opportunity he would rush out and do whatever it was. Just to prove some stupid thing.'

'It's kind of you to say it,' he answered. 'But I know it was my fault.'

'Did you push him?' she asked directly.

He stared at her. 'Of course not.'

'Well then.'

'But as good as. I drove them to it. Both of them.'

'Don't tell me Mark jumped. He liked himself too much for that.'

'No. He fell.'

'So it was an accident.'

'Yes, but . . . '

'No buts,' she took his hand in hers, hardened and reddened from work, nails bitten down. 'Let them rest. Let you rest.'

Liam's eyes filled with tears. 'I loved him,' he said. 'I loved him.'

'We all did,' the woman replied and held him to her. And after so many tears, the tears still fell and mingled.

'God help him,' she went on, 'I don't know that he deserved so much.' They laughed together then and then she poured them both another cup of tea.

'It must be hard for you now,' he said. 'I'd like to help you. If there are any jobs needing doing around the house, the garden, that sort of thing.'

'That'd be grand, Liam,' Sarah replied and smiled.

For some weeks, Francis, feeling the need for intense physical work, had been helping to dig up the potato crop on the farm attached to the monastery. One night after a hard day he felt the overwhelming urge for a pint or two of beer and company other than that of the austere brown-robed monks. So he sneaked out like a child in a boarding school and walked the several miles to the nearest village. The pub he found had live traditional music and a jolly crowd. He was hit by a culture shock that started to wear off after half of the first pint of creamy black stout that slid down his throat like nectar.

After two pints, he changed to whiskey – *uisce beatha* – the water of life. The more he drank, the clearer his eyesight seemed to become, the faces around him suddenly vivid, pulsing, eyes gleaming, teeth.

The merry dance music of reels and jigs stopped to allow the whistle player and the piper to perform a slow air. It seemed to him, grown sentimental from drink, resonant with the beautiful, barren landscape, the flight of a bird across a lonely waste, the tragic history of his country. He looked around at the faces and love welled up in his heart for the poor human race that could still, nevertheless, make so much that was good out of so little.

He was drunk but not incapable. In fact, his perceptions were heightened. Everything was suddenly so clear. He could even, it seemed, see through things and out the other side. Now at last he knew the secret of life, he knew what he wanted, what he must find, if only he could remember, if only he never forgot.

It was a night of such clarity. The sky was white with stars. He walked with his head up staring into infinity, slipping on the icy road, stumbling over roots and rocks along the path that was a shortcut back, clutching at brambles to steady himself so that the next morning he wondered to find his palms covered in blood.

Arriving at the monastery at last, he looked at the grey mass, with its windows like numerous shut eyes. There was a Greek myth, wasn't there, about a monster with many eyes that Odysseus or someone, had to creep past on his long, long journey home, a monster that never slept until Odysseus blinded him. The Cyclops, that was it, but on second thoughts didn't the Cyclops have only one eye?

'I'll have to find that out,' Francis thought to himself, falling asleep, dreaming of a peacock with its tail fanned.

It was early December when Maeve gave birth to her seventh child, a girl finally after so many boys.

'Now at last Fionn can tie a knot in it,' she said to Ruth when she came visiting, bearing a bottle of wine for the mother and the pinkest of suits for the baby.

'We can allow ourselves a bit of sexual stereotyping for once, can't we?' she laughed.

'This child is going to be one big frill,' Maeve said. 'And fuck them all.'

The girl was to be called Snaoibhe – a princess. Meanwhile she gurgled and yelled as if she were ready to burst and generally asserted herself.

'Tom was in,' Maeve said, indicating a large bunch of yellow roses.

The colour of cowardice, Ruth thought.

'Is he in Dublin then?'

'Would you care?'

Ruth thought. 'No,' she answered honestly. 'That's all past and gone.' It was sad in a way, like a death, but nonetheless true.

'Well, you've more important things to be concerned about, with your exhibition and all.'

'Yes,' said Ruth, still looking at the two-day-old child and thinking, but you're nice, too. And that she would also like to have another child some time, not too far in the future perhaps. Only not conceived on a gravestone but properly, in a bed.

'Anyway, he's not in Dublin. Just passing through. Nuala's got him where she wants him. She won't let go of him again.'

Strutting like a peacock through his dreams, Argus, the hundred-eyed watchman, that was it, sent to deadly sleep by the sweet music of a flute. Francis awoke with a terrible thirst but no other bad effects. With a sense of well-being that caused him to smile as he washed in the cold water in the cold morning. But then it came to him that he couldn't remember the important thing he had discovered the previous night, in among the songs and the stars, the key to understanding everything. He had picked it up and carelessly dropped it again. All he knew was that the time had come for him to leave. Suddenly he felt closed in, stifled by this life of renunciation and abstinence. It wasn't for him. Certainly not. And he knew that he could no longer wait for things to happen. He would have to act for himself. He would have to forge and change and build and rebuild.

'You'll be glad to see the back of me,' he said to the father abbot, who received his news blandly.

'I hope you've benefitted from your stay,' the man replied.

'Yes thank you, Father.' The appellation ran off his tongue naturally although he had consciously avoided using it for months.

'And many thanks for your help in the farm and for your financial contribution,' the abbot said courteously.

It had been unnecessary. The monks had not looked for money but Francis had paid his way anyway out of a little savings account that he had always kept separate from his current money. Marion was unaware of the existence of this account, although it had not been opened with a view to deceiving her but to have a little something in reserve in case of unforeseen emergencies. Francis felt guilty in using up the fund only on himself but justified it by the nature of the crisis.

Now he couldn't wait to get out of the place. Even the father abbot was astonished, though he concealed it well, at the haste of the departure after so long. The two men grasped hands briefly as if the monk knew that anything else would have been unacceptable.

Francis shook the dust of the monastery from his shoes and set his face towards the east.

Liam's mother stirred. Something had woken her as she snoozed in her armchair in front of the television, a bottle of stout nearly finished by her side. Something that wasn't the sound of the slime monster oozing out of the drains to terrorise the city or, on the other channel – and she couldn't remember which she had finally decided to watch – the screams of the beautiful young woman as she was carried off by the unspeakable villain, to be hung over a snake pit by a thin thread that the slightest movement could break. It was a careless tune that cut through the synthetic noise. Her son was whistling, unconsciously content after so long.

She dragged herself out of her chair and took herself to the source of the sound, the kitchen. Every surface was covered in newspaper. Liam was painting something extraordinary, a doll's house of all things, and whistled merrily as he worked.

'What's that?' his mother asked.

'Oh, you're awake,' he actually smiled. 'I peeped in but you were dead to the world.'

'I wasn't. I was just resting my eyes.'

She was still staring at the wooden house.

'It's for Sarah's little girl for Christmas.'

'Who?'

'You know Sarah, Mark's . . . wife.'

'Oh, the nurse.'

She knew Liam had been going round there. She half-wished he'd bring the woman back, so that she could quiz her about her worsening chest pains. On the other hand, she didn't want to encourage the friendship. The last thing Liam needed was to wind up with someone with three little ones to support.

'I'm pleased with it,' Liam said, painting the roof bright red and smiling that stupid smile. 'It's turned out really nice, hasn't it.'

'Has it?' his mam said and lurched back to her programme.

It was a fanciful idea but the more Ruth thought about it, the more inclined she was to go along with it. Like making magic.

Sonya had returned from Italy with a pile of books, bottles of wine and olive oil, cheeses and Siena cake and a handsome young Italian to help her to carry it all.

'Giovanni,' she introduced him. 'I want to have a party for him.'

That they were in love was beyond dispute, whispering and touching, full of secret smiles. They made a strange but attractive couple, she with her short bright red crest of hair, looking in the tightly bodiced blue velvet dress suddenly like, Ruth thought, a wan Renaissance madonna by Piero della Francesca, while luscious black curls hung down over Giovanni's shoulders, his white teeth gleaming in olive skin, like the incarnation of a Mediterranean summer.

'He's so sad because everything here is grey,' Sonya said. Giovanni spoke little English but it seemed that Sonya was able to gabble away freely in Italian. When Ruth commented that she was unaware that her friend knew the language, Sonya replied, 'Oh, I just picked it up.'

She had got the idea from the memoirs of the clown Grimaldi that she was currently reading as part of her studies.

'You see,' Sonya said, 'his father, Joey Grimaldi's I mean, was an Italian living in London. He bought a garden because he wanted to see colours again, flowers growing. London was such a gloomy and terrible place in those days, you know. But he bought it in the middle of winter and the garden was as grey and gloomy as everywhere else. Then he had a brainwave. He would fill the garden with artificial flowers and fruits and turn winter into summer. And that's what he did.'

And that was what Sonya wanted to do. To effect a metamorphosis. For her Giovanni.

'And we'll invite everybody to come.'

When Francis boarded the ferry at Rosslare, he had no clear idea of where he was going. In the bar, he got into conversation, if that was the word, with a dour lorry driver who offered him a ride to London which, since it was offered, he accepted. Had the driver been going to Edinburgh or Birmingham or Southampton or Tibet he would probably have accepted just as readily.

The journey along the motorway was fast and dull. The only moment of drama was when they crossed the Severn bridge, riding up up into the sky.

''Twill fall down one of these days,' the lorry driver remarked as they swayed in the wind.

'Not today, please God,' Francis replied laughing nervously. He had shut his eyes in terror.

'Arh,' the man said.

Once they stopped to eat, in the middle of Somerset, Francis thought, but it could have been anywhere. The driver wasn't anxious to talk and Francis soon gave up the attempt to pay for his ride by providing a diversion. He had become hypnotised by the monotony of the long, flat yellow road. It seemed to be going nowhere, just on and on for ever. But that of course was a fantasy. They had to arrive and in due course did. London was larger than he remembered, even more anonymous. It was the rush hour and people with tense faces pushed along the streets and poured underground. It oppressed him unbearably after the emptiness and stillness of the countryside, the measured walk of the monks. But he was here. Where else could he go?

Hampstead. That was where Charlotte Isabel's friend was living, he remembered from the postcard she had sent him with her address on it before he had left home all those months previously. She'd hardly still be there after so long but Hampstead sounded green and calm to him. A refuge. He found the postcard – a view of Kenwood House – thrust into his address book and treated himself to a taxi.

'She's out,' the old man said on answering the door, looking with curiosity at the stranger in front of him. Francis had grown a beard that was already crinkly and thick, unlike the hair of his head that straggled over his shoulders but left his pate bald. After the journey, with his rucksack and his loose, grubby clothes, he looked undeniably disreputable. Certainly not the sort to invite into a nice home.

The old man asked him to come in and wait.

'She won't be long,' he said. 'The shops have closed.'

The living room was heavy with dark wooden furniture, well-polished. Hardly by Charlotte Isabel, whose domestic accomplishments Francis knew only too well. By this old man then, buffing his furniture, dusting his books, caring for the relics of his life.

Some record was playing. Songs to a piano accompaniment. Francis sank thankfully into a soft chair and realised how long he had deprived himself of his music.

Chance. How strongly it influences our lives. A path among so many, lightly chosen or even taken at random, that determines everything coming after. The decision to go out or stay in, to turn left or right, to smile in encouragement or frown, to say yes or no, to risk or play safe. Francis hurrying to avoid Sonya on the cliffside had only hastened their meeting. So was it chance or was it not rather inevitability? Could he have avoided her and led a different life. Logic said yes – and yet he wondered. Were certain events destined? Everything had ensued as a result of that meeting. Or no, coming to think of it from before. From when a piece of music was overheard in a dusty junk shop or before that, when he waywardly started to follow a peacock feather bobbing in front of him in a crowded street, eye to hypnotic eye, or before that again, long before, at the moment of his conception perhaps, the chance meeting of two sets of genes. And was everything connected by thin threads? Or rippling out from a first cause? There was a story he had once read, a science fiction story in which a time-traveller back in prehistory strays from the path and crushes a butterfly, thereby changing the whole of subsequent development. So then at what point was the pebble tossed into the pool? And towards what meeting was he even now being impelled?

And what made him think of any of it? That heart-tugging tune, the tune he was hearing now, so familiar, was surely the one played in the junk shop by the old woman in the silky purple dress.

'What is it, the music?' he asked Charlotte Isabel's friend.

'Schubert. *Winterreise*. Winter Journey. It's beautiful, isn't it.'

'Very melancholy.'

'Ah well you see it's about a wanderer who in his despair renounces human companionship, loses the will to live and journeys towards nothingness.' The old man smiled. 'Typical romantic rubbish,' he said.

Charlotte Isabel was delighted to see Francis after she had ascertained that it was indeed him under all the hair.

'Has John told you my news?' she asked.

'No.'

'About my book. It's getting published. And you, my amanuensis, will be receiving a nice little cheque from me for all your help.'

'That's great. Not the cheque. I don't want anything. I mean, your success.'

She patted his hand. 'And I'm writing another . . . Well, I'm thinking about it.'

'She hasn't got very far yet.' John remarked. 'She spends all her time shopping.'

'No . . . I go to the shop; that's different. I don't buy much.'

The old man looked at her affectionately. She took his hand.

'Don't believe what people say to you,' she told Francis. 'It isn't over until your toes curl up.'

Francis was pleased when they invited him to stay. 'But only for a few days. I have to move on soon,' he said.

'Where to?' Charlotte Isabel enquired.

'I don't know.'

'Then stay.'

'I can't. I have to go . . . It's like I've lost something and have to find it . . . I nearly did once, find it, I mean, only . . . ' He looked into her old face that tried to understand as he tried to explain.

'I can give you a loan, an advance if you're short of money,' she said.

'Oh no, I have a bit left.'

London seemed to him more friendly now. Just from knowing that empathy was back there in the house that smelt of polish and old books. He walked the streets of the city as he had walked the boreens around the monastery. It would be so easy to stay.

Another Christmas was coming. The streets were hung with coloured lights, shop windows were filled with tinsel and artificial snow. Francis got himself a job as a Santa, needing no false beard – just plenty of talcum power and padding for his thin frame – and sat telling greedy children he would try to bring them whatever they wanted if he could, then presenting them with cheap mementos – colouring books with wax crayons, magic pads that you could draw on and then make your picture disappear, plastic babies for girls, action men for boys, a bag of dinosaurs, a trumpet that played only one note.

The gross materialism finally depressed him but he would be off in the New Year, hitching across Europe and leaving it behind as soon as possible, either heading towards Africa or Asia, his own private odyssey, leaving the itinerary to chance.

Amaranthus. That's what it was called, the picture Ruth was

working on, a huge oil bursting with abstract curved shapes or the close-up of petals in all shades of purple, the immortal flower that never fades.

There were now several completed oils to add to her collection of ink drawings for the exhibition. She was working in a fury of energy, red-hot colours in wide sweeps, all the greens of spring, a soil that had lain fallow blooming into life again.

The piano had arrived at last, brought in fact not by the man but by the women in the van, Amazon Removals, an all-female company that Ruth had found in an alternative directory. And along with the piano were books, a bureau, an inlaid coffee table, a mountain of bed linen, still starched the way her mother had always done them, towels and hand-embroidered tablecloths and a chest of carefully packed old crystal glasses that Linda had known Ruth coveted.

The tiny front room of the artisan cottage was stacked full. Starveling picked her way over to the piano and stood in front of it reverentially. Ruth unlocked it, put the key down and lost it for ever.

She looked at her strange child. Whatever happened, she thought, she would never let go of her hand. If necessary she would accompany her down whatever winding paths the child trod. Starveling touched the keys, then clambered up on to the stool and started to play.

'She's good,' one of the removal women said, bringing in a bag of sheets and stopping to listen to the polka. Then the other woman came in and the two of them started to dance around on the only spot of clear space as the music got faster and wilder.

'John and I are going over to Mary's for Christmas. She's having a surprise party,' Charlotte Isabel told Francis one evening after he had staggered back from work.

'How can it be a surprise if you know about it?' he asked.

'Well, that's what the letter says. A surprise party. I suppose we're going to be surprised by it.'

She looked at Francis, so exhausted.

'Why don't you come too?'

'Ah no,' he said. 'I have to be moving on.'

'Are you sure you're going in the right direction?' she asked.

'It's over between Sonya and me. It never started. Not really.'

'I wasn't thinking of Mary.' She looked down at her old hands with their dark red nails and heavy gold rings. 'Sometimes to find what you're looking for you have to go back.' She glanced across to where John sat snoozing in his favourite armchair.

Go back? He thought with dread of Marion and her recriminations, of his daughter's contempt, of his son's sad empty room, the pathetic little life snuffed out, of Liam's guilt-haunted despairing face, of his own room, loveless and hollow, that was more a mockery now than a sanctuary, of the piano that he could play only haltingly, murdering the incomparable harmonies with his clumsy fingers, that, let's face it, he would never play properly. Impossible. Going back was back to failure. He would never go back.

And yet the very next day, walking in the rain of a chilly Yuletide street that tried to be cheerful but only succeeded in being frantic, he paused at the sound of a hurdy-gurdy and at the sudden sight of the entranced face of a child staring up at the man winding a cracked tune out of his machine.

The child. How could he possibly have forgotten the child? She must have peeped in so many times from the corners of his unconscious, huddled in the dark, lost and longing to be found, but he had ignored her or missed her or turned away. Once yes he had seen her but then he had been drunk.

Wasn't that after all what the Buddhists said, what Charlotte Isabel said, that to find yourself you simply have to stop and look. Dorothy at the end of the Yellow Brick Road who could have gone home at any time, she only had to wish to make it happen. And there at that moment in the tawdry street of a dirty and corrupt city, among people endlessly chasing elusive rainbows, it was revealed to him that it wasn't necessary to go to the top of a mountain, to an African bush, to a remote island or even a monastery to find what you sought. That it could be here, now, always in the palm of your hand.

The child applauded the hurdy-gurdy man enthusiastically as her mother at last pulled her away. Francis dropped a pound coin into the damp felt cap on the ground.

'Cheers, mate,' the man said.

It was very cold. Ruth's, Steve's and Sonya's fingers, ungloved because they needed to be flexible, had stung painfully as they secretly tied the dozens of bright flowers and fruits to bare branches in the old orchard and burnt and throbbed when they came back into the warmth of the house.

People were invited for the afternoon. The sky was dark grey, weighted down. Gradually the visitors started to arrive, Starveling gravely eating the crisps and nuts that she was supposed to be passing around. The big house was noisy and cheerful but – just past the solstice – it would soon be getting dark outside. Sonya decided she could wait no longer for Charlotte Isabel and her friend to arrive. She went into the garden, leading a stumbling Giovanni whose eyes had been blindfolded and summoning the curious guests to follow. A surprise party.

The bright train of people entered the orchard to gasps of delight. Sonya dramatically removed the blindfold from Giovanni's eyes and he exclaimed in flamboyant Italian at the sight of the winter garden turned into summer for his benefit. He kissed Sonya and then, clowns that they were, they stood on their hands and kissed again to general cheering with Starveling dancing around them clapping. Maeve sat under a flowering tree with her new baby girl, tightly swaddled against the bitter cold.

Ruth thought that she would like to paint the scene. It could hardly be more beautiful or strange.

But she was wrong.

'Snow!' someone shouted and Ruth looked up. It was true. Light flakes started down out of the ashes of the sky, getting thicker fast. People laughed, splashing red wine on the snow as it settled.

Steve fetched his mandolin and twanged a sad gay melody, his own. The guests stood still and listened while Starveling stared at his hands.

This was the strange picture that met Charlotte Isabel and John as they followed the sounds into the garden, an unlikely *fête champêtre* in the whitening world.

'The flight was delayed by freezing fog,' she apologised to her granddaughter, hugging her to her furry coat. She looked around. 'It's lovely,' she said. 'But why try to make it what it isn't? Winter is beautiful too.' And she pulled John by the hand and introduced him to Sonya. John, who had been a prisoner of war in Italy, immediately started chatting to Giovanni, fluently if inaccurately, hands flying.

Ruth and Starveling were catching and studying large and intricate flakes of snow before they melted on their hands. Suddenly the child stared into the darker shadows where a spare figure was standing awkwardly just behind Charlotte Isabel and John.

'Daddy!' the child cried, 'Daddy!'

She hurtled across towards him. And as Ruth looked on

astonished, the stranger swung Starveling up in his arms and held her tightly and kissed her crinkled face.

'Francis?' Sonya queried, at first not fully recognising the bearded man.

The black dog which had been howling in the room in the extension for some time was released at last and bounded across to his master with at least as much joy as the child.

'Francis,' Sonya led him into the group. 'This is my darling Giovanni.' And the Italian embraced him warmly.

'Remember,' Sonya whispered, hoping he wasn't hurt, 'Scapino.' Madly in love with someone new every day.

Francis held the child and smiled because after all it wasn't for Sonya that he had come back. And then the tableau in the snow, the figures in the summer garden froze, as Francis looked across for the first time to where Ruth was standing and she looked back at him. And though it was impossible because they had never met before and in fact had been barely aware of each other's existence, they later both agreed that it was in that instant as the snow fell on the vivid paper flowers, on the shining fruit, on the still, smiling people, that at last, at last they truly recognised each other.